BUNDERLIN

I've worked in the chemical industry and in town planning. I've been a barman and a parson. I suppose I have been a historian as well because my first book, *Counting the Days to Armageddon,* was a history of a fringe religious group. At heart I'm a storyteller and Bunderlin is my first novel.

I live in South Wales with my wife, Margaret, and three dogs.

Robert Crompton

BUNDERLIN

ROBERT CROMPTON

For Judith
with regards
Robert Crompton

Published by Solidus
www.soliduspress.com

For Margaret and Ben

Prologue

Peter Bunderlin was in the garden but he wasn't standing up. He was sitting on his seat between the poplar tree and the big tangled hawthorns. It was good here because he could see across to the school and down the lane and into the field where the animals went to graze. Nobody ever saw him. They could have done if they had looked, but they didn't look so it was really quite easy for him to hide without being hidden.

Down the other side of the garden there was a very high solid fence which the neighbours had put up because they didn't like very big people like him and Franz who could see over the tops of things. That was silly really because there was nothing interesting in their garden, so that wasn't why he sat down. He once frightened a little girl. He didn't mean to. He had gone to the garage to get one of the goats down from the roof when the girl looked up and saw him. She screamed and ran away crying and he didn't like that. Her mother had probably taught her to be frightened of animals as well which was silly.

So he just sat on his seat and watched and read and read and read his poetry book. He knew all the poems now and he often read them in his head. Read in his head and ready for bed. But when he did that he played with them and made them different and funny. So he read them in the book as well. And then he would give the donkey and the goats apples and carrots and things when they came to him. And sometimes when the pigs began to squeal in the afternoon he would go into the house and help his mama fill their feeding bowls.

That was a long time ago. Now he has to wait in the corners again and watch and hope to see the man he is looking for. He still keeps his camera in his pocket but he has to be careful not to do anything that will make people want to send him back to prison. Some of the people in prison are not nice and there are no animals so it would be silly to go back.

Part One

One

I shouldn't have to be doing this, Martin Latham told himself. He pulled up behind the white van outside the vacant shop. A traffic warden eyed him suspiciously but moved on.

Bit of a comedown, squire,' said the van driver as he and his mate carried Martin's desk into the flat above the shop.

'Just a stopgap,' he responded defensively. 'As soon as my new place is ready I'll be out of here.' He tried to sound casual but the man's remark needled him. He resented feeling he had to explain to a complete stranger why he was moving to this dingy place from the house he'd worked so long and hard for. It didn't help that the man hardly listened. Ah well, he told himself, at least the move meant that he would be able to carry on with his research undisturbed for the rest of the summer.

They soon finished unloading the few pieces of furniture and Martin sat down to take in his new surroundings. How many other transient tenants had stared at these walls and felt as deflated he did just now? What pictures and posters had brightened up the place? Who else had sat here and resolved to move on as soon as possible? As he looked around he noticed a greeting card amongst the junk mail he'd picked up on the way in. Who would have sent that? Not Julia, surely? Emma, maybe. But it wasn't from either of them. 'The photos will be ready next week,' it said inside. So it must have been meant for someone else, the previous occupant, perhaps, or somebody whose plans to take the flat had fallen through. He dropped it into the waste bin and went to move his car before that traffic warden came back.

When he returned he began to unpack the small selection of his books and papers—the rest were in boxes in his sister Jean's garage—and arranged them on the shelf unit by his desk. He set up his computer and felt reassured when it bleeped as it came back to life. With a sudden burst of determination he opened the file on *The Pre-Maccabean Origins of Proto-Daniel.* It wouldn't nag him any more. He'd have the chance to get on with it and finish it before the next invasion of new undergraduates. He left the title page on the screen and went to sort out his kitchen and make a meal.

He felt a little self-conscious in the Wheatsheaf that evening. A smart-casual fifty-year-old with well groomed hair and neatly trimmed beard. Perhaps he should cultivate a more carefree look, let the hair grow a little, touch up the grey and merge into the background. He smiled ruefully—just being away from Julia might... No, he shouldn't start on that line of thought.

A young woman in a short skirt and a low top approached him. 'Looking for business, sweetheart?'

'No. Just drinking.'

On Monday morning another card arrived with a photo processing receipt. 'You can collect the photos from Ann Bates's shop,' it said. But still there was no indication of the sender and nothing to suggest that it was not meant for someone else.

He began to make himself some breakfast but was interrupted by a loud hammering at the street door. He turned out the grill and went downstairs. And there, in chopped-off, frayed jeans and tie-dyed tee-shirt, was Emma, his daughter. Her long brown hair was about to get tangled in the straps of the huge rucksack she was wrestling to the ground.

'Here, let me get that. Didn't expect you for a few days yet.'

He led the way upstairs and into the living room where Emma flopped into an armchair. 'Something smells good. Am I in time? I'd just love a bacon sandwich. But don't worry I'm not stopping. Well not long. Thought I'd crash out here for tonight and get a lift to the station tomorrow. That's OK, is it?'

'Yes, of course. When do you need to be there?'

'About one o'clock. We need to pick up Sally on the way. She's at her folk's place in Farnworth. And, by the way, Mum says will you have Samson?'

'But I can't have the dog here. There's no garden for a start. And your mother's got all that space for him.'

'Not any more, she hasn't. She's moving in with Barry, remember? Anyway, I said I'd collect him later today so it's too late to say no.'

Emma tucked in to a bacon and egg sandwich whilst Martin made himself some toast. 'It's nice, this place. It'd suit me. If I was planning on coming back, which I'm not, of course.'

'Have you got any ideas yet for after finals?'

'Come off it, Dad, that's months off. I'm not even beginning to think about it yet. I'll make us a coffee. Don't suppose you've got any decaff, have you? But not to worry, I've got a jar somewhere in here.' She began to search in the many pockets of her rucksack.

'Try the cupboard first. You'll find some in there.'

'Oh, right. Tell you what, when I've had this drink, can you drop me off at Auntie Jean's? I want to see this new Shetland pony she's got. I'll pick Samson up on the way back. And you'd better give me a key in case you go out.'

He handed her the spare key as she started to poke about among the clutter which was already beginning to accumulate on the mantelpiece.

'Give me a tenner as well and I'll get us something nice for supper.' She picked up the card which had arrived that morning. 'I'll get these photos for you while I'm at it.'

'But I'm not sure that they're anything to do with me.'

'Course they are. Must be. No one else lives here, do they? You'd better give me another fiver. No, make it ten.'

Emma returned late that afternoon with Samson, a brown and white bull terrier with a black patch over one eye. As soon as he saw Martin he went wild with excitement. It should have been great to have the dog around but Martin groaned inwardly at the prospect of trying to exercise him adequately, particularly once the new term began.

'I'll get supper for us tonight,' said Emma breezily. 'Hope you like Thai food. Well, you'll have to, cause that's what I've got. Anyway, come and look at these photos. Don't know why you go to that Bates's place. Right at the far end of Chorley Road, for goodness' sake. How many photo shops do you have to pass to get there? I suppose you fancy Mrs Bates. Is that it?'

'Don't be daft. I don't even know the woman. Or her shop. They're not even my photos, remember?'

'If you say so. But they've got your name on the packet so let's take a look at them.'

One by one, Martin took them from the packet and handed them to Emma after a quick glance. 'There's nothing special here. Just general views from round and about the town centre and the park. One or two from a bit further afield.' The last one surprised him. 'Oh. This one's, er...'

'What is it?'

'Well, here, take a look.'

She took it from him and examined it carefully. It was a picture of Martin himself at the front door, probably on the day that he moved in.

'So what do you suppose this is about?'

'Haven't a clue.'

'Well, maybe if we have another close look at them all we might spot something. So here goes. First one.' She put the picture on the table in front of him. 'Tell me about it.'

'It's the bandstand in the park. Looks a bit dilapidated. There's nothing else. Trees in the distance.'

'And this one.' She began to spread them out on the table.

'The rose gardens and the old café. Some of these are prints off old negatives, of course. It's ages since the café was demolished. And the bandstand as well, come to think of it.'

'What about this one?'

'Shops on Chorley Road. Recent, I should think.'

More shops, Saint James's Church, Victoria Square, Barton Lane School, a reservoir, probably Rumbold Lake. 'Oh, wait a minute. Some of these ring bells, not all of them, but some of them do. So I think I might know whose photos these are. Yes, of course I do. A big guy, enormous guy.' It was the lake that had brought it back to him. 'These are all places he had some sort of connection with. Looks like he's back in circulation.'

'And he's been looking for you?'

'Watching and waiting, I should say, knowing him.'

'So, tell me about him. Why doesn't he just knock and say, Hi, remember me? Come to that, why would he want to look you up again after however many years?'

'That's what I'd like to know. First time I met him was when I was a kid at primary school. The headmistress tried to warn me off. Came across him again years later and a girl who knew him tried to warn me off. And the last I saw of him was when I visited him in Strangeways shortly after he'd begun a life sentence for murder. I'd given evidence against him.'

Two

It began here, a long time ago.

'I'll take it to Mrs Bundy,' Martin said, even though Colin and his young sister said he shouldn't. 'She'll know what to do. We can't just leave it here.'

He picked up the injured cat and walked towards the goat lady's house. 'Martin! Just put it in her garden and then come away,' suggested Colin anxiously. Like a lot of the children, he still believed this lady with the funny voice and the story-book hairdo was a witch.

Martin took no notice and went up to the strange detached house next to the school. Well, the house wasn't strange exactly, although it did look dark and forbidding. It was the people who lived there, Mrs Bundy who wasn't really a witch and Old Bundy the giant. And some folk said there was another giant as well. They were like a sinister family from a fairy story. His mam and dad were quite friendly with Mrs Bundy and always stopped for a chat on the way to and from the allotment, but they never saw the giants and Martin wasn't sure that they were real. So he had grown out of the silly ideas of the infant school about these odd people, but he still felt a bit nervous and excited as he knocked at the dark green door. The ginger cat squirmed in his grasp but didn't try to escape. A dog inside the house began to bark. The cat writhed again but Martin held on to it.

Presently the door creaked open and Mrs Bundy appeared. She wore a long flowered skirt and a blue blouse with the sleeves rolled up. Her long brown hair was plaited and tied in grubby white ribbons. She looked down at Martin and smiled and he knew that really she was quite friendly.

'Please, Mrs Bundy, it's this cat. He's hurt. Can you help him?'

She opened the door wider. 'Bring him inside.' Warily, he followed her into the front room of the house where she took the cat from him. She felt its injured leg, not too gently, Martin thought as the cat yowled loudly and the dog in the back of the house started barking again. 'He is your cat?' Mrs Bundy asked.

Martin shrugged his shoulders. 'Don't know whose he is. Just found him outside.'

'I will look after him for you and he will get better. You will come and see him next week?'

Martin promised to return in a few days and Mrs Bundy showed him to the door.

He called at the house several times over the following weeks to visit the cat. The cat recovered and began to wander further about the house and the surrounding area, but Martin's visits remained confined to the front room with the dark landscapes and the two tall clocks. He was aware that there were more animal members of Mrs Bundy's household but, other than the goats, which had a habit of climbing on the outbuildings at the back, and Kaspar, the Alsatian, who had befriended the nameless cat, he never got a good look at any of them. He only ever heard them scrabbling about behind the high fence at the back and, occasionally, what may have been the braying of a donkey. But he didn't see anyone else, neither giants nor ordinary people.When eventually Martin did meet the rest of the menagerie, it was the climbing wandering goats that brought it about. It was a Thursday afternoon and the class, some of them at least, were listening to their teacher reading from *The Adventures of Huckleberry Finn*. Suddenly a young voice called out, 'Goats, sir! Sir, sir! Mrs Bundy's goats are in the playground.'

The teacher removed his glasses and looked around the class to see who had interrupted his reading. 'I'm sure they are doing no harm. Just ignore them.' But the distraction was too much and Mr Jenkins and Mark Twain together could not compete with two small goats hungrily feeding on the bushes and plants growing around the edge of the playground. He put the book down and walked over to the window to take a look for himself. 'All right then. I think this is a job for you, Martin. You'd better run along and ask Mrs Bundy to retrieve her animals.'

Martin ran across the playground, out through the main gates and down Barton Lane to the now familiar house next to the school. 'Mrs Bundy, it's your goats,' he said when she came to the door. 'They're in the playground eating the flowers.'

'Oh, my naughty children! Always they are up to mischief. Wait there.'

She disappeared into the house and returned a moment later, followed by someone else. It was one of the giants. Not Old Bundy. It was the other one and he had to bend his head slightly as he came out through the door, a bit like stepping out of the little cupboard under the stairs. He wasn't really a giant, he was just a very very big man with reddish hair and a wispy beard. He was a grown-up but not as old as people's dads. More like Martin's big sister.

'You go with Peter,' said Mrs Bundy. 'He will show you how we bring the goats home.'

Martin walked alongside the big man towards the school gates and Mrs Bundy followed. When they reached the playground the goats were eating the wallflowers that grew in the borders and Mrs Scattergood, the headmistress, was standing at the door.

She strode towards them. 'Get those animals out of this playground!' she called. 'Do you hear me? Get your animals away from here! This is a school, not a farmyard.'

'Who is that?' Mrs Bundy asked.

'It's Mrs Scattergood.'

'Scattergood, chattergood, Scattergood, fattergood,' the big man responded. 'We plough the fields and Scattergood.' He walked up to one of the goats which had stopped eating. 'Scatter goats, gather goats, porridge oats,' he chanted as he bent down to lift the animal which was making no move to avoid him. He picked it up and placed it across his shoulders with its legs hanging round his neck like a scarf and looked around for the other wandering animal.

Mrs Scattergood grasped the top of Martin's head and turned him firmly towards the school door. 'Back to your classroom,' she ordered.

On his way home that afternoon, Martin turned into the lane between the playground and the houses, intending to take the short cut by the allotments. Mrs Bundy was in her front garden cutting back some overgrown bushes. She looked up as he approached and called to him, 'Come here! I want to show you something.' She let him in through the side gate in the high fence. 'You want to see my other animals? Come with me.'

At one end of the garden were two ramshackle sheds and an Anderson shelter. Along the far side were what appeared to be various feeding troughs and an old zinc bath full of water. In the middle of the garden a donkey was standing motionless, facing the house and looking at nothing. Suddenly a small reddish-coloured pig ran out of the Anderson shelter squealing and shrieking and began to crash around the troughs. It sounded as though it was in terrible pain. 'What's wrong with it?' asked Martin.

'He's hungry. Come with me. I will show you what we do.'

He followed her into the kitchen and so did the pig. In the corner was a large copper boiler like the one his mother used for washing clothes. Mrs Bundy lifted the hinged lid and stirred the thick soupy contents with a big stick that looked like an old rounders bat. She picked up a jug and began to fill a bucket. The pig squealed louder and louder. She filled up one of the troughs and the pig and its more docile mate set about noisily and messily emptying it.

'Now come with me. I will give you some lemonade.'

He followed Mrs Bundy back into the house and she showed him into a large room adjoining the kitchen. There were cardboard boxes piled up everywhere, leaving just enough space to move between them. By the window was a dining table with boxes and cases crammed underneath it and more stacked on top. Only the sideboard and the mantelpiece were free of boxes. On these were displayed a huge collection of clocks. Clocks of every description: carriage clocks, bracket clocks, cheap alarm clocks, an enormous black and gold clock which seemed to Martin to be in the shape of the Town Hall with its great columns at the front entrance. And on the walls all around the room were an assortment of cuckoo clocks.

He had been staring open-mouthed for several minutes at all the clocks before he realised that there was somebody else in the room. In the shadows of the corner between the fireplace and the window Peter was sitting in a leather armchair and squashing its arms outwards. The ginger cat was on his knee. 'Hello,' said Martin and went to stroke the cat.

The big man made no response but continued staring absent-mindedly. Kaspar was lying on the rug at his feet whilst a black and white kitten played games with his tail. Mrs Bundy came into the room and handed Martin a glass of her home-made lemonade. 'A drink for my little friend,' she said.

'Please, Mrs Bundy, why have you got so many clocks?'

She laughed. 'My Franz. He makes the cuckoo clocks. Always he is making clocks. And people bring him clocks to mend.'

'My sister's got a cuckoo clock,' said Martin.

He drank the lemonade and looked for somewhere to put the glass down. 'I'll have to go now. My mam will get cross if I'm late home.' He said goodbye to the young man in the armchair but still he made no response. Outside, the pigs had finished their feed and were basking in the spring sunshine. One of the goats was on top of the Anderson shelter eating leaves from the overhanging trees and the donkey was now standing motionless facing the troughs and still looking at nothing.

As Mrs Bundy was letting Martin out at the back gate, Father Spencer cycled slowly past on his way from the allotments, his cassock gathered around his knees. He looked from Martin to Mrs Bundy, and from Mrs Bundy to Martin and, without a word, rode on. Before Martin reached the road, he saw that the elderly vicar was cycling towards the main school building.

The following day, as Martin's class were marching in single file back to their classroom after morning playtime, a familiar shrill voice called out, 'Martin Latham! Come to my office.' It was Mrs Scattergood. He followed her up the stairs to that part of the school which pupils only ever saw if they had been caught in some particularly dreadful wrongdoing. On this occasion, however, the headmistress did not appear at first to be especially angry.

'Now then, Martin,' she began as she seated herself at her desk, 'are you going to tell me about yesterday?'

'Yes, Miss.' He thought she winced when he addressed her as 'miss' but he could do no other. When first she had come to Barton Lane Primary School two years before, she had tried to insist upon being addressed as *Ma'am* as befitted her position as head of the school. But Martin, in his innocence, had protested in front of the whole school at morning assembly, 'But, Miss, you're not my mam so I can't call you mam.' And so she remained *Miss* just like the newest and youngest recruit to the school staff.

'Well?' she prompted.

'Please, Miss, what am I to tell you about?'

'Why did you go to that animal woman's house?'

'Mr Jenkins told me to go. Her goats were in the playground and they were eating the flowers.'

'Yes, I know about that,' she said impatiently, 'I mean after school. You were seen there after school, so tell me why you had gone back.'

'She asked me to go in and see her animals.'

'And then what?'

'She fed the pigs.'

'Yes, and then?'

'Gave me some lemonade.'

'What else?'

'That's all really, Miss.'

'Are you sure?'

'Yes, Miss.'

'Absolutely sure?'

'Yes, Miss.'

'Very well, then. Now listen to me, Martin. You are not to go in there again. Do you understand me?'

'No, Miss. Why can't I go in there if I want to?'

It was not the response that Mrs Scattergood expected. 'Because these people are not to be trusted,' she snapped angrily. 'Do you hear me?'

'But she's quite nice really,' Martin protested.

'Don't you dare answer me back! Those people are not "quite nice really". Do you realise that while your father was away fighting in the war, there were some people who had to be taken away for fear they were Nazi spies? You know what that means, don't you?

'Yes, Miss.'

'People who wanted this country defeated in the war. And Mr, what's his name? Anyway, him, he was one of them. So don't you dare tell me they are "quite nice really", because they are not.'

'But my mam and dad let me go there.'

'Enough! I will have no more of this!' She took a ruler from her drawer. 'Hold out your hands.' She hit him hard, twice on each palm. 'Now go back to your classroom and don't you dare let me see you ever again going into that house. Go on, away with you.'

On his way back to school after lunch time, Martin saw Mrs Scattergood coming out of Mrs Bundy's front gate, looking very righteous and satisfied. He would have tried to avoid her, but it was too late. She looked down at him and said, 'She won't trouble you again, Martin. I've seen to that.'

He thought that perhaps he was supposed to say, 'Thank you,' but he would not. Mrs Scattergood strode on to school.

On the way home that afternoon, he took his usual short cut along the lane and when he came to Mrs Bundy's side gate, it was slightly ajar. She looked out as he drew near. 'Your teacher, she is not a bad woman. One day she might understand. You must do what she tells you. I know bad people. Really bad people, but they are not here. Cannot hurt us any more.' She handed him a small cardboard box. 'This is yours. You are still my friend, no matter if teachers tell you not to come.'

'I'm sorry, Mrs Bundy.'

'You must go home. Always you can wave to my goats when you walk in the lane. And your cat, he will watch for you.'

'And I'll listen for the donkey.'

He walked home sadly and told his mother what had happened. 'Don't worry too much about it,' she said. 'You can always visit her again when you start at the Grammar School. Now then, what's in the box?'

He opened it and took out a cuckoo clock. 'Oh, it's just like the one our Jean had for her room in college,' said his mother. 'She went and chose it from the shop in town. Now then, where shall we put it?'

A few days later, everyone filed into the school hall for morning assembly but Mrs Scattergood was nowhere to be seen. Instead, Mr Jenkins came to the platform and announced solemnly that the Headmistress had been taken into hospital and would be away from school for a few weeks. In the meantime he would stand in as Deputy Head. 'Quiet!' he shouted as the assembled school seemed about to erupt into cheering. 'We will sing hymn number twelve, *New Every Morning*.'

At the end of the afternoon, Martin approached Mr Jenkins on his way out of the classroom. 'Sir, is it all right if I go and see Mrs Bundy's goats on the way home?'

'Of course it is. You don't have to ask me. Never have done before.'

'Thank you, sir.'

He stopped by occasionally over the next few weeks and helped to feed the pigs. Konrad, the donkey, soon became accustomed to him appearing at the gate and would slowly approach and nuzzle him, waiting for the titbits that Mrs Bundy let him feed to him. Like the Alsatian, he held an honoured position in this strange household. Kaspar and Konrad were the only two animals who had been given names. Even the ginger cat remained unchristened. Mrs Bundy always spoke of him as Martin's cat so perhaps he should give it a name. 'Mrs Bundy,' he said one day, 'I think I should like to call my cat Prowler.'

In those few weeks when he was again free to visit Mrs Bundy, Martin never went further into the house than the kitchen. He never saw Old Bundy and imagined that he was hidden away somewhere making clocks. And he hardly ever saw Peter again except once when he was walking home from school along the

lane. As he was going past Mrs Bundy's garden he look
the fence and Peter was there, almost hidden between the trees.
Martin stopped. 'Hello,' he called.

But Peter said nothing. It seemed rude to walk away, so he
waited a little more. Still the man said nothing. 'Hello,' Martin
called again.

'You said that already,' the big man replied.

Martin carried on home not really knowing whether Peter
Bundy was funny or just very silly.

It was coming towards the end of term, when all of Martin's
class would leave Barton Lane for good. Everyone supposed that
Mrs Scattergood would not return now until after the summer
holidays and all the class were quite openly glad to think that
they had already seen the last of her. One Friday, however, when
Mr Jenkins was dismissing them at the end of the afternoon, he
announced to the departing rabble, 'You will be very glad to learn
that Mrs Scattergood will be back on Monday. So I want you all
to let it be clear how orderly and disciplined you have remained
in her absence. No fighting in the playground, no rampaging
through the streets, no talking in the school corridors or you will
send the poor lady straight back to hospital. And we don't want
that, now do we?'

On Monday morning gloom descended on the school. Mrs
Scattergood, who had arrived very early, as was her habit, came
into the playground a few minutes before the whistle was due.
Some children noticed her in the doorway and became rather
more subdued and orderly but a group of boys who were marching
around bellowing an assortment of playground chants had not
seen her. As they came to where she was standing they began
to chant, *Webster cuts your hair, Webster cuts your hair, ee aye
addio, Webster cuts your hair.* Would they dare to sing the next

verse? They did. *Creepy grabs your bum, Creepy grabs your bum, ee aye addio, Creepy grabs your bum.* The Headmistress grabbed the boys and hauled them off to her study.

Morning assembly was a little late starting. Everybody was waiting for the Headmistress to come in but she did not. Mr Jenkins slipped out and returned a few minutes later with four boys whom he sent to join the rest of their class.

Then Mrs Scattergood marched in, took her place at the lectern and glared at the assembled school. 'It has become immediately apparent,' she began sternly, 'that during my absence discipline in this school has suffered greatly. I will not have it. This morning I have heard the most appalling language in the playground. I will not have it. Now let me tell you this—things have got to change. And let me warn you that you must be very careful out of school. There are bad people around. Very bad people. But there are bad children as well and when bad children start going to bad people terrible things can happen.'

Martin had thought at first that this was just about the chanting in the playground but now he supposed it was also about him going to visit Mrs Bundy. He tried to hide behind the boy in front of him.

'So you must be very careful. Do I make myself clear? Very well, we'll say no more about it. But think on. We will now sing hymn number twelve, *New Every Morning.*'

On the way home that afternoon, he waved to one of the goats, which was standing on top of the Anderson shelter and looking into the lane. But he did not go in through the gate.

Three

Years later Martin had forgotten about the goat lady.

Martin reached the corner, hesitated and walked on as far as the post office. Then he walked briskly back towards the used car dealer's yard. There was a big man with unkempt greying red hair and a long beard sitting on a low wall at the street corner. A brown and white terrier was lying at his feet. It was the same vaguely familiar man he had spotted a couple of times over the past few days and he began to feel a little uneasy. Was this guy following him? Surely not, he thought. Must be coincidence.

He walked along the line of used cars and back again. But the one he wanted wasn't there. Circumstances had conspired to make up his mind for him. He would not buy the car after all, he had dithered too long and it was gone. 'See anything you fancy?' said the flabby man in greasy overalls leaning against the door post.

'No. There was one last week, but I guess you've sold it. Sunbeam Talbot.'

'That one, yeah. Sold. Got a nice Zephyr Six down there. Good car, pull the birds, know what I mean?'

'Not what I was looking for.'

'Fuck off then.'

So he did. As he came out of the yard, the big man emerged from behind a Commer van and his dog trotted at his side. 'Caveat emptor, caveat empty.'

'Er, yes, whatever you say,' Martin replied warily.

Jesus wants me for a sunbeam,' said the man and walked on towards the row of shops further along the street, laughing as he went.

'Daft bugger,' Martin muttered to himself. That was when he realised who it was. Peter, Mrs Bundy's giant in the dark corner and he'd been watching Martin—closely enough to know which car he'd been interested in.

He was in the Haymarket a few days later. Martin had gone in for a game of pool and there he was, at the far end of the bar. What on earth is this guy up to, why is he following me? Martin thought. But what do you do? Go up to him and demand an explanation? Don't be daft, Martin told himself. You're being paranoid. He made his way to the bar where the man was standing and caught his attention as he pushed past. 'Oh, hello again,' he said.

'Moonbeam, hornbeam, sunbeam. Been and gone.'

'Yes, gone. Already sold,' Martin responded.

'Try, try and try again. Try a Triumph. Triumph Renown. A much better car, if you ask me.'

'A Renown?'

'Renown. Renown. Renown.' He pronounced it as if mimicking the impatient revving of an engine. Then, with a laugh, he added, *'John Gilpin was a citizen of credit and renown.* But not Crediton. London. *A train band captain eke was he, of famous London town.*'

Was this guy serious? Martin wondered, but before he could respond and before he'd managed to buy a drink, someone called from over by the pool table, 'Hey, Martin! You're on.'

By the time he had lost his second game and, with it, the table, the list of waiting players had grown and the early evening group were ready to move on. 'I'll catch up with you,' Martin said and went back to the bar. He was not going to pass up the chance of getting his hands on a Triumph Renown—even if the guy selling it was completely bonkers.

'So, a Renown, you say. You know of one for sale? Where?' he asked the man.

'Elsewhere, dear boy. Are you interested?'

'Could be.' He tried to sound casual. But ever since his dad had owned a Mayflower, Martin had wanted to move up to the bigger and better and more impressive Renown.

'Could be. Would be. Should be.'

'It's yours, is it? You want to sell? Is that it?'

He made no response but seemed to be staring thoughtfully at the disclaimer notice behind the bar. Martin wondered whether he had heard him and was about to repeat himself when the man spoke. 'The menagerie will not be held responsible for cats, goats, armadillos left unattended on the premises.'

'The car you mentioned just now,' Martin repeated. 'Are you selling?'

'No, I am drinking. Then I shall be buying and then I shall be drinking some more.'

Martin groaned inwardly. If he was going to play clever-dick games and make conversation difficult he would go and catch up with the others and leave him to talk to himself. 'Well, if you do want to sell, I might be interested in taking a look at it.'

'And so you shall. Now let me get some more drinks.' Without asking what Martin preferred, he called for two pints of mild. Then, satisfied that the barman had heard his order, he said, 'You go and claim that table over there.' Before Martin could move, however, he added, 'No, wait a minute. This really is awkward but my wallet has slipped inside the lining of this confounded jacket and I can't fish the thing out. I'll have to ask you to let me get the next round.'

'So, this car, when can I see it?' Martin asked when he took the drinks to the table.

'Soon. I'll bring it into town one evening.'

Martin knew what his father would have to say about this. *If you buy a car from a stranger in a pub you're crackers. It's just asking for trouble.* But the guy wasn't a complete stranger and, besides, Martin could rely on Terry, his friend from work, to come and have a look at it and say whether he thought it was worth buying. That was not all, however. He shouldn't be thinking of buying a car at all, not if he was going to go ahead with his harebrained idea to give up a good job and go to university. But if there was the chance of a Renown then, daft or not, he would take it.

As he was talking about his plans, Martin became aware that the man was paying little attention to him. Something or someone in the crowd at the bar had caught his attention. 'Look, dear boy, let's move to that table over there.' He picked up both drinks and went to the other side of the room. Martin followed.

'Which university? Oxford, Cambridge, Heidelberg or up the road?' he asked. So he had been listening, though his attention still seemed to be elsewhere.

'Up the road.'

'*The rolling English drunkard made the rolling English road.* Don't let them talk you out of it. Follow your heart. Excuse me a moment.'

Martin assumed that he had gone to the gents, but he went in the wrong direction. Almost as soon as he had disappeared from sight, a young woman came up. 'Look, when your friend comes back tell him to lay off, for God's sake.'

He looked up in surprise. She was in her early twenties with long fair hair and a slightly freckled face. Quite attractive, really, Martin thought. 'Sorry? I don't understand.'

'No, I don't suppose you do.' She glanced round, perhaps to see whether the man was returning, and then sat down. 'Look, I didn't mean to be, well… Anyway, he's a decent guy but he's really started to piss me off. Did me a favour once, and now I can't get him off my back. Always hanging about. And give these back to him, tell him I don't damn well want them.' She slapped a wallet of photographs onto the table. 'He's a useless photographer anyway. Pointless, fuzzy photos of a gang of layabouts. What for, for goodness' sake?'

'So who do I say..?'

'Veryan.'

'Sorry?'

'Veryan. With a V. As in Cornwall. Oh God, here he comes. I'm out of here. Just tell him to leave me alone.'

As she rejoined her friends at the other end of the bar, the big man came back. Martin handed him the photographs. 'From Veryan. She, er, says she doesn't want them.'

He took the wallet and stuffed it into his pocket without saying a word.

'So what's that about, then? The photos, I mean. Mind if I ask?'

'Ask and it shall be given you, seek and ye shall find.'

'You're…' No, better not say it, Martin thought. He noticed that Veryan and her friends were leaving the pub but the man continued to be preoccupied with someone or something at the far end. He sipped his beer and carried on watching. Eventually a stocky man of about sixty with a severe military-style haircut pushed his way out of the crowd and headed for the door. The man took a long drink of his beer and put the glass down half empty. *'The time has come, the walrus said.* We shall continue our conversation another time.'

What conversation? Martin wondered.

'Meet me tomorrow evening at the top end of Lostock Road, near the Wheatsheaf. About seven o'clock.'

Four

He should have said no, made some excuse or simply not turned up. But he wanted to see that car. And the big man fascinated him. What was he? Dangerous psychopath or harmless eccentric? Or just a daft great clown who was probably best avoided?

Martin waited at the corner near the pub from seven until nearly half past, expecting him to drive up in the Triumph. After the long dry summer, the lightest of breezes stirred up the dust and Martin's eyes were beginning to feel gritty and his throat dry. He needed a cool beer or two but still he waited. He gave up at last and was about to walk back towards the town centre when somebody caught up to him from behind. 'What on earth do you think you are playing at?'

It was Veryan, the young woman from the bar the previous evening, and she was furious. 'This really is getting intolerable. If you don't leave me alone, I'm going to call the police.'

'OK, I'll go. Honest, I will. I never meant to… Well, I don't know. What I mean is…' In fact, Martin was not at all sure what was going on.

'Look, I'm sorry,' said Veryan. 'I don't suppose you knew what he's like any more than I did. But you were supposed to be meeting Bird, right?'

'Bird? Er, yes, but how did you know?'

'Because he's just bloody well phoned me, damn him. Said would I slip out and tell you he can't make it. Oh God, I can't believe I'm doing this. He said he'll see you in a couple of days.'

Martin was momentarily lost for words. It had been a mistake to come here and he ought to have known it.

'Known him long, have you?' asked Veryan.

'No, not really. I saw him a couple of times years ago when I was a kid and he lived next to our school. I've seen him around a fair bit lately, but I hadn't spoken to him before last night.'

'Well, for what it's worth, watch out. Bird, well that's what I call him, he never lets go.'

Martin set off in the direction of the Haymarket but as he waited to cross the road a familiar large form emerged from an alleyway between two blocks of shops and stood in a shop doorway. Too late to slip away without being spotted, Martin approached him. 'So you made it after all.'

The man looked at him vacantly.

'You came after all,' Martin repeated. 'Veryan said you had…'

'I don't know what you're talking about,' he replied. And with that he turned and walked away.

'Daft bugger,' Martin muttered and carried on to the Haymarket. It was not until late the same night that Martin began to wonder if perhaps the man he had met was not Bird but somebody else. If so, the resemblance was striking, and more than just striking, for he'd had no doubt whatever at the time that it was Bird. He was dressed like Bird and he spoke like him. He was as big as Bird and he moved like him. There couldn't be someone else just like him, surely? Only the passage of time allowed room, though not very much, for doubt. It was Bird—of course it was—playing the sort of silly game that might be expected of him. Though he was certain, or almost certain, that it was just a silly game, Martin was beginning to feel apprehensive. He had become one of the pieces in this strange man's game and he didn't like it.

Bird made no contact over the next few days. He no longer hung around in the Haymarket or in any of the coffee bars where Martin had noticed him so frequently over the previous couple of weeks, but if he felt relieved to have shaken off a potentially troublesome hanger-on, he was also curious to find out a little more about the big man called Bird. He looked out for Veryan. Cautiously, of course, for he had to avoid allowing the impression that he was playing Bird's game. But she also was no longer to be seen in the Haymarket.

There were other things to think about, which began to push Bird and Veryan from his mind. Except that, crazy or not, the man had a car which Martin might be able to buy for a reasonable price. And he had seemed to talk considerable sense or, more correctly, what Martin wanted to hear when he had spoken of his plans to leave the chemical industry and go at last, as a late entrant, to university to read History. Most of the guys at work thought he was mad to contemplate the change, and his father insisted that it was foolish to waste the qualifications he had already obtained, and downright disloyal to the firm that had already invested so much in his education. Bird, on the other hand, had said he should follow his heart and Martin liked to hear that because it confirmed that he was doing the right thing.

A month passed and Martin was coming to think that maybe he should wait until he was settled in at university before buying a car. He had almost forgotten Bird when he received a picture postcard of a Norfolk landscape. 'Dear Martin, *Summer suns are glowing over land and sea, happy light is flowing bountiful and free.* But light does not flow and neither do the Broads so I must hurry home to humdrum haunts. I will contact you upon my return. P. Bunderlin.' It was postmarked Manchester.

P. Bunderlin was Peter Bundy, quite obviously. But what was disconcerting to discover was that he knew Martin's surname and his address. How did he know? How long had he known? And, what bothered him more, why had he taken the trouble to find out?

He had assumed that if Bunderlin had been paying too much unwelcome attention to Veryan, it was probably the case of a man approaching middle age who had become infatuated with a younger woman, and there was nothing too unusual about that, of course. But he was beginning to realise there was much more to it and he felt uneasy at the thought that he had now become the focus of Bunderlin's attention.

His misgivings subsided, however, as Bunderlin appeared far from eager to make contact despite the postcard, and it was another fortnight before their paths crossed once more. Whether by chance or design, Martin was never sure. He could only guess. It was a Saturday afternoon in August and he was walking through Rylands Park on his way to the library. When he emerged from the formal gardens and began to cross the field opposite Rylands Hall, he noticed a solitary figure standing underneath the horse chestnut tree in the hollow. The figure began to run lumberingly towards the empty bandstand, stopped a few yards short and walked slowly around it. As Martin came close, the man emerged from the far side and he saw that it was Bunderlin, but as Martin began to approach him, he turned and walked away, disappearing into the clump of trees at the far side of the field. Martin carried on to the library.

He came back through the park on his way home and stopped at the café near the rose gardens. No sooner had he taken his coffee to a table than Bunderlin appeared outside with his dog. He said something and the dog sat, facing the door. Bunderlin came inside.

'Martin, dear boy, how good to see you.'

'I saw you earlier on. By the bandstand.'

'When?'

'Earlier this afternoon.'

'Not me. Only just got here, dear chap.'

'I was sure it was you. Looked just like you.'

'Just like me, just like you. But what is justice? Tell me what you've been doing while I've been away. Absent. Absence makes the heart grow fonder. Absinthe, on the other hand, makes the art profounder. Now let me get us some tea.'

He went to the counter before Martin could point out that he already had a coffee. The assistant wasn't there so, he called loudly, 'Can you bring a large pot of tea and some scones out here, please.'

He returned to the table. 'Actually, dear boy, I shall have to ask you to pay for this. Left my wallet in the car.'

A young waitress brought a tray to the table. 'There you are, Mr Bundy. Nice and strong, how you like it.' She set out the cups and Bunderlin put Martin's coffee onto the tray for her to take away.

Martin shook his head. 'They seem to know you here,' he observed.

'If she didn't know I was here she wouldn't have brought the tray.'

Daft bugger, Martin thought.

The waitress returned, bringing a more robust chair. 'Here,' she said to Bunderlin, 'Bit more comfy for you.'

'I take it that you've been to Norfolk for a while,' said Martin, trying to steer the conversation to something intelligible. 'Did you have an enjoyable time?'

'*Time and Fate of all their vintage prest.* We must arrange to get together this evening.'

'I'll probably be in the Haymarket with friends all evening.' Martin responded.

He'd meant it as an excuse, but it didn't come out that way.

'No. Not the Haymarket. Meet me in Victoria Square at nine. Nine o'clock would be a very enjoyable time.'

'OK,' said Martin but he thought that perhaps he might avoid that part of town that evening.

'About nine o'clock at the feet of Queen Victoria. Which reminds me—why do you never get a full length portrait of the Queen on bank notes?'

'I haven't a clue,' Martin replied, but he refrained from adding that he didn't much care.

'It's so that you can't counterfeit.' With that he stood up and, picking up the scones and, hooting with laughter, walked out of the café leaving his tea untouched. Martin watched through the window as they headed towards the main gates, the dog dancing excitedly at his side, catching the pieces of scone that Bunderlin tossed to him as they walked away together.

It was well after nine and Martin was still in the Haymarket playing bar billiards with some friends from work. They were near the end of a game when he became aware of someone standing in the corner watching them. It was Bunderlin. He approached as soon as the game finished. 'You were not there,' he said, almost accusingly.

'Er, no,' Martin admitted. 'Can I get you a drink?'

'I bought you one at nine o'clock in the Swan but I drank it myself. Then I bought you another.'

Martin looked at him, puzzled, not really sure that he understood what he was saying.

'Come along, then,' said Bunderlin a little impatiently.

'No, I can't. I'm with friends.'

'Dear boy, I will have you back with your friends within half an hour. So do hurry along or Kenneth will have our drinks.'

He was beginning to feel embarrassed so, not wanting too many people to know what kind of oddball company he was beginning to mix with, he slipped out with Bunderlin to the Swan and hoped that he would be able to shake him off and return to his friends as quickly as possible. Or, of course, if he could see the car at last, he might change his mind about not buying just yet.

The Swan was a dismal, smoky pub sandwiched between the back of the shops on Victoria Square and the newspaper buildings. At this time on a Saturday evening it was crowded with night workers taking a break. 'Ah,' said Bunderlin as they went in, 'our drinks have gone. Drinks are drunk, drunks are drinking. But not to worry.' He sat on a tall stool at the bar and motioned to Martin to take the other one. 'Two pints of mild, please, Harry,' he called to the barman.

'So when do I get to see this car you think I might want to buy?'

'As soon as you wish. But look, you're a studious, thinking person, right? You see, I need your opinion on something that's rather important to me. Meditation. Does it work? Or is it harmful?'

'I wouldn't have thought it could be harmful. But whether it works, well, I suppose that depends on what you expect to gain from it. It's not really something I know much about.'

'But you should. Definitely you should. People need to know about these things.'

'You should try it. See how you get on.'

'Get on, get off, get in, get out, *about it and about. But evermore came out by the same door as in I went.* Yes, I've tried it.'

Martin made no response. He didn't know how to. The barman brought their drinks and Bunderlin pulled a fat roll of banknotes from his pocket, peeled one off and gave it to the man. Then he led the way to a corner table without waiting for his change.

After a few moments of silence Martin said, 'Look, about this car—maybe it's best if we just forget about it for now. In fact, I'm not really sure I want to go ahead with buying a car just yet. So, sorry if I've wasted your time.'

Bunderlin didn't answer. It was almost as if he hadn't heard.

'Well, I must get back before the others move on.'

Still nothing. A black and white mongrel came up to them and sat looking up at Bunderlin. After a few seconds with no response from the big man, he pawed his knee. Bunderlin reached into his pocket and produced a dog biscuit which he threw towards the mongrel, which jumped up, caught it, ate it greedily and sat once more, staring expectantly into the impassive face. After giving the dog three titbits in this manner without a word, Bunderlin showed him his empty hands and the dog walked away.

'Seems to know you,' Martin ventured but gained no reply. A scruffy man of about thirty approached them, looked directly at Martin and sat down, saying nothing. After a few minutes Bunderlin pulled out a handful of change from his pocket and gave it to the man.

'Cheers, Mr Bundy,' he said and went to the bar.

Martin waited a little longer, not really expecting an explanation and not getting one. 'Oh, well, I'll be away now. Cheerio.' He left the Swan and walked quickly back to the Haymarket.

Five

It was a warm and windless Friday afternoon in July and a strong smell of hydrogen sulphide still hung in the air from a leak earlier in the day. Arthur, the laboratory assistant, had already cleared up and gone home and Martin and Terry were trying to finish the *Guardian* crossword whilst waiting for the final batch samples of the day to be brought in for testing before they could pack up for the weekend. The phone began to ring and Terry picked it up.

'Outside call for you,' he said, pushing the phone across the desk.

It was Bunderlin. 'Martin, dear chap, I really need to see you.'

Martin hesitated. He had hoped to be able to avoid the big man and had not seen him since the evening, a couple of weeks ago now, in the Swan. 'Well, I'm not sure…' he began.

'No, of course. I won't keep you but I did want to get in touch because it really is very important. So I'll see you later.' He hung up without trying to say when and where. 'Daft bugger,' Martin muttered and recalled uneasily that Veryan had said Bird never lets go.

'By the way,' Terry said, 'I forgot to tell you, the same chap phoned this morning while you were down at the spray dryers. Sounded a bit loopy, if you ask me. It's not that weird guy who hangs about in the Haymarket, is it? The big scruffy chap?'

'That's him.'

'You're mad. Rule number one: never give your phone number to anyone who might use it. And did your mother never tell you about talking to strange men?'

'Don't be daft. Actually, I had been thinking about buying his car.'

'Then you are the one here who is being daft. That, Martin, my friend, I can assure you. Daft as they come, or even dafter.'

Martin was not going to be drawn into the sort of banter that Terry so much enjoyed. He left him to wrestle with the last three crossword clues and went to set up the equipment for the last job of the day.

By half past four he was cycling home along Middleton Road when a black Citroen Safari estate drew level with him and slowed to his pace. It stayed alongside him for a hundred yards or so before pulling ahead and stopping suddenly right in front of him. Unable to swerve to pass the Citroen, Martin braked sharply and came to a halt with his front wheel touching the car's bumper. He dismounted to stop himself falling. From the rear window of the car a dog barked at him.

'What on earth do you think you're...' he began as the driver emerged. It was Bunderlin. 'You'll cause an accident driving like that, you idiot.'

'Martin, dear chap,' he began, ignoring his protestations, 'I really must have a word with you. Let me put your bike in the back of the car.'

'But I can't... I need to get home.'

Before Martin could remount and ride on, or do anything to stop him, Bunderlin lifted the tailgate and began to manhandle the bike inside.

'There we are. Hop in and we'll get on our way.'

Reluctantly, he got into the passenger seat as Bunderlin squeezed his great bulk into an arrangement of angle iron, plywood and cushions where the driver's seat used to be. The dog, denied its comfortable place in the back, climbed over onto

Martin's knee. They continued along Middleton Road and Martin assumed at first that he was being taken home to his flat. But they drove past the top of his road and headed out towards the moors.

'Where are we going?'

'I have something to do. It won't take very long.'

At the top of the long climb they reached open country and pulled into a lay-by above Rumbold Lake. Martin waited for Bunderlin to explain himself. And he waited.

'How long are we going to sit here?'

'As long as may be fruitful.'

'So what are we waiting for?'

'Nothing, dear chap. Nothing at all. Just look and drink in the peace and beauty.' He wound down the window and inhaled deeply. 'Doesn't it make you want to sing for joy and soar like a bird?'

'Not at this time on a Friday afternoon, it doesn't.' But, in fact, the sweet fresh air did lift his spirits for it was a welcome change from the noxious fumes he had tolerated all afternoon.

'Ah, my poor, dull-spirited earthbound little friend, you must learn to rejoice. Sing out for joy!'

The daft bugger actually means it, Martin thought as the big man began to sing in a tuneless and strangely high pitched voice, *Oh, for the wings, for the wings of a dove.*

Suddenly he became almost sensible again. 'I need you to do something for me.' He was staring intently ahead across the lake. 'Will you help me? Please tell me you will help me.'

'Depends what you want, of course.'

'One volunteer is worth ten Preston men. I need you to volunteer.'

'So tell me what you want me to do and I suppose I might do it for you if I can.'

'I need you to go to a meeting. Just go there and tell me about it later. That's all. Nothing more than that. Nothing at all. Nothing.'

'What sort of meeting? Where is it? You don't mean now, do you? There's no way I can go anywhere right now.'

Bunderlin made no reply but resumed his fixed gaze straight ahead. 'It's getting late,' he said after a few minutes. Must get you home. But can you just do one thing before we go?' He rummaged amongst an assortment of papers in the door pocket and found a small book, which he handed to Martin. 'Open it at page four five one. There, can you read the poem in the middle?'

Martin opened it and found the page. He read through the poem quickly and offered it back. 'There, I've read it. What now?'

'No. Outside.' Bunderlin reached into the back of the car and pulled an old yellow and green cake tin from the junk underneath Martin's bike. 'Come with me,' he said, opening the door. The dog ran off into the copse a short distance away and Bunderlin headed towards a stile at the side of the lay-by and down the footpath towards the lake. Then, standing at the water's edge, he asked Martin to read the verse again.

'*Remember me when I am gone away,*' he began.

'Louder. It has to be louder,' said Bunderlin. 'As if you're calling to the birds at the other side.'

He tried again.

'That's better. That's very good. Do it like that. When I say ready, you start reading.'

Martin began to recite the poem to the distant moorhens and Bunderlin, who had taken the lid off the cake tin, was throwing handfuls of whitish grey powdery stuff over the water.

'*Remember me when I am gone away,*
Gone far away into the silent land;
When you can no more hold me by the hand,
Nor I half turn to go yet turning stay.
Remember me when no more day by day
You tell me of our future that you planned:
Only remember me; you understand
It will be late to counsel then or pray.

Yet if you should forget me for a while
And afterwards remember, do not grieve:
For if the darkness and corruption leave
A vestige of the thoughts that once I had,
Better by far you should forget and smile
Than that you should remember and be sad.'

When he came to the end of the verse, there was still some of the powdery stuff left. Bunderlin simply tipped it into the reeds growing at the water's edge and shouted across the lake, 'Sing for joy, gentle spirit! Soar like a bird!'

He pulled a grubby rag from his pocket, wiped the inside of the cake tin, and led the way back to the lay-by calling as he went, 'Kenneth! Come here!' Eventually the dog came running up. Wet, very dirty and smelling almost as foul as a leaky chemical plant, he resumed his place on Martin's knee as they drove back into town and straight to Martin's flat. 'What did we do just now?' Martin asked as he pulled his bike from the car. He was pretty sure that he knew the answer, but why a cake tin, for goodness' sake?

'We did something very special,' Bunderlin replied. 'Thank you. You have been very kind to me.'

Martin wanted to press him for an explanation but there was a tear rolling down the big man's face. It could wait until another time.

Six

Later that evening, Martin set off to walk into the town centre and join the usual group around the pool tables in the Haymarket. Just outside the flats, however, a black Citroen Safari estate was waiting. Bunderlin called from the open window, 'Martin, dear boy! Over here.'

'What now?' Martin asked.

'I'm striking while the ironing board is hot. Carpet Diem. No time like the present, no tense like the pluperfect.'

'What are you talking about?'

'It's that very special favour you so kindly agreed to do for me. Come on, in you get and I'll take you.'

'Take me where? Anyway, I didn't actually agree to anything.'

'For goodness' sake, dear boy, don't stand there talking and asking questions all day. Get in or you'll be late.'

'I can't. You'll have to… well, I don't know, but I can't. I have other things to do,' Martin replied and began to walk away. Bunderlin drove on slowly and stopped a little ahead of him, but Martin carried on towards the end of the road. This time Bunderlin drove off, turned the corner and disappeared. Relieved, Martin hurried on in the direction of the town centre but when he came to the petrol station the now all too familiar black car was waiting on the forecourt. Bunderlin was standing with the passenger door open.

'Don't be difficult, Martin,' he called. 'I really must ask you for this one favour.'

'And then will you leave me alone?'

'Of course I will, if that's what you want. Now hurry up. We still have time.'

Once again, with even less eagerness than before, he got into the car and Bunderlin pulled forward to the petrol pumps. As he was about to start filling his tank, the woman from the kiosk came up to him. 'Oi, you, you clumsy great twerp! Let your friend do that for you for God's sake.'

He handed the nozzle to Martin. 'She thinks I might spill some.'

Martin filled up and Bunderlin handed him a roll of banknotes. He went to the kiosk.

'Friend of yours, is he?' said the woman at the till.

'I suppose he is really.'

'Aye, well, he's a barmy sod. Harmless, of course—except when he's filling up. Gets more on the tarmac than in the tank. I've told him I don't want him coming here again, but does he take any notice? Does he buggery.'

Martin got back into the car and they drove into town, turned into Eastgate and went to the far end where the shops were all very shabby and run down. Bunderlin braked suddenly outside a radio and TV shop and pointed to a window in the upper storey. 'There. That's where it is.'

Martin looked up. A board in the window advertised the Suhija Meditation Centre.

'So what are you asking me to do?'

'See that door between the shops? You go in there and up the stairs. Just tell them you're interested in how they do things. That's all you need to say. It'll only be about an hour. Then when it's over, come back and find me in the Swan. And bring a friend.'

Martin hesitated, not quite sure what he was being asked to do. 'OK then. I suppose I might as well. But at least tell me why you can't go yourself.'

'Because I am Bird and you are Martin. And a martin is only a small bird. Now hurry up, they'll be starting. Or redstarts or starlings.'

Martin got out of the car, went up to the door and rang the bell. A tall thin man let him in. 'Come in, my friend. New, aren't you? Who recommended you?'

'Er, Peter Bunderlin.'

'I don't know him. But come on in anyway. Top of the stairs and go through the door.'

Martin walked into the room and, closing the door behind him, stood for a few moments looking round. It was thickly carpeted and furnished with armchairs, settees and coffee tables. The air was quite clear but there was a hint of incense. There were about a dozen men but no women in the room. Nobody paid any attention to Martin so he went across to an empty armchair on the far side. A few people were talking but most were just sitting silently looking vacantly into the centre of the room. After a few minutes a young, fair-haired man in shorts and a t-shirt came across and sat on the coffee table beside Martin.

'Hello. I'm Sayeed. This your first time here?'

'Yes.'

'Let me introduce you, then. I don't know everybody. Just a few actually.' He waved a limp arm around, presumably picking out the few whose names he knew. 'That's Edwin in the corner. Oswyn. Coniston. Torquil. That's Ingleby who's just come in. And the guy by the window is David. He's new as well. And you are?'

'Martin.'

'Martin,' Sayeed repeated to the room in general. 'We'll all be going into the latihan in a little while. Once you're initiated, if you decide that's what you want, you'll be able to join us. Usually takes about three weeks. Then, if we feel you're ready, we'll do the necessary and you can be a full member. David is going to be initiated tonight.'

He left Martin to sit staring into the middle of the room, wondering why he had let himself be persuaded to come to this odd gathering. After about twenty minutes a bell rang and Sayeed stood up without a word and one by one everyone else stood also. As they filed out through the door at the far end, more incense wafted into the room. When the last person had left, six or seven women came in. Last in the line – and Martin realised at once that he should have expected her – was Veryan. She went to sit down almost opposite but then, having spotted him, she came across.

Martin held up his hands. 'Look, I had no idea you would be here.'

She smiled wryly. 'I take it Bird sent you. Where is he?'

'Says he'll be in the Swan later tonight.'

'Well, that's an easy place to avoid.'

'Does he still bother you? Follow you about, I mean.'

'No. Haven't seen him for weeks, thank God. Of course, he doesn't need me now, does he?'

'Oh? Why not?'

''Cause he's got you.'

'I hardly think so,' Martin replied.

'Don't kid yourself. He's got you all right. That's for sure.'

Veryan appeared rather more relaxed and friendly than she had been when Martin had seen her before. Relaxed, friendly and attractive. Bunderlin's words came into his mind: 'Strike while the ironing board is hot. Carpet Diem.'

'I wonder if... Well, I thought maybe... Would you like to come out for a meal some time?' he asked.

'No way,' she responded at once. 'So long as you're Bird Bunderlin's poodle, I don't want to know you.'

Veryan's emphatic rejection him stung far more than Martin could have thought it would. It was not just that she had turned him down. That was something everybody experiences and learns to shrug off. It was being called Bunderlin's poodle that he really disliked because it wasn't true and it wouldn't ever be true. He was in control and for anyone to suggest otherwise was simply uncalled for. After a short while he slipped out.

Seven

It was well after midnight when he returned home, relieved to have been able to avoid Bunderlin for the rest of the evening. He would come looking for him sooner or later, that was certain, and it would be difficult or even impossible to avoid him completely, but in future Martin would say no and mean it, and would not allow himself to be cajoled into doing the big man's bidding. Pity about Veryan's all too definite put-down, but he would not give up. Quite apart from anything else, it would be interesting and useful to find out what she knew about their mutual acquaintance. Time and a different approach, that was all it needed.

The door bell rang and Martin groaned. 'Who the bloody hell…? Surely not?' He walked quietly to the door and looked through the spy-hole. It was Bunderlin. Well, he would not open the door to him, especially not at this time of night.

The bell rang again but still Martin did not answer it. The letter box rattled. 'Go away. For God's sake, go away,' Martin muttered silently through clenched teeth. Then he heard a knocking at the flat next door. He looked through the spy-hole just as his neighbour opened her front door in her dressing gown.

'No, he's not gone away,' she was saying. 'Heard him come in not long since so he must be in there. Here, let me.' She gave three short rings on the bell and began to call through the letter box.

'Mr Latham! Are you in there? There's somebody wants to see you, so look sharp. Disturbing the neighbours at this time of night. Wake up, Mr Latham!'

'Damn the stupid woman,' Martin muttered and opened the door.

'I'm going to complain to the Housing Association,' she called whilst closing her door. 'One o'clock in the morning, I ask you.'

Bunderlin stepped inside unbidden, closely followed by Kenneth, his fox terrier, and handed Martin a bottle of white wine. 'Fetch a couple of glasses, there's a good chap, and you shall have an explanation.'

'I don't need an explanation and I don't want your wine, thank you very much,' Martin replied, handing the bottle back to him. 'I just need a peaceful night's sleep.'

'Don't talk such nonsense. Of course you want a glass of wine. *A loaf of bread, a flask of wine and thou beside me. And wilderness is paradise.*' He went to the tiny kitchen where Kenneth had already begun his own exploration of the flat by upending the waste bin and sorting through its contents. Bunderlin began to open cupboards and drawers, apparently looking for glasses and a corkscrew.

'OK, if you really must,' said Martin. 'Ten minutes and one glass. And then I want you out. Do you understand me?' He took the bottle from Bunderlin and barely half filled two small glasses. 'Right, come and sit down.'

'It's so kind of you to invite me in. But I realised I simply had to come and tell you.'

'Tell me what?'

'Patience, dear boy, patience. You're very stingy with the wine, you know. Partial abstainer, are you? Here, give me that.' He took Martin's glass and his own and went back to the kitchen. He returned with the bottle tucked under his arm and both glasses filled to the brim.

'Now, let me begin.' He thought for a moment as if wondering where to start whatever it was he wanted to say. 'In a churchyard not very far from here, there lies interred…' He stopped and tried to stifle a laugh. 'I'm reminded of… Oh dear.' He gave way to a burst of uncontrollable hooting. 'I'm reminded of an unfortunate old man from north of the border. You must know of the one.' He began to recite a limerick.

'*There was an old man of Strathclyde,*
Who collapsed in a toilet and died.
His unfortunate brother
Collapsed in another.
And now they're interred side by side.

'But that is beside the point. Let me start again. In this churchyard there lies, I think we had better say buried. There lies buried. But the lies are not buried. They resound from the rooftops. And it is, of course the brambles that are berried. Ah, this tangle of words. The words crawl in, the words crawl out.' He drained his glass and clumsily refilled it, spilling wine onto the table.

He resumed his tale. 'I've found a way through the verbiage. In the churchyard, down amongst the graves, there reposes in a shallow plot a small casket of the sort used for the ashes of cremated bodies. The one I speak of is different from all the rest. You see, the priest, he spoke such nonsense. So when he told me that I must have the ashes placed in hollowed hallowed ground, I told him I would keep them in a hollow in the house. But he was a stubborn old fool so I gave him the casket and we buried it in his churchyard and he recited an ancient Hebrew poem over it. What he doesn't know is that I kept the ashes and what he buried was shovelled out of a bonfire in my garden.'

Despite himself, Martin laughed. Told by Bunderlin, the story was even plausible, though he was not completely sure whether to believe him. 'You're having me on.'

'Indeed I am not. My story is truer than anything that priest has ever told from his pulpit. His sermon was rubbish, he should pulp it. I would like to have used the remains of one of her animals, but they all died long before she did and we didn't keep them.'

'Who?'

'My mother, dear boy. A fine lady. A princess. A Rhine maiden.'

'And what did you do with the real ashes?' Martin asked, suspecting that he already knew the answer.

'We scattered them upon the water this very afternoon. For which, dear boy, my thanks.'

He had suspected as much, of course, but he had hoped it was one of the animals, one of the goats. But no, it was the goat lady herself and Martin wished he had known when they had done it.

'And now I shall leave you,' said Bunderlin. 'You can tell me about the incense burners another time. Rest in peace. Dressed in pieces of clothing.'

Martin closed the door, heaved a sigh of relief, and went to the kitchen to tidy up after the dog and to make himself some cocoa. Kenneth, however, had stayed behind, sneaked back to the kitchen and had resumed his task of sorting out the rubbish. He looked up at Martin and wagged his tail.

Martin lay awake, unable to get the day's events out of his mind. Bunderlin's story was, in turns, hilariously funny and deeply disturbing. It was the material of a barely believable comedy but it called up images of bodies buried on the moors, their whereabouts known only to the tortured and twisted souls who had put them there. Most irrational of all, perhaps, as he lay there tired but unable to sleep, Martin began to feel strangely drawn to that mad giant who had loped into his world like a gangling playful puppy that could not understand the word *no*.

The doorbell was ringing and Kenneth had begun to bark. Martin reached for his watch. Six o'clock. Post already? Surely not. Why can't he just leave the packet or whatever it is on the doorstep? He pulled on a pair of trousers and went to the door.

It was Bunderlin, looking even grubbier and more unkempt than usual. He was grinning broadly and holding up something wrapped in a black plastic bin bag. Kenneth, on seeing his master return, suddenly sprang to life and came running up letting out a noise that combined howling and barking. He jumped and pranced around Bunderlin, wagging his tail so furiously that he could barely stay on his feet.

'Come in, for heaven's sake, before you wake the neighbours for a second time.' Martin went back to his bedroom to find a shirt. When he came out again, Bunderlin had gone into the kitchen and was triumphantly unwrapping his package. 'Here we are,' he said gleefully. 'If you didn't believe me last night, there's your proof.' He placed a very muddy box on the draining board and began to clean it off with a jug of water and a scrubbing brush.

'What on earth have you got there?' Cautiously, Martin stepped forward for a closer look. It was a wooden box, about a foot square and six inches high. It looked like oak but was almost blackened by moisture. A metal plate on the lid was still perfectly legible. *Greta Bunderlin. 1920 – 1970.*

Martin tried to control the rising panic. 'What is it? Where did you get it? What have you been doing, for God's sake?'

'Just retrieving what should never have been left where it was. Doesn't belong there, you see. That's all,' Bunderlin replied cheerfully.

'From the…? You mean you went and dug it up?'

'From the churchyard. Yes, that's right.'

Perhaps it was a good thing that the dog had stayed behind, Martin thought. 'But you idiot, that's a criminal offence. It must be. I mean, digging up human remains. For heaven's sake, man, get it out of here.'

'Not human remains at all. Like I told you. Here, let me show you.' He took a large screwdriver from his pocket and began to prise off the lid of the casket. 'They're only buried a foot down, these things, you know. Here we are, it's coming now.' The lid came off and revealed a dark grey lumpy stuff that had caked solid. He began to poke at it with his screwdriver to loosen it up. 'Ah, look at this! This is what I gave that silly old priest to bury. I'd been burning various things so if I'm right there should be...' He chipped away at a lump of the stuff. 'And there it is! Take a look at that.' He handed Martin a dusty lump of something that looked at first alarmingly like a fragment of bone. 'That didn't come from the crematorium. It came from a bonfire in my garden.'

Warily Martin brushed away the dust and ash with a finger. It was not bone at all. It was part of the charred spine of a book with the burned stubble of the pages on one side and the stitching on the other. 'OK, you've made your point. I believe you. Now I think you'd better go and clean yourself up and I'll make a pot of tea. And then you and your dog can get this junk out of here.'

Whilst Martin was making the tea, Bunderlin came back to the kitchen wiping his still muddy hands on a towel. 'I've been thinking,' he said. 'I'll leave all this stuff here. Just to be on the safe side. I mean if the police decide to come and tell me that some ghoulish vandals have been digging among the graves, I wouldn't want them to find that casket. So I'll let you get rid of it for me.'

Martin said nothing. And Bunderlin fell asleep on the settee with Kenneth resting his head in his lap.

Eight

Bunderlin had gone away again but this time there was no picture postcard. Instead, it was a hurried note scribbled on a torn-off scrap of brown wrapping paper and, as before, posted in Manchester. He was on his way to Scotland and had to rush to catch the post before his train left. He would return in a few days.

Martin tried to recall when it was that he first realised the big man who had been following him was Peter Bunderlin. That time at the car dealer's clinched it when Bunderlin spoke and immediately began to play about with the words. Until then he was just an exceptionally big man who didn't seem quite so awe-inspiring to an adult as to a small child.

The next time that Martin visited his parents, instead of going by the direct route, he took a detour past his old primary school. The house on the corner was now even more neglected than it had been years ago. From the road he could see that much of the paint had flaked away from the window frames which were, in some places showing signs of rotting away. Grimy curtains hung in tatters at the upper windows and the front garden was thoroughly overgrown. Outside, parked at a crazy angle half on the pavement and half on the road, was a black Citroen Safari estate.

He stopped to take a closer look. From the gate in the lane at the side of the house, the back garden appeared much the same as he remembered it, except that there were no longer any pigs or goats to be seen. Long grass was beginning to cover the once bare earth and the bushes at the end were starting a slow advance towards the rusting Anderson shelter. The doors of the garage were almost off their hinges and were propped in place with a felled tree trunk and a wooden railway sleeper.

Whilst Martin was still peering over the broken gate, the back door opened and a large old man with a walking stick shuffled into the garden. 'Who are you? What do you want?' he shouted.

'Mr Bunderlin?'

'Yes, I am. I am Franz Bunderlin. What do you want?'

'I'm a friend of Peter's,' Martin ventured. 'Is he at home?'

'No. Peter is not here.'

'Sorry for troubling you. Cheerio.'

He continued on his journey and a few moments later Franz Bunderlin drove past in the Citroen. If he hadn't known already, Martin could have mistaken him for Peter.

Later in the day, on his way home, he took the same route but did not pause at the house. About a mile further on, however, he spotted a familiar large form leaning against a telephone kiosk. 'Hello,' he said, dismounting from his bike. 'I thought you were in Scotland.'

Bunderlin made no reply but continued staring fixedly ahead. 'You never asked me about what went on at the meditation centre,' he tried. Still no reply. Martin remounted his bike without moving away.

Several minutes seemed to pass and then Bunderlin suddenly said, 'It's late,' and set off at a brisk pace, turned down an alleyway between the houses and disappeared in the direction of the railway station.

'Daft bugger. Don't know why I bother,' Martin muttered and rode on home.

A couple of days later, when Martin arrived home from work one evening in mid September, Bunderlin was waiting in the main doorway of the flats. 'Good day and greetings, dear boy,' he called as Martin approached. He held out a plastic shopping bag. 'I brought you some dinner. A souvenir from a far country.'

Martin looked into the bag. Inside was a round brownish speckled thing which seemed to be fastened at top and bottom with staples. 'What is it?'

'A haggis,' replied Bunderlin. 'A hag is a witch, but a haggis is not a witch. Which should you eat? No, you should eat the haggis.' He hurried away down the path, across the parking area and on towards the main road.

As Martin turned the haggis over in his hands wondering what he was supposed to do with it, he noticed that it was beginning to go mouldy. He smiled, wondering how long Bunderlin must have had it. So, that was it? A not very convincing attempt to prove that he had, after all, been to Scotland and that whoever it might have been by the telephone kiosk the other day, it could not have been Bunderlin? Martin dropped the haggis into the waste bin and began to prepare a chicken curry, hoping that Bunderlin would not return some time later expecting to share a portion of haggis.

He did return about two hours later but if he'd had any thoughts of eating they seemed to have been forgotten. As he drank tea in complete silence, Martin noticed a distinct smell of petrol. Careless, as usual, at the filling station, he thought.

'So did you enjoy your trip to Scotland? Where did you go?'

'Glasgow, Stirling, Falkirk, Edinburgh, Dundee, Ayr, Glasgow, Dundee. I didn't go to Inverness. I've never been to Inverness. I'll go to Inverness next year.' He began to laugh. 'Invernext year. Invernext. Nessnext. But not Aberdeen. I won't go to Aberdeen. Aberdeen, gabardine, mackintosh. It rains all the time.'

From the distance there came the sound of an emergency vehicle siren and for a brief moment Martin wondered if Bunderlin had, in his carelessness, set fire to the filling station. 'Listen!' said

Bunderlin. 'They're here! Must go and see what's happening.' He hurried out but Martin let him go without making any attempt to follow.

There were at least two more sirens before Martin grabbed his jumper, draped it around his shoulders and set off to walk to the Haymarket. When he crossed the top end of Clayton Lane he noticed a blue flashing light reflected in a shop window so, curious at last to see what was going on, he took the slightly longer way to the pub. Coming round the bend of the road he saw two fire engines and a police car by the row of shops opposite the old Grammar School. A small group of people had gathered on the opposite side of the road to watch and, separated from them by a few yards, was Bunderlin.

Martin approached him, not at all sure whether he would be capable of intelligible conversation. 'What's been going on?'

'Obvious, dear boy. There's been a fire at Webster's barber shop.'

'Anyone hurt?'

'Probably. They took someone away in an ambulance. Old Webster, I should think.' He sounded quite unconcerned for the barber's welfare. 'Didn't think he would be there at this time of night. *Come into my parlour, said the spider to the fly,* said the Webster to the firefly. *Oh what a tangled web we weave.* Tangled webs woven for Webster.'

'Poor old guy. Anyway, I'm not going to stop here. I'm going for a drink. I'll see you around.'

Just as he was about to walk away, a Morris Minor drew up. The driver leaned across and wound down the window as one of the bystanders approached him. She returned to say something to her friends and then got into the car. As it drove away a buzz of chatter began and the message was relayed from the front of the crowd to the back. A woman in front of Martin turned around and said, 'Hear that? He was dead when they got him there.' Before turning back to her friends, she paused. She looked puzzled, disturbed even. Had she noticed the smell of petrol? Martin wondered.

Bunderlin turned his back to the woman and whispered something which Martin could not quite make out. But he thought it might have been, 'Serves him right.' He began to chant softly, '*Webster cuts your hair, Webster cuts your hair, ee eye addio, Webster cuts your hair.*'

'For heaven's sake, shut up, you idiot,' Martin hissed.

'Shut up shop. *The man recovered from the bite, the dog it was that died.*'

'I'm going for a drink,' Martin said and waited briefly to see whether Bunderlin would respond. He said nothing.

'What's up with you, you morose get?' said Terry late the following afternoon. 'You've been moping around all day like an undertaker's donkey. You're supposed to be happy, for God's sake, leaving this place. Realised it's all a big mistake, have you?'

'No, of course not. It's something else.'

'Well, go on then. Spill the beans.'

'No I can't. I'm probably completely wrong.'

'Since when did being wrong stop you sounding off?'

'Well it does now. I'm going down to the filters to collect the samples.' He took a palette knife and a sampling iron and went out onto the plant. But the filtration was not finished so he would have to return later. More waiting around doing nothing and, most probably, a late finish, which was especially irksome on a Friday.

Terry was making tea when he returned to the lab. 'Not ready yet? Come and do this crossword. Hey, did you hear about that fire last night? Dirty Sam Webster got frizzled.'

'Yes, I know.'

'Well I'll be buggered. Except now we won't, of course. Must be someone somewhere who'll miss him.'

'I think I know who did it,' Martin blurted out. 'Well, no, I don't. It's got to be completely wrong. Can't be right, but I can't help thinking... well, what if..?'

'Come on, then, tell it all. What do you reckon? Someone you know, was it? Someone I know?'

'No. It's got to be wrong.'

'But it's not wrong, is it? Oh, God, it's not that daft sod you thought you were going to buy a car from, is it? Told you not to speak to strangers—and they don't come stranger than him.'

He should have kept his unfounded suspicions to himself, and he should have known that if he did not, Terry would constantly harp on about his duty to inform the police. Really, Terry didn't nag, but it felt like that to Martin and he decided to give the Haymarket a miss that evening. A quiet evening in front of the television with a couple of cans of beer would help to erase his error in letting out what he should not.

But the television was just as bad as Terry. An item on the local news reported the police's difficulties in apprehending persistent offenders who were shielded within a culture in which grassing on a friend or neighbour was the ultimate offence. And later the early evening news reported the death of Jimi Hendrix. He died on the way to hospital apparently, and that reminded Martin of Sam Webster. Then a brief tribute referred to Hendrix's setting fire to his guitar at the Monterey Pop Festival. Thinking he might as well put up with Terry's nagging, Martin drained his glass and went to the Haymarket.

Nine

Martin waited near the meditation centre but when, at last, people began to emerge, Veryan was not among them. He tried sitting in the café near the Wheatsheaf in case he should see her walking past, for didn't she live somewhere nearby? Perhaps he should simply go straight to the police with his suspicions as Terry insisted he ought, but he was not entirely convinced that he was right and wanted to speak with Veryan first. She probably knew Bunderlin fairly well, after all, so perhaps a chat with her would help him to clarify his thoughts.

Eventually he spotted her one Friday evening in the Haymarket with a group of women he recognised from the meditation centre. He crossed his name off the pool table list and went over to her. He was prepared for her to be mad at him for approaching her but she remained calm and friendly, even if she was not pleased to see him.

'Look, I wouldn't do this if I didn't have to, but, well, I really do need to speak with you. It's about Bird. I'm worried about him.'

'Well don't say I didn't warn you. What's he been up to?'

'Is this the big chap who used to hang about outside the centre?' asked one of the others.

'The same. OK, ten minutes. What's the problem?'

'No, in private. It's a bit, well, delicate, really. Rather complicated in a way.'

'Oh well, if you really must. You'd better phone me.' She wrote her number on a beer mat and handed it to him. Then, slightly closing the circle round their table, she picked up the conversation which Martin had interrupted. He took the hint and left them.

Veryan was willing enough, though in a resigned sort of way, to meet him the following morning in the Buttery coffee bar. She arrived just a few minutes after Martin but wanted to go somewhere else right away.

'There's something I want to show you,' she said. 'If you want to know what sort of guy Bird is, you should see this. If it happens.'

He took a mouthful of coffee and followed her out. 'Where are we going?'

'You'll see. I didn't realise till I came past just now. Otherwise I would've suggested it when you phoned.'

She led the way down a side street, which emerged behind the Town Hall. Further along, they came to a launderette nearly opposite the Pelican. 'There we are,' she said, pointing to the pub.

'What? I don't get it. What's this got to do with Bird?'

'My guess is he'll show up in a little while. To meet a couple of friends, you might say. See those beer crates and the notice?' The crates were apparently intended to reserve an unloading space outside the pub, for the notice read, *Please keep clear. Delivery this morning.*

Martin and Veryan went into the launderette and sat on the bench in the window. 'I can't imagine why you've brought us here. But, look, I just wanted to get your reaction, I suppose. I'm worried about Bunderlin. Bird. This will sound crazy, but you heard about the fire at the barber's shop?'

She looked startled. 'Do you know something about it?'

'I'm not sure. I hope I'm wrong. But, well, I suspect Bird might have done it.'

'Bird? Why, for heaven's sake?'

He told her briefly about his suspicions, the smell of petrol and Bunderlin's almost gleeful reaction to the news of Webster's death.

'This is too much to take in. I can't imagine that you're right. It's just not him. OK, he might have been sloshing petrol around but haven't you ever seen him fill his car, the clumsy oaf? Always does manage to get it all over himself. If he started a fire he'd set himself alight as well. Mind you, if it was him it would take a weight off my mind. 'Cause while you've been worrying about him, I've been worrying about someone else.'

'Someone else? Well, that would… Who?'

'I'm not saying. No way. I've got no reason to link him to the fire. It's just that he really hated Webster. I mean really hated him. But I suppose plenty of others did as well.'

'Why?'

'Because he was too fond of letting his hand wander up small boys' trouser legs. Don't see Bird ever getting that treatment somehow. But how would I know what turns a guy like that on?'

'Gosh. I never knew. I knew the old playground chants, of course—*ee aye addio, Webster grabs your bum*—but I never thought it was for real.'

Before he could pursue the significance of this, Veryan interrupted his thoughts.

'Look. The pub.'

A dray, pulled by two immaculately turned out sleek brown cart horses, had drawn up outside the pub. Three men got down from it and whilst two set about preparing to deliver the pub's order, the third stood with the horses. Martin and Veryan watched as the men began to unload the barrels and crates.

'There!' said Veryan after a little while. 'I knew it. Over there by the bus stop. Come to meet his friends.'

It was Bunderlin, with Kenneth, watching what was going on but showing no sign of wanting to approach the draymen. He stayed at the bus stop until they had finished unloading. They closed the cellar trapdoors and went into the pub and the third man left his horses and joined them. Bunderlin approached the horses. Did they recognise him, or was Martin imagining it? Bunderlin came close to the offside horse and stood directly in front of it. The animal raised his head, seemed to snort, and then Bunderlin stepped a little closer. The two, man and horse, stood nose to nose for several minutes and Kenneth sniffed around the dray, raising his leg at each wheel in turn. Bunderlin stroked the horse's muzzle and produced some titbit from his pocket. Moving to the other horse, he repeated the ritual. Finally, he turned and walked slowly back to the bus stop and the horses tried to follow for a few steps before jerking to a halt.

'So, is that the guy you thought you knew?'

'Oh, sure it is,' Martin replied. 'I knew his mother when I was kid. She shared her house with an assortment of livestock. Goats, pigs, you name it.'

'Well, that fits. The only way I could understand him was to think of him as one of the animals. It's how he relates to people— or doesn't relate. Either you're his dog, or he's your dog. Nothing else works. Which makes him one big pain in the neck and I'd be glad to see no more of him. But I'm sure he's basically harmless. In fact, he can be incredibly kind and generous. Really helped me out when I needed it. Then when I'd got settled into my flat he gave me his mother's old sewing machine. A rather good Singer, it was. Maybe that was just an attempt to buy friendship. I don't know. I can't cope with him and sometimes I feel a bit guilty about it because he's a good guy, really, in his own silly way.'

'Well, perhaps you're right. It was the gleeful relish when he was there just after the fire which did it for me. But maybe that doesn't mean very much at all.'

Martin expected Veryan to leave but instead she went for coffees from the drinks machine. She returned as Martin was watching Bunderlin walk away in the direction of the Town Hall,

Kenneth close at his side. 'So, tell me about yourself. You've got to have more going on than just meeting Bird now and again. Or trying not to,' she added with a smile.

It hadn't helped very much. When he thought of the daft bugger who communed with horses, whose closest friend was his dog, who contrived that bizarre ceremony for the scattering of his mother's ashes, Martin was pretty sure that Bunderlin was no arsonist. But when he thought of the big man smelling of petrol, so gleefully flippant just after the fire, and as excited as a small child waiting to meet Santa Claus, he was just as sure that the fire was Bunderlin's doing.

Veryan had taken him by surprise. Always threatening to call the police to get him off her back, to put an end to his insufferable pestering. So he had been quite sure she would say, shop him and serve him right, the dangerous old sod. He wasn't expecting that underneath her exasperation and anger with the big man she would have any warmth of feeling for him. And he wasn't expecting her hand on his arm as she stood up to leave the launderette, and the lovely sweet smile. 'Don't let him needle you,' she had said, and then she was gone. But he still had the beer mat with her phone number. And hadn't she said to him, one way or another, that she was ready now to accept that invitation for a meal together?

Ten

Jack Latham had achieved the modest success which, south of the railway line, was as much as anyone could easily comprehend. Being a time-served tradesman, an electrician, he already belonged to the working class elite, but his five years in REME during and just after the war had given him sufficient extra qualifications and experience to leapfrog the ultimate goal of foreman by the age of fifty. He dithered for ages and had already let a couple of chances slip by until at last, encouraged by Dorothy his wife, he applied for the post of Third Engineer. His surprise and delight at being appointed were to stay with him throughout the rest of his working life but he didn't let it go to his head. He remained loyal to his roots and when they decided to move out of their council house he insisted that they should buy a property south of the railway line.

To Martin it seemed that his father could not understand why anyone should fail to be content with modest success. A man—women didn't come into the reckoning—had a duty of loyalty to his firm and to his roots. Having gained his Higher National Certificate, Martin ought to be satisfied with that and trust that one day, when his turn came around, he might rise to the level of Plant Superintendent. Anything beyond that should be left to the hoity-toity brigade. For a working class lad to want a university degree, though if it was a BSc that might just have been OK, was like cats wanting to be dogs.

In fact, Martin had misunderstood his father completely. He had been fiercely critical and unsupportive when first he had said he was going to apply for university entrance and he remained so until his place was secure and he had resigned his job at Merrion Dyestuffs. Then it was, 'You'll do us proud, lad. I can see it now—you'll be one of them professor johnnies before we know it. Who was that chappie on the television? I know. A. J. P. Taylor. Now there was a clever man for you. And I can see you, our Martin, you'll be just the same. First of the Lathams to go to proper college.'

'There was Jean, Dad. Don't forget our Jean.'

'Aye, but that's different. Schoolteacher be buggered. She only ever wanted to be a farmer. Can't say that I blame her. If we'd stayed in Cheshire when we got wed, your mam and me, Jean would have gone to work on Pickvance's farm when the time came and she'd have been happy as the day is long and never mind your college nonsense.'

Martin followed as he systematically made his way around the garden, picking off dead flower heads as he went. They went into the greenhouse where the leggy tomato plants, stripped now of much of their foliage, bore a good crop of late ripening fruit. After a quick inspection of the plants and a poke here and there to test the moisture of the compost, Jack pulled a couple of stools from under the staging and lit a cigarette.

'I've decided not to get a car just yet, by the way,' said Martin, wanting to turn the conversation to the Bundy household.

'Just as well.'

'But you remember I said I was thinking about a Triumph Renown?'

'Oh aye. Now there's a decent car. You could do worse than a Renown, if you ask me.'

'The chap who was selling it is Peter Bunderlin. Remember him? Son of old Mrs Bundy, the goat lady from beside the school.'

'Well, that's the main thing. Know who it is you're buying from. I should think he'd be a pretty reliable sort.'

'Bit of an odd character, really. Can't make head nor tail of him. In fact, he seems completely batty at times.'

'Always was. Never said a word to anybody. Just stood there like piffy looking gormless. Solid, though. Good solid young chap.'

'That's him. I'm a bit worried about him, actually. Remember the fire a few nights ago at the barber's shop? I might be completely wrong but I can't help thinking he might have done it.'

'Shouldn't worry about it if I were you. Not your concern, is it?'

'Well it would be if I was sure about it.'

Suddenly Jack became quite serious and firm. 'Listen, Martin, you've let them down once before. Remember when that teacher put her oar in? What was her name?'

'Mrs Scattergood.'

'Aye, that one. A right name for her, that was. Scattergood all right. She says jump, so all meek and mild you jump. And you never went to see the lass again. Well, it isn't right. So don't do the same again. Remember who your friends are.'

'But if he really did do it…'

'I've just bloody told you. It's no concern of yours. If he did it, that's between him and his conscience and the police. You just keep out of it. Besides, the world's a better place without the likes of Sam Webster, the smarmy great poof.' Then he added, 'And don't say anything to your mam about this. She was very fond of that young goat lass. She didn't have it easy when she came over here. Not by a long chalk. So you just keep out of it.'

He set off to cycle home, no clearer in his mind than when he had come. His father had said just what he wanted to hear – leave it alone – but in doing so he had made Martin realise that he could not. He needed to be sure about what he believed had happened, and he needed to act appropriately. And he ought to make up his mind one way or the other fairly soon because within a few days he would be starting his university course.

The Citroen was parked outside Bunderlin's house when Martin rode past. He slowed down by the school gates and wondered if perhaps he should see whether the big man was home but decided not to. At that moment a brown and white dog appeared further along the pavement heading towards the house. It was Bunderlin's dog.

'Kenneth,' Martin called, stopping at the kerbside when it came near.

The dog stopped, looked up, and ran over to him, wagging his tail furiously.

'Where's your master?'

Kenneth cocked his head first to one side then to the other as if trying to make out what Martin was saying.

'What are you doing, out on your own?'

He sat and looked intently at Martin, waiting for him to say something intelligible. Martin guessed that he should probably not have called to the dog for he would most likely try to follow him once he set off again. Kenneth, however, glanced back up the road from where he had come and set off running towards Bunderlin who had appeared from round the corner. He ran back and forth the diminishing distance between Martin and Bunderlin before suddenly turning tail, running home and clearing the garden wall at a leap.

'Martin, dear chap. Greetings.
When all the world is young, lad,
And all the trees are green;
And every goose a swan, lad,
And every lass a queen;
Then hey for boot and horse, lad,
And round the world away,
Young blood must have its course, lad,

And every dog his day. '

Martin could think of no response.

'Look, dear boy, I need to see you later. Meet me in the Wheatsheaf in half an hour.' He raised an arm and set off towards the house.

It was before eight o'clock but a small group of hardened drinkers had already begun their evening session. Martin, who always felt a little guilty whenever he came to the pub so early, bought only a half pint of bitter and determined to make it last until nine. He picked up an evening paper which had been left on the bar and went over to a table near the window, as far away from the fruit machine as possible. A few minutes later Bunderlin came in with Kenneth, who jumped onto the bench seat beside Martin and thrashed the upholstery with his tail as he watched his master buying drinks at the bar.

The big man came to the table with two pints of beer. 'Greetings, dear boy,' he said. He picked up the empty ashtray, wiped it with a corner of his jacket and poured what remained of Martin's half pint into it. He placed it in front of Kenneth who lapped noisily and messily at it. Martin picked up the pint glass which Bunderlin had brought him and glanced at the clock. Five past eight. He would make this drink last until nine.

Gradually the bar filled up. The tapes playing softly in the background gave way to the juke box which was playing only Abba records. And at times the noisy fruit machine joined forces with Dancing Queen to make intelligent conversation quite impossible. From time to time Kenneth pawed Bunderlin's arm and he responded by reaching into his pocket for a dog biscuit. Nine o'clock came and Martin had managed to keep his intake down to two pints. Time now to stop counting.

The juke box and the fruit machine called a ceasefire and in the brief silence Martin took the chance to suggest moving somewhere quieter.

'Dear boy,' Bunderlin replied, 'if thine ear offend thee, pluck it off. Tis better to enter a pub deaf than hearing music be cast into hell fire. So let us go.' He stood up. Kenneth jumped down from the seat and ran to the door and Martin hastily finished the last of his beer.

Kenneth ran ahead of them and led the way to the Swan. He sat at the door and looked back to check that Bunderlin was still following. Then, while they were still some distance away, the dog took the first chance to go inside when the door was opened. A few moments later they followed him in but Martin could not spot him and Bunderlin seemed unconcerned. When they took their drinks to a table, it was a different dog who approached first, possibly the same mongrel Martin had seen there once before.

The Swan was smokier and grimier than the Wheatsheaf but its atmosphere was more conducive to conversation. There was something that had been nagging at Martin's conscience for a few days now, nothing to do with the fire, and he thought it was about time he spoke up. 'Look,' he began, 'you probably don't realise this but I used to know your mother years ago.' He didn't think it right any longer not to mention that he had visited their house all those years before. Openness. It was all about being open. Bunderlin just looked at him.

'I remember Kaspar and Konrad.'

The mongrel had been waiting long enough for his titbit and pawed at Bunderlin's knee. At once he got his biscuit.

'Do you remember Prowler?' Martin asked. 'The ginger cat.'

'Run, run as fast as you can,' Bunderlin replied. 'You can't catch me, I'm a ginger cat.'

'Yes, well, it was me who brought him for your mother to look after. Just thought I should tell you. My dad knew her as well.'

'And your mother.'

'Well I should imagine so, yes. We used to have an allotment at the back of your house. And I used to go to Barton Lane School.'

Bunderlin's only response was to raise his glass and empty it in one long draught.   A middle-aged couple, incongruously smart for the Swan, approached them.

'Hey, there,' the man said to Bunderlin. Remember me? New Street. About a year back.'

Bunderlin said nothing.

'Come on, you must remember. Cold as hell and two hours to wait for the train.'

'Not me,' said Bunderlin. He turned to Martin and asked him to wait ten minutes and then buy him another drink. 'I shall return anon. Or even sooner.' And then he left the pub.

'It's got to be the same guy,' said the middle-aged man after Bunderlin had gone. 'Can't be many others quite like him. Friend of yours, is he?'

Of course he was a friend. Why wouldn't Martin call him a friend? But something about the man made him feel a little wary. 'Well, I sort of know him a bit.'

'Right. New Street Station, it was, like I said. We got talking while we waited for the train. Anyway, I just wondered if it might be the same guy.'

'Could be, I suppose,' said Martin.

'Spoke to him last week, didn't you?' said the woman. 'When you saw him in the town centre. But he said it wasn't him then as well.'

'Well, there you are, then.'

'No, but… Well, I mean, a big bloke like that. Can't be many of them around.'

'Maybe he'd just forgotten seeing you. Does happen. He'll be back in a few minutes so you can ask him yourself.'

'Sure. Just curious, that's all,' said the man. 'If it's the same guy, he's weird, I can tell you that. Well, takes all sorts.' And with that, they left the pub.

An hour went by and still Bunderlin did not return. Kenneth, who had spent most of the time curled up near the cellar door, came and lay underneath Martin's table. If it wasn't for the dog he would have given up on Bunderlin and left ages before but he couldn't simply walk out on Kenneth. He couldn't believe that Bunderlin would do that either. To leave him behind at Martin's flat was one thing, but to leave him in the pub was another.

Martin bought another drink—it would be his last before closing time—and returned to his table. The barman called time and draped his glass cloths over the beer pumps. Kenneth came out from underneath the table and looked up at Martin. 'Looks like you're going to have to come home with me tonight.' He drained his glass and stood up. 'Come on, Kenneth.' The dog followed obediently as if he was used to going home with Martin.

Kenneth went into the flat ahead of Martin, who stopped to pick up a newspaper that had been pushed through the door. He went into the kitchen to make a mug of tea and put the newspaper down beside the kettle. That was when he noticed the scribbled note beside the headline: 'Martin. Look after Kenneth. I may be delayed.' And the report read: 'New lead in arson probe. Police today issued descriptions of two men they want to question in connection with the fire which killed barber Sam Webster...'

Eleven

Martin elbowed his way through the crowd shambling out of the lecture theatre and headed towards the underpass where he had chained his bike. What a start to his university course. Not the three lectures in one morning—it was to be some time yet before he would enter so thoroughly into university life that he would regard such a full morning as an imposition. It was not even the fact that he was obliged to take a third course—Politics, he'd not very eagerly opted for—in addition to the English and History that he really wanted to study. It was that interview with the police, four days ago now, which still nagged and dominated his thoughts and was already crowding out all he'd taken in of the introductory lectures.

He knew he should have come forward sooner with his suspicions. So he had gone to the police station expecting to be treated as an accomplice and he still felt that is how he was regarded even though both officers interviewing him had shown no hesitation in accepting his account of things. He wasn't charged, he wasn't arrested, he wasn't suspected in the least. He was just an innocent bystander doing his civic duty. But it didn't feel that way. And he felt really shabby after telling why he'd thought Bunderlin guilty. He cycled home to take Kenneth for a walk and to feed him. He'd let Bunderlin down but he would not let Kenneth down.

The afternoon following his visit to the police station, he had taken Kenneth back to the house expecting that Franz would be there to take him in. But there was no reply and the dog had been so confused when Martin had to bring him away again. Next time he would check at the house first and only take the dog back if he knew that Franz was going to be there. But he was never there.

He still wasn't there near the end of term or through the Christmas vacation. And then, shortly after the start of spring term, when Martin learned that the trial had been fixed for a date just before Easter, Jean called at the flat with Bill, her husband.

'Hey, guess what, our kid. We're moving.' For a long time they had been looking for a house nearer to their parents with enough land for Jean to indulge her long held wish to keep goats. At last they had found the ideal place near Kearsley. 'So, dearest brother, we'll be able to take this scruffy old mutt off your hands. Give him somewhere decent to run. It must've been a bit of a drag having him in this place all this time.'

It wasn't a drag at all. He'd got used to it and so had Kenneth but it was against the Housing Association's regulations to keep pets and Mrs Perry, the caretaker, had begun to remind him of the rules. 'Yes, I know. I'll see to it,' he'd told her more than once. He saw to it about half way through the spring term. He tried not to let anyone see how much he missed that dog. Just the trial now, and then the whole episode would be over.

The foyer of the Crown Court was busy as Martin entered and he had to remind himself that only a few, if any, of the people milling around had any interest in Bunderlin's case. Nervously he made his way to the witness room to which he had been directed, and felt a surge of relief as he stepped into the quiet and cool waiting area. Two others were already there. A police officer was reading his notes and a middle-aged man in a grey suit sat with his legs crossed and stared at the ceiling. The attendant handed Martin a copy of the statement which he had given to the police and suggested he read through it to refresh his memory and to check that all was in order.

Those preliminaries took no more than a few minutes. Martin tried to make himself comfortable and pulled the paperback book from his pocket. *Leviathan* by Thomas Hobbes. If he had to miss lectures, at least he would take whatever chance he had for reading set texts.

The three witnesses sat in silence throughout the morning and Martin was relieved when the lunchtime recess came and he could go, still in complete silence, to the cafeteria. Things speeded up after lunch. First, the police officer was called and, maybe an hour later, it was the turn of Dr Parkinson, whom Martin supposed was a forensic scientist. On his own in the witness room, Martin continued to wade through Hobbes until the usher came into the room and said that he could go home. 'Be here at ten o'clock prompt in the morning.'

The following day he settled in for an equally boring but anxious wait. The morning came to an end with an early lunch recess. And then, at last, he was called.

As he stepped into the witness box, Martin glanced across to the public gallery. There was small group of middle-aged men and women at one end. Webster's neighbours. On his own at the other end was a white haired old man and Martin thought that perhaps he ought to recognise him. Behind him, also on her own, was Veryan.

'… and nothing but the truth,' he heard himself saying. For a moment he felt a surge of panic as he feared that he would somehow lose track of what was going on. He confirmed his identity and looked at Bunderlin sitting in the dock staring vacantly at the ceiling. He wanted to say something to him. Anything—just 'Hello' would do.

'Relax, Mr Latham,' the surprisingly young-looking prosecuting counsel was saying. 'We just need to hear from you your answers to a few simple questions. Would you tell the court, please, what happened on the evening of Thursday the seventeenth of September last? From when you arrived home from work.'

'When I arrived home Bird was waiting for me outside the block of flats where I live.'

'Bird? Who is Bird?'

'Oh, Bunderlin. Peter Bunderlin.'

'It would help the court if you would refer to the defendant by his name,' said the Judge.

'Sorry, yes Bunderlin was waiting.' For a moment he felt flustered. Perhaps he should have said, 'Your Honour' or 'My Lord.' He had forgotten which. High Lord, Circuit Honour, that's what the attendant had said. And this was a High Court Judge, of course, because it was a murder case. Should he apologise and repeat himself? But his omission went unnoticed and the barrister continued his questioning.

'How long were you with him at that time?' the barrister asked for a second time.

'No time at all. Only a minute, if that. He had just returned from a trip to Scotland and had brought me a gift. Then he hurried away.'

'What did he bring you?'

'A haggis. A fairly old one, I think—it was beginning to go mouldy.' That was completely unnecessary, of course, but he had included it in his statement. He had thought at the time that Bunderlin must have bought it on a previous occasion and used it now in an attempt to establish the fiction of a trip to Scotland. Counsel did not pick up the point and Martin felt guilty for mentioning an irrelevant failing.

'Did he return later?'

'Yes. About an hour later. About seven o'clock.'

'And when he returned at seven, did you notice anything unusual about him?'

'He smelled of petrol.'

'Indeed, Mr Latham. He smelled of petrol. Was this just a slight smell or was it fairly strong?'

'It was fairly strong.'

'Strong enough for it to linger in the room after he had left?'

'Yes.'

'What happened next?'

'He told me about his trip to Scotland and then he left.'

'Were you aware of anything that prompted him to leave?'

'We heard sirens and he hurried off to see what was happening.'

'And you went with him?'

'No. I went out a little later. I met him near the barber's shop.'

'There was a crowd gathered, is that correct?'

'Yes. There had been a fire. Two fire engines and a police car were still there and lots of people were standing around watching.'

'And was Mr Bunderlin one of those people?'

'Yes.'

'When did you hear that Mr Webster had died?'

'While we were standing near the onlookers.'

'And how did Mr Bunderlin respond to that tragic news?'

'He began to recite an old playground chant about Webster.'

'And how would you describe his manner? Would you say he was upset by the news or not?'

'No, he was not upset.'

'He was not upset to hear that Mr Webster had died?'

'No. I didn't think so.'

'Thank you, Mr Latham. That is all.'

Prosecuting counsel sat down and Martin felt agitated. There was much more to be said. Those answers needed to be qualified, put into context but, presumably, that would be the job of the defending counsel.

'Do you wish to cross-examine the witness, Mr Mosscrop?' asked the judge.

'No, thank you, My Lord. I have no questions.'

'But…' Martin began in protest.

'That is all, Mr Latham. You may leave the witness box.'

Frustrated, he left the courtroom. 'Is that it?' he asked the usher. 'Don't I get a chance to add anything?'

'No, that's it. You can go home.'

'Can I go to the public gallery?'

'If you want. But remember you mustn't talk to anyone about the trial until it's all over.'

Martin made his way to the gallery to listen to what remained of the trial and took a seat at a discreet distance from Veryan. He was aware that she had looked towards him when he came in but he did not meet her eyes. As he sat down Bunderlin came to the witness box. Is that usual? Martin wondered, feeling fairly certain that it would be unwise to allow him to give evidence in his own defence. The Prosecution would tie him in knots.

It seemed at first that his counsel wanted to show only that Bunderlin did not intend the death of Webster, not that he was innocent of arson. 'When you went to Mr Webster's shop on that evening, did you intend that any harm should come to Mr Webster?'

'*I knew no harm of Bonaparte and plenty of the Squire.* No harm.'

'Would you simply answer yes or no, please, Mr Bunderlin. Did you think that whatever you might do to his shop, he would be perfectly safe?'

'Safe as houses. Safe as a bug in a rug. Simply yes.'

'Why did you think he would be safe?'

'He wasn't there.'

'Why did you think he was not there? Had you seen him somewhere else that same evening?'

'Yes.'

'Where?'

'In the Haymarket.'

'Are you sure? Are you sure that he had gone to the Haymarket Tavern?'

'No.'

The barrister looked surprised and appeared for a moment to lose his composure. But he quickly recovered. 'So why did you believe that Mr Webster was in the Haymarket?'

'Because he always goes to the Haymarket on Monday, Tuesday, Wednesday, Thursday and Friday evenings.'

'You heard Mr Latham tell the court that when you visited him that evening there was a strong smell of petrol on your clothes. Is that correct?'

'Yes.'

'Will you tell us why you smelled of petrol?'

'I had been using petrol.'

Behind the barrister, Bunderlin's solicitor looked to the ceiling, but again the barrister recovered his direction.

'What for?'

'For my car.'

'Did you spill some petrol while you were filling your car? Is that what happened?'

'Yes.'

'Do you often spill petrol?'

'Yes.'

'Is it true that you have been banned from using Barton Filling Station, near your home?'

'Yes.'

'Why?'

'They don't like the smell of petrol.'

'And you are very clumsy. You spill quite a lot. Is that it?'

'Yes.'

So far, so good, but where was it going? Martin found himself jumping ahead. So Bunderlin had been at the shop for some as yet undisclosed reason but without intending any harm to Webster himself. And the petrol on his clothes was there simply because of his normal carelessness—as Martin had originally thought and as Veryan had suggested. He sat on the edge of his seat waiting to hear why Bunderlin had been at the shop just as the fire was started. But then defence counsel said, 'No further questions,' and sat down leaving Martin thinking he must have missed something. Where was the rest of this defence?

The prosecution barrister stood up and with a faint smile and a slight bow to defence seemed to be saying thank you for a spectacular own goal. 'Do you enjoy watching a fire, Mr Bunderlin?' he began.

'Yes.'

'Some weeks before the tragic fire at Mr Webster's shop you had a big bonfire in your garden. Is that correct?'

'Yes.'

'In fact, you were burning things for several days.'

'*The worm dieth not and the fire is not quenched.*'

'Quite. You told the court you intended no harm to Mr Webster. You believed he was not there? Is that correct?'

'Yes.'

'My Lord, I should like to bring back the exhibits numbered one to thirty-two.' The judge assented and the usher fetched the requested items. 'Mr Bunderlin, will you look at these photographs and tell me what they are.'

'Photographs of Webster.'

'Did you take them?'

'Yes.'

'Why?'

'I was watching him.'

'You were watching him. Take this one, please. Number six. Will you describe the photograph.'

'It's Webster walking along Clayton Lane.'

'Will you read the words on the back, please.'

'Clayton Lane. Sunday seventh of June. Eight p.m.'

'Who wrote that?'

'I did.'

'And did you write something similar on each of them?'

'Yes.'

'Why?'

'I was watching him.'

'You were carefully observing his movements over a period of four months between the beginning of June and the evening of the fire. All during this time you were planning your attack on him and his shop. You were in a better position than anyone else to know that at the time you poured petrol around that room and started the fire, Mr Webster was elsewhere in the shop. You intended everything that happened on that fateful evening. Is that the truth?'

'No. I didn't intend the haggis to go mouldy.'

The barrister, who had looked as if he was ready with another question to fire at Bunderlin straight away, stopped and smiled. He turned to look at defending counsel, who was looking into his lap and shaking his head. It seemed like minutes before the next question. 'You intended everything that happened at Mr Webster's shop. Deserved it, did he?'

'Yes,' Bunderlin replied without faltering.

'And you did it, did you?'

'Yes.'

'No further questions.' Prosecution sat down looking smugly satisfied and Bunderlin's team held their heads in their hands.

It was the middle of the following morning when the court usher announced that the jury were ready to return. The same few people as before made their way towards the public gallery. Martin hung back until Veryan had gone in. He was not sure whether she had seen him. He went in and sat down near the exit.

Guilty. Martin watched as Bunderlin was led away and then slipped out before the others began to leave also. He paused briefly on the concourse and watched as the small group of neighbours headed for the main entrance, heads bowed. As Veryan passed by on the far side of the concourse she looked across to him and smiled thinly but did not stop. Martin turned to walk away but someone took hold of his arm.

It was the white-haired old man who had been there throughout the trial. He had not recognised him before. Close to, he realised it was Mr Jenkins, the school teacher from years before. 'We failed him, Martin. He had such a wonderful feeling for words. For verse. Loved it, you know. It was always a delight to read poetry when Peter was in class. It was the rhythm, he loved the rhythm, you see. But nobody ever had the patience to listen to him. Or just be quiet with him. And we failed the others as well, you know.'

'Others?'

'Not a mention in the trial. Not a mention. All those boys who complained about Webster. Didn't listen to them, see. No wonder someone among them bore a grudge. A terrible grudge, Martin. All because we didn't listen. Wouldn't believe them. Ethel Scattergood believed them but we told her, good God, woman, get a grip. Corporal in the Fusiliers he was. And six months later she lost her marbles, so that was it, see. All those boys, terrible it was. And now Peter Bundy goes to prison.'

They walked slowly and silently towards the main entrance and paused at the top of the steps. 'I'll not ask after yourself today, Martin. Not the proper time. Another time maybe.' He began to walk away but then turned back. 'Never had a short back and sides, you know. Not Peter Bundy. Think about that, Martin. Well, cheerio.'

Martin hurried home. He had course work to catch up with and a dog to visit. And maybe in a couple of weeks he would ring Veryan.

Twelve

Two heavily made up young women in tight jeans were smoking and chewing gum. A middle-aged man with tattooed knuckles and wearing a leather-belted white boiler suit thrust his hands into his pockets and stared at his feet. Martin had expected many more than this. The small door in the large solid gateway opened and a prison officer stepped out whilst his colleague watched from behind him. He glanced at the waiting people, looked up and down the approach road and beckoned everyone inside.

From the main entrance they walked along the side of an open yard and went into a dismal room at the corner. First the women and then the man submitted sullenly to the brief search, handed over various possessions to be collected on the way out, and disappeared through the door at the far end of the small room. Martin stepped forward. No, he had no tobacco, drugs, chewing gum, knives or other weapons. He dropped his loose change, wallet and notebook into the box and joined the others, to be led to the visiting room.

It was set out with enough tables and moulded plastic chairs to accommodate far more visitors than the four of them. Martin took a seat at the table he was directed to and waited. A few minutes later Bunderlin was escorted into the room. When he was seated, the officer escorting him went to sit at the side of the room, just a few paces away.

'How are you?'

The big man smiled faintly but said nothing. Conversation with Bunderlin was never easy. Today, Martin thought, it would be harder than ever.

'Are you reasonably comfortable?'

Still no reply.

'I tried to take Kenneth back. Tried lots of times but Franz was never there.'

'Shopping. Always shopping.'

'My sister Jean is looking after him now. She's good with animals. Has a dog of her own. Border collie. And a Shetland pony. She's got a decent field, about an acre, behind the house. They run free all day. Seem to enjoy it.'

'Send me a photograph. They won't let me have Kenneth in here, but I think they will allow me a picture.'

'Of course.'

Bunderlin began to stand up and immediately the prison officer barked, 'Sit down!'

Meekly, he sat. 'Sit down, eider down, down derry down. Among the leaves so green oh.'

Martin laughed. 'What do they make of you here?'

'They make rules, they make little wooden boxes, they make tea. But they never make love-in-a-mist or hay while the sun shines.' He began once more to stand up.

'Bunderlin! Sit down! And stay sat down till I tell you to stand up, or you will go back to your cell!'

Again he obeyed and slowly the seat gave way underneath his great weight. Its flimsy legs splayed and Bunderlin sank to the floor and looked set to stay there for what remained of the visit.

'Bunderlin! Stand up, you idiot!' barked the officer. 'Go and get that wooden chair from by the door. And don't bloody well break it.'

Meekly, Bunderlin did as bidden and lowered himself carefully onto the sturdier chair. He smiled but said nothing. Martin soon gave up the attempt at conversation but he couldn't just get up and leave. Not after only a few minutes. So he sat and waited for half an hour and then Bunderlin looked up at the clock on the wall. 'They will tell you to go now,' he said. 'Your time is up.'

'Sure. I'll come again whenever you want me to.' Martin stood up.

'I will take care of you,' said Bunderlin.

Martin wrote twice, maybe three times, during the next few months but never had any reply. He sometimes wondered whether he should try again to see Franz but before he could make up his mind the house was boarded up. And then Veryan's phone number became unobtainable. Kenneth, though, seemed set to go on forever so Martin never quite forgot about the big man.

Part Two

Thirteen

Back to Martin's flat. Bunderlin is watching and waiting.

After dropping Sally and Emma at the station, Martin drove to Rylands Park and left the car by the now disused library. Samson trotted a few yards ahead of him as he made his way towards the formal gardens and out the other side.

So much had changed. The café had gone and in its place stood an incongruously proud and ugly public lavatory. The bandstand had gone but, worst of all, Rylands Hall had gone save for its portico, which remained as the entrance to a newly laid out garden in memorial of some otherwise forgotten local councillor. Well, forgotten by Martin at any rate. And also forgetting Samson for a moment, he walked into the garden. Already it was beginning to show signs of neglect and he felt a wave of sadness as he recalled the awe in which his generation of children used to hold the old Hall. Someone great had lived there, so they thought, but they didn't know who. Colin, his friend, would have known, of course, because Colin's dad was butler to Lord Whoever-it-was and they lived in a flat at the Hall. Actually Colin's dad was caretaker and the original owner, who had left his estate to the Borough, was a nineteenth-century industrialist, but never mind the details.

Bunderlin remained, or had returned, and one day soon could be expected to show his face. 'Hey, that's scary,' Emma had said and Sally had agreed, even seeming to find it exciting to think that her friend's dad had once grassed up a dangerous criminal who had now come back to settle old scores. The fact was, he tried to reassure them, if Bunderlin was free it was as a lifer on parole. And that meant he could be returned to prison for the merest hint of inappropriate behaviour. A single phone call would bring him under judicial scrutiny.

What Martin didn't tell the girls was that he would almost certainly never make that phone call. It was not simply that he was fairly sure Bunderlin was no threat. The suspicion that he really did intend to settle old scores lingered in his mind. But the old feelings of guilt had come back. The feeling that he was betraying a friend when he told the court of Bunderlin's behaviour and the smell of petrol on his clothes on the evening of the fire. And his frustration when the prosecuting counsel would not allow him to elaborate on his evidence and, worse, when the defence lawyer had declined to cross-examine him.

He had assumed that Bunderlin's mental state would allow a defence of diminished responsibility, but he had sat through what remained of the trial with mounting disbelief as the perfunctory defence offered nothing to give the jury cause to doubt his guilt. So it was Martin's evidence, it must have been, that sent the big man to jail and once again, all these years later, he was beginning to feel guilty about it. He shouldn't. He knew he shouldn't. After all, Bunderlin had caused the death of the barber and had got no more than he deserved. Had he, though? After all these years Mr Jenkins's brief comment as they were leaving the court still echoed. Jenkins had obviously believed Bunderlin to be innocent and Martin still flitted back and forth between doubt and certainty.

So what if..? What if he really was seeking revenge for his years in prison? How would he do it? Didn't they say that an arsonist was always liable to try again? Would Bunderlin think of setting another fire? Martin shuddered and called to Samson. Where was he, the silly old dog? He called again and waited, fancifully half expecting Mr Seddon, the old Parkie, to appear from behind a tree and give him a telling-off for allowing his dog to be off the lead in the gardens. After a few minutes Samson came crashing through a beech hedge and for a moment the thought of his defenceless dog caught in a fire was unbearable. But almost at once the mood lifted, for one thing was certain: whatever harm Bunderlin might be capable of inflicting, he would move heaven and earth to protect an animal.

On the drive home, he made a detour by way of Barton Lane to see whether the old detached house on the corner by the school might offer a clue about Bunderlin's current preoccupations. He slowed as he drew near, causing the driver who was too close behind to pull out sharply and hoot angrily as he went past. Martin was more interested in the house, which was now beginning to look derelict with its upper storey windows boarded up. It was evidently not abandoned, however, for as he was passing a man emerged from the side gate and looked up at the sound of the car horn. He was maybe a bit less than average in height, quite thin and had long straggly grey hair and a droopy overgrown moustache. His shabby tweed jacket with rolled up cuffs was several sizes too big and completed the picture of a miniature Bunderlin. Martin carried on to his flat, left Samson inside and drove to the university library to collect some papers that he had ordered.

Late that afternoon as he was passing the seedy café nearly opposite his flat, he noticed the same scruffy man sitting inside at a table by the window. On an impulse, he went in but as he approached him, the man seemed hardly to respond. Odd, Martin thought, who had expected some reaction from him when directly confronted by the one he must have been following for several weeks.

'Excuse me. Do you mind if I ask, are you by any chance an associate of Peter Bunderlin?'

'Who?'

'Bunderlin. Sometimes calls himself Bird. Are you a friend of his?'

'You've got me there, squire. Don't know who you're talking about.'

'You were at his house this morning. I'm sure it was you.'

'No, not me. You got that one wrong, squire. Quite wrong.'

'Well, thanks anyway. Sorry to have bothered you.' Only half convinced, he left the café. Maybe it was a mistake after all, a coincidence that, of all the places where he might have seen him, wearing what could have been Bunderlin's cast-offs, it just happened to be at Bunderlin's old house. Could be a squatter, of course, and Bunderlin could be living in a probation service hostel. But as he came out onto the street and walked past the café window, he noticed that the scruffy man was using the pay phone by the counter. And looking across the road, he realised that it was from about here that the photo of him at his doorway would have been taken.

He went to the flat and looked out across the street. He had an unobstructed view of the café but the scruffy man had disappeared. Martin knew Bunderlin from years ago, however, and remembered how he had tried to push him into keeping tabs on Veryan. He knew precisely what the scruffy little man was up to.

He went back outside and looked up and down the street. He went to the corner and looked down Lostock Road towards the Town Hall but the man was nowhere to be seen. Before returning to his flat he went into the shop below, which now appeared almost ready for opening. The woman he had seen there fairly often was adding the finishing touches to the paintwork.

'Hi, I thought it was maybe time to introduce myself. I'm Martin. From up above.'

'Yeah, right. Seen you round. I'm Maureen Tong. You any good with a paint brush?'

'Hardly. Nearly ready to start trading, are you?'

'This weekend. Drop in for drinks Friday night if you like.'

'Might do that. So what sort of place are you going to be running?'

She looked a little amused and puzzled. 'Oh, didn't you know? Magazines, videos, a few toys, leather goods. Things like that.'

'Well, best of luck with it. What I wanted to ask, though... There's a guy hangs about round here. Thin, scruffy chap with long hair and a coat that would go round him twice. I wondered if you'd noticed him?'

'You must mean Scobie Sharples. Does odd jobs for beer money and dosses in a lock-up near the bus station. Why are you interested?'

'Oh, it's probably nothing. Just that he seemed to have been following me.'

'What, Scobie? I suppose he might if he thinks you're good for a touch. If you want him, you'll always find him in the New Zealander.'

'Right. Well, thanks. Better be off now.'

'See you then. Hey, if you do go in the New Zealander, you should watch your back.'

'Oh, why?'

'Well, talking posh like you do. They'll get ideas—specially if they think you're looking for someone.' He would have taken Maureen's hint and avoided the New Zealander but his curiosity was aroused so he went there early that evening. It was a grubby place, which had probably not been redecorated in years. Even this early, whilst it was still fairly empty, a strong smell of stale tobacco hung in the air. Martin took his drink to a table in the corner and watched in bemused fascination as gradually the place began to fill up with customers who matched their surroundings.

Scobie Sharples came in and looked almost directly at Martin but appeared to take no notice. He went through the door to the back room. Two heavily made up girls in very short skirts and low-cut tops approached Martin.

'Looking for business, sweetheart?'

'No. Just having a quiet drink.'

'Well sod you, then.'

He soon became aware that people were glancing towards him and a couple of times he heard, in accents probably intended to mimic his own, *Just having a quiet drink*. He was wondering whether to go and find Sharples as he had first intended, or simply to leave when Maureen Tong walked in. She was served right away and evidently picked up the talk about the odd guy in the corner for she turned at once and looked directly at him. She came over, smiling.

'Smart dude, you are, aren't you? And you stick out in here like a sore thumb. Did you know that?'

'Well, I had gathered that, yes.'

'Know what these punters think about you?'

'I don't think I care to know.'

'Well some of them reckon you must be somebody's probation officer and so long as they think that they'll leave you alone. But if anyone puts it about that you might be a Social Security snooper, and they will, you can bet on it, you'll have an accident on the way home. What do you do, by the way?'

'I teach.'

'Might have guessed.'

Just then a grossly overweight, sweaty man sporting tattoos on every inch of exposed skin approached their table. Without a word, he placed a drink in front of Maureen and returned to his friends. 'Join the queue, pretty boy,' he called, and gave Martin a two-finger salute. Maureen picked up the glass, took it back to the man and emptied it over his head.

'You, you sodding great lump of shit, you couldn't afford me even if you saved up all year.'

'Come on, smart guy,' she said when she returned. 'Drink up and you can take me to the Gaiety.'

Much later that evening, after a tour of too many of Lostock's town centre bars, Maureen climbed into a taxi and Martin walked home rather more drunk than he had been for months. He was vaguely aware that, having been seen around the town in Maureen's company, he was now less likely to be regarded as some sort of official threat to anyone engaging in the alternative trades. But he had not appreciated that there would be some who might speculate and draw other conclusions about Maureen Tong's new escort.

Fourteen

The phone began to ring. It was Nigel Coulson, the young, newly promoted Reader in Modern History. 'Martin, are you free this evening?'

Of course he was free. 'Well, I'm not sure. I'll have to check.'

'Mary and I are having a bit of a do and we thought you might like to join us. Nothing special. Just dinner and drinks.'

He was about to make an excuse but told himself not to be so silly. 'Sure, I'd love to come.'

The call was well timed for Martin had spent the first half of the morning nursing a mild hangover and gradually feeling more and more sorry for himself. As the dismal walls of the flat closed in on him and squeezed his spirit, so did the town centre. Years ago he loved this place. He knew every street, every café, every pub and had friends, well, acquaintances, in each one. Now he was thrown back into that same world but he didn't belong there any more. And didn't they let him know it, those unlovely regulars in the New Zealander and the other dreadful places where Maureen had dragged him the previous evening. He had no wish to linger in their seedy company.

But neither did he still belong in his own world for it was a world of couples with no room for single males. 'Have a flat warming party,' Emma had said when, in an unguarded moment, he had confessed to loneliness. Perhaps when he moved into the cottage at Borrinsmoor he would do that, but not at this grotty place. That really would show everyone how far he had fallen.

Feeling a little brighter at the prospect of getting back into the social life he had almost left behind, he took Samson for a longer than usual walk. Before they were half way round the park, however, he was not so sure that he should have allowed himself to be so easily cheered up. It was a last minute invitation, after all. A fill-in because of a late drop out. That's what he was. Or someone had said, Mary most likely, 'What about poor old Martin, all on his own now? He's sure to need cheering up, so don't you think we should invite him too?'

'Stop being an old grump,' he told himself. He would summon all the good grace he could muster and he would go to Nigel and Mary's and enjoy the evening.

By the time he returned to the flat he had decided to leave it until the next day to resume work on his paper. After all, with the library closing early during the vacations, there was really very little point in driving out to the university after lunch. He opened the door and unclipped Samson's lead. The dog ran up the stairs ahead of him and Martin, still not brimming with vitality, plodded a little wearily behind him. He let the dog in and immediately went back down to the street to buy a loaf at the corner shop and then renew his road tax.

He returned about half an hour later but Samson, who would normally be waiting to greet him at the door, was not there. He was in the living room—sitting contentedly on the sofa beside Peter Bunderlin. Martin blinked. Was he dreaming? Was he going mad? The big man smiled faintly and stroked the dog. He looked old and rather heavier than Martin remembered. What little hair he had left hung over his shoulders and his beard rested on his chest and shed dandruff onto his shirt. His smile broadened into a wide grin, revealing a set of teeth like a derelict graveyard.

'What on earth do you think you're..? How did you get in here?'

Bunderlin raised a hand to wave him to silence. 'Questions, Martin, questions. First, I need you to do something for me.'

The man was just outrageous. 'Do something for you? You have me followed—you have done, I know you have—you break in here, and the first thing you do is ask me to do something for you. I'm doing nothing. I want you out of here. Now.'

'I can't go until you do me the one favour I ask.'

'You're impossible. If you don't leave here right away I'll call the police.' He took his phone from his pocket. 'In fact, I'm going to do that now. This is a serious matter. It's breaking and entering... It's... You do realise, don't you, the position you're in?'

'Martin, dear chap, it would be so easy for you just to pick up my stick. I dropped it over there when I came in.' He pointed to a walking stick lying on the floor by the table. Martin picked it up and handed it to him. He had another at his side and with the two he struggled to his feet. 'I like Samson,' he said.

'How did you know my dog's name?'

'He's a good dog. He's friendly. He welcomed me in and, do you know, he asked no questions. Ha, no. He did. He asked me, where's my apple? Where's my apple? You want to ask why your fine dog let me in? He knows me. When you take him to the park I am there and I hear you calling, Samson, Samson, but he comes to me for biscuits and pieces of apple. He's my friend. You don't see because you don't watch. But I watch. You're my friend, Martin. You want to ask why I have come? I just told you—you are my friend.'

Even if he had the number, Martin probably would not have called the police. He just wanted Bunderlin out of the flat. 'How did you get in here? Tell me that. I know I didn't leave the door open, so how did you get in?'

'I come in like you do, Martin. I use my keys.'

Martin looked at him, open-mouthed.

'*There was a door to which I have the key. There was a veil past which just I could see. Some little talk awhile of me and thee there seemed—and then no more of thee and me.*'

'What on earth are you talking about?'

'Old Bundy is Old Khayyam. No, you thought Franz was Old Bundy. He was. But now Franz is gone and Bird is Old Bundy and Old Bundy is Old Khayyam. You knew that. But you didn't know, you didn't even guess. All your questions and still you didn't know you are living in my shop.'

Was this crazy giant telling him that he owns the shop and the flat? That he must have been keeping tabs on him for weeks? That it was he who had responded so quickly to his half-hearted request for information about flats to let? And lured him here with the offer of no deposit and a low monthly rent? How on earth had he managed that? Was the man sinister and dangerous —or just daft?

As he had done on every other occasion years ago, Martin caved in. 'Oh, sit down again, you daft bugger. I'll get us a drink.' He went out to his kitchen and made a pot of tea but then, so that it would not last too long, he topped it up with a little cold water. It might be wise to appear friendly, just long enough to find out what Bunderlin was up to, but no more than that.

'Now, are you going to tell me what you want with me?' he asked when he returned.

'I told you but you forget so soon. You don't listen. Now you tell me about yourself. And Emma and Julia.'

'How do you know about my family?'

'It's no secret. You don't have secrets.' He slurped his tea. 'But let me give you a word of advice. Advice from an old man—you should wait for the water to boil. A washed kettle never boils. And a kettledrum never boils at all. Now I must ask one more thing—look through the window and tell me what you see.'

Martin began to feel more uneasy. He looked out not knowing what he was supposed to be looking for. 'I see shops, traffic, a bus, pedestrians.'

'No, no, dear chap. Down below.'

'An old green van parked just outside. Is that it? What's going on?'

'It's my driver. I shall go now, but come and see me on Friday. Three o'clock outside the Haymarket.' He struggled to his feet and shuffled to the door. He handed Martin his sticks and gestured at him to go down first. Then, turning around and grasping the handrail, he backed slowly and painfully down the stairs.

When they got outside Martin saw Scobie Sharples waiting beside the green van. He held the passenger door open and Bunderlin struggled into the seat. As they drove away, he wound down the window and called, 'Friday. Don't forget.'

Martin came back inside, but had no time to heave a sigh of relief before two men burst out of the shop and pushed their way in behind him. 'Hey, what's going on?' he protested.

'Just get up the bleeding stairs, smart guy,' said the older man and the two followed menacingly close as he went up to the flat.

He didn't get a good look at them until they were inside. Both were smartly but casually dressed. The older, shorter man had close-cropped grey hair and tattoos round his neck. The younger man had slicked down black hair and sported large gold rings on every finger.

'Just a business call, squire,' said the older man. 'I think you and me can help one another. Know what I mean?'

Martin said nothing. Samson, sensing that the men were far from friendly, bared his teeth and growled and Martin bundled him into the bedroom. Then, thinking that was probably a mistake, he stayed close to the door just in case he should want to let the dog back in again.

'Yeah, just needed to ask you something really. Then we'll be on our way. Know what I mean? And you want to watch what you're doing with that dog. Bleeding dangerous animal, that is.' The younger man stood to one side and slightly behind, and stared at Martin whilst glancing occasionally towards the bedroom door as Samson kept sniffing noisily underneath it.

'Well, go on. Ask me, then,' said Martin nervously. 'What did you want to know?' He edged towards the bedroom door and unfastened it so that Samson could paw it open.

'Tony Lullaby,' said the older man. 'You know Tony Lullaby, don't you?'

'Never heard of him.'

'Hear that, Gerry. The gentleman says he's never heard of Tony Lullaby.'

'Bollocks,' said Gerry and then let out a ridiculous little cry of alarm when Samson crashed the door open and sidled up to Martin.

'Yeah, bollocks, that's what I think. So let me remind you. Nice man, Tony. Very nice man. Maureen's nearest and dearest. Doesn't like other geezers messing with his lady. Know what I mean?'

'Except paying guests, of course,' said Gerry.

'Well, of course. Except paying guests. But you're not a paying guest, are you, Mister Smart Guy? No, course you're not. And you know what that says to me? It says you're working for our very dear friend Tony Lullaby. Else you really did do him in that time, you and the grieving widow downstairs. Better take a look around, Gerry.'

Gerry wandered round the flat poking into drawers and cupboards but as he did so he began to sniff and sneeze and splutter and kept glancing over his shoulder to see where the dog was. 'Hey, do you mind?' Martin protested. 'There's nothing in here that's any concern of yours.'

'No, no. No offence, mate,' Gerry replied. 'Just... er, just looking, that's all.'

'Either way, you see, Mister Smart Guy,' said the older man, 'I reckon you can help me and my nice young friend here. Cause when Tony did the Houdini trick he forgot to pay out my dividend on a little investment. Well, he couldn't really. Not at the time, see, cause I had to take an unexpected holiday. A few months on the Costa del Strangeways. Know what I mean? So all I'm asking, my friend, is for you to tell Tony that his mate Dave is back. And Dave says, please, pretty please, could he have his documents back and his share of the payout?'

'What if the gentleman can't come up with anything, Dave?' said Gerry, wiping his nose and his eyes with his hand. Martin tore off a couple of sheets of kitchen towel and handed them to him.

'Cheers, mate.'

'Well, if he can't help us we would have to think about what we could do,' said Dave and then turned to Gerry who was sneezing more and more into the paper towel. 'What's wrong with you, you snivelling little prat?'

'It's that bleeding dog. They always do this to me.'

'Oh shut up, you're fucking useless. Now then, Mister Smart Guy, we're going to leave you. But we'll be back and I'm sure you won't let me down. Know what I mean? No, don't trouble yourself, we can see ourselves out.'

Martin went to the window to check that the two men had left the building then, once they had driven away in the red Mercedes that had been parked opposite, he went down to the shop to see Maureen.

'Hi, Mart,' she said as he walked in. 'Those two heavies been to see you as well?'

'Yes. So what's it all about?'

She bolted the door and went through to the back. Martin followed. 'Park your backside. I'll make a drink. Coffee OK?'

He sat on one of the many boxes lying around the storeroom and waited for Maureen to volunteer something about the two heavies. She sat down but said nothing. The kettle began to sing. She got up and picked up a jar of coffee. 'Fucking bastards! Absolute fucking bastards those two.'

'So who's this Tony Lullaby they were talking about?'

'Even worse. Made them two look like angels. Sugar?'

'No, thanks.'

She made the coffee then picked up a knife and began slitting the parcel tape on some of the boxes. 'Wish I could do this to Dave Brierley and Gerry Mason. My stock, this. Supposed to be my ticket out of all that shit.'

'And where does Tony Lullaby come into it?'

'Doesn't, not any more. He's dead, thank God. Two years ago. Best Christmas present I ever had when the lady pig took me to identify him. Said I couldn't be sure. But it was him, I know it was. Seemed a good idea to let people think he might have done a bunk and left some other poor sod in the mortuary.'

'So how did you get involved with him?'

'Started working when I was fifteen. It was great for a few months 'cause I was earning really big money. But then Tony decided he was my agent. Took everything I earned, the bastard. Made me take punters who like to rough their girls up a bit. Said he was protecting me. So he was, in a way, I suppose. I could go anywhere I wanted—anywhere he wanted—and the others wouldn't dare object cause Tony wouldn't let them. Only had to cut a couple of the girls and word soon got around that nobody messes with Maureen Tong.'

'Charming character.'

'Fucking bastard. Course, eventually he got a couple of years for dealing. That's when I thought of this place, see. I was keeping all my money again and I thought if only I could set myself up before the bastard gets out. Didn't dare to think how he might have an accident.'

Martin wasn't sure that he ought to hear any more of this story. But he didn't let caution trouble him too much. 'So then what?'

'Had this really great punter. Well, he was a fucking barmy geezer actually. But nice sort of barmy, not nasty. Big chap. Saw him every week. Didn't always want to screw, sometimes we just sat and talked—or didn't even talk. He could sit for ages saying absolutely nothing. And then he'd come out with something completely dotty. Anyway, he said he could help me get a shop to rent. I thought I was made. Trouble was, they let Tony out. He beat me up really bad and took everything I'd got. They should've thrown the key away.'

'But you managed to bounce back?'

'Yeah, right. When the lady pig came and took me to the mortuary. They said I didn't have to look at his face 'cause he was pretty bad but that's why I wanted to see. I remember looking at him and thinking, hallelujah. But then I thought what if it's some other poor sod? Anyway, he'd still got his steel bracelet on so I knew it was him.'

'What had happened?'

'There was a fire in his shop. They reckoned it was a gas heater that blew up. And he was too pissed to get out.'

Fifteen

Nigel Coulson could be tiresome on occasion and that evening, Martin thought, looked set to turn into such an occasion. It began inauspiciously with Nigel deflecting Martin's belated congratulations upon the publication of his latest monograph, with the observation that his publisher could have timed things to very much greater advantage. Martin, who had little experience of such frustrations, would have sympathised if he'd known how to or if he'd not thought sympathy would only bring out the worst in Nigel.

Martin glanced around the room looking for somewhere to escape. Helen Parkinson was already in conversation with Jim O'Neill from German. She could always lift academic shop talk from the stuffy to the fascinating with her enthusiastic defence of vernacular history and accounts of her current projects piecing together the lives of Lancashire's cotton workers as if they were her own friends. Yes, it's all very well, some dreary old fart had once said, but it's too entertaining for serious work. Tim Parkinson and Lesley O'Neill were poring over what was either Nigel's most recent addition to his collection of rare volumes or else a book club edition of a coffee table picture book.

Before he could begin to feel excluded, however, Mary came to his side. 'Come along now, Martin,' she said. 'Let's go and find you a drink.' She steered him towards the kitchen, where a tall thin dark-haired woman of about forty was waiting to resume her conversation with the hostess. 'Martin, let me introduce you to Carol. She's an expert, and believe me I mean expert, on interior design and décor.'

'Well, not really. Not any more.'

'Carol, my dear, you really must believe me—something will turn up for you. Now why don't you get Martin a drink. Give him the Riesling. I know it's one of his favourites. That's right, isn't it, Martin? Oh, and by the way, Carol's son, Teddy, is starting at Warwick next week. That's where your Emma is, isn't it, Martin? Anyway, you two get to know each other. We'll be starting to eat in a minute or two.'

As soon as Carol had poured the wine, Mary was back and was coaxing them to the dining table where she made sure they sat together. Jim opened his napkin with a flourish and spread it over his lap whilst Nigel went round topping up everyone's drinks. For a few moments there was an awkward silence as everyone appeared to be waiting for their host to formally open the meeting. If that is what he did, he did it by addressing Martin.

'So tell us, how is your latest project coming along?'

'Progressing slowly,' Martin responded, hoping that he could avoid having to elaborate.

'So what is this one?' asked Jim.

'Just some thoughts on the origins of apocalyptic. Well, Daniel in particular.'

'He means Daniel of lions' den fame,' added Nigel.

'Oh gosh, still on that one?' said Helen, sounding a little surprised. 'Isn't that what you were doing last Easter?'

'The same.'

'Wow. Must've grown. I thought it was just a brief note you were doing. I really love it when something that starts as just a critical note or whatever suddenly opens up and ends up as a whole monograph.'

'It's the jaws of those lions opening up, I'll bet,' said Nigel. 'Quite a one with the animals, is our Martin. Brings his dogs to lectures, would you believe?'

'Actually I've only ever done that once. And nobody would have known anything about it if that stuffy little Religious Studies major hadn't complained.'

'I like dogs,' said Carol. 'Really cute things. They're lovely.'

Nigel and Jim looked at her almost as if she was a small child who was not expected to make any attempt to join in the grown-ups' conversation.

'I used to have a dog,' she continued, 'Well, not for years now of course. But my dad once bought me a puppy. A lovely little Bedlington Terrier.'

'A Bedlington?' said Jim. 'What's a Bedlington Terrier?'

'It's a cross between a sheep and a poodle,' replied Martin without thinking.

Carol looked startled as if offended that her favourite breed should be described in such a flippant way, but then she relaxed and giggled. 'Actually that's quite a good description. They do look a bit like that. Popty—that's what we called her—was just like a sweet little lamb.'

'Popty? What sort of name is that?' asked Jim.

'Actually, it was the name of the lady we got her from. It was like this, you see. We were on holiday in North Wales and there was this lovely little bread and cake shop. And the lady who owned it, Popty Meredith, that was the name over the shop window, she had some puppies for sale...'

Martin thought Jim was about to ask whether they were amongst the bread or the cakes, but he just raised an eyebrow and said nothing.

'Well, Dad had already promised to get me a dog so I begged and I begged and eventually he gave in and got one. Anyway, she was such a lovely lady I wanted to name my puppy after her. So I did. I'm sure dear old Popty Meredith would be absolutely mortified if she realised we'd named the dog after her. But she was such a lovely cute little thing. The dog, I mean. Well, so was Mrs Meredith, actually. As far as I can remember, that is. It's a long long time ago. I was only ten, I think. We had her till long after I'd got married. Dear little Popty Bed. That's short for Bedlington, of course.'

Jim turned to Tim Parkinson and asked, 'When do we all get to see this new boat you and Helen have bought yourselves? You must throw a party, you know.'

Later in the evening, when Martin was firmly resisting the temptation of another glass of wine, Mary brought him into the kitchen with the simple device of a request for help with the coffees. Carol was perched on a high stool at the oak dresser and all too obviously brightened up when she saw him come in. 'I was telling Carol,' Mary said, 'she needs to start getting out more. Course, you know all about this, don't you Martin? I mean with the new place you're having done.'

He wasn't really sure what the connection was between getting out more and buying a cottage at the foot of the moors, but he could see quite clearly what Mary was trying to do.

'From what Nigel tells me, you're practically having the place rebuilt from scratch.'

'Gosh, that sounds exciting,' said Carol.

'Must be,' said Mary. 'I really envy you, in a way. I mean getting the house just how you want it. You're going to be needing all sorts of things to give it just the right atmosphere.'

'Well, maybe.'

'There's no maybe about it, Martin. Take my word for it. And you could do worse than get Carol to give you a hand there. You're pretty good at that sort of thing, aren't you, Carol? Helping folk with décor and finding the right period pieces to create the ambience they want. Look, why don't you two just natter while I take these coffees through.'

'So what sort of ambience did you have in mind?'

'To be honest, the only thing I really want at the moment is for the builder to finish my kitchen so that I can move in. Then if I can just enjoy the view of Winter Hill, that's all I ask.'

'Right, I get it. The Pennine Magic. Yes, I can see it now. It's really exciting.'

Sixteen

From the Buttery Café, Martin had a clear view across the square towards the Haymarket. He had been there for about half an hour and it was now nearly quarter past three. There was no sign of Bunderlin and Martin half expected someone to approach him with a message, but it was a quiet day and the café remained empty. Five more minutes, then he would leave. A young couple who were walking past paused to study the menu in the window, momentarily blocking his view. They moved on after a few minutes and Martin looked once more across the square. There he was, on one of the seats in front of the Town Hall looking intently in the direction of the pub. Martin walked over, telling himself that he would keep this brief.

'You made it then.'

Bunderlin looked at him and smiled but said nothing. Martin sat down and waited for him to speak.

At last he broke the silence.

'*A chap from Newcastle on Tyne,*
found a dog and a cat in a mine,
a pig in a poke
with a sorrowful bloke
and a vinegar fly in the wine.'

He chuckled briefly. Not the raucous laughter of years before, just a quiet contented chuckle.

Martin shook his head. 'I don't understand you. Will I ever?'

'Always, Martin, you are asking questions. But you never asked me about... about being in prison.'

'Not had the chance yet. So, OK, tell me about being in prison. How was it?'

He did not reply at first, appearing to be carefully considering his words. But then he said, 'You saw Maureen. She's good. Be kind to her, Martin.'

'You know her, then? Well, another tenant of yours, I suppose.'

'Tenant of mine, tenant of yours, *Tenant of Wildfell Hall.*' He was just as daft as ever, making it nearly impossible to hold a sensible conversation with him.

'After you'd gone the other day,' Martin tried, 'I had a visit from a couple of pretty shady characters. They seemed to think I know something about a chap called Lullaby.'

'What?' Was there a hint of alarm in Bunderlin's voice? 'Lullaby, hush-a-by, don't you cry.' He stayed silent for a few minutes and then struggled to his feet and began to walk slowly in the direction of the car park. He stopped at the top of the passage between the pub and the Post Office and appeared not to want Martin to come any further. 'You came once,' he said. 'That was kind.'

'Well I couldn't leave you to struggle out here to no purpose.'

'I mean before. When I was in Strangeways. You came once. Remember what I said to you—I will take care of you. And I will. Old Bundy keeps his promise. Now I am going home.'

Martin watched as he began to walk away. He had only gone a couple of yards when he turned and said, 'It wasn't... ' He didn't finish the sentence

Martin waited a moment before asking, 'What wasn't, well wasn't whatever?'

'The fire.'

'So why...? Why did you not put up a decent defence, for heaven's sake? Are you planning an appeal now? Is that it?'

'Appeal. Peel, peel, apple peel, John Peel, Robert Peel.' He reached into his pocket and produced an apple. 'Here. Give it to Samson. It's a Granny Smith. He likes Granny Smiths.' He raised a stick and pointed towards the far end of the alleyway where Scobie Sharples was waiting. 'The twin. Always think of the twin,' he said and began to walk away.

When Martin arrived home the shop front was transformed. No longer vacant premises, it was Discreet World and a notice on the door, just a shoulder's width from his own letterbox, advised him not to enter if he was under eighteen or easily offended by material that he might consider obscene. He had wanted to call in to see Maureen but it could wait. He went up to the flat.

'Questions, Martin,' Bunderlin had so often chided. Little hope now of avoiding them. What did he mean by the twin? His own twin brother? Or younger brothers? Was he talking about the real arsonist? Did he serve a prison sentence to protect someone as close as a twin brother? A brother who was even dafter than him and had to be hidden away most of the time? Or was it just another example of his silly playing around with words?

Martin recalled those few occasions years ago when it was just about possible that he had met Bunderlin's exact double. Not the vacant episodes—he was thinking about the times when he had spoken with him but Bunderlin had later insisted he had not been there. And the couple in the pub that time, who thought they had met him on a railway station somewhere but he had told them he'd not been there. Martin wasn't convinced then and he wasn't convinced now. But maybe, just maybe. Or what about the time when he had seen Franz Bunderlin? He was old, much older though. Wasn't he? Staying in the shadows, perhaps, the two could be mistaken for each other or could even be twin brothers. But close up, close enough to speak to, the difference would be clear. And Franz had come out into the light. He could be an older brother though, of course.

It was only six o'clock when the sound of music and laughter began to come from down below and Martin groaned at the thought of a party starting so early. He had been wondering whether it might be worth finding out what Maureen knew about Bunderlin. Almost certainly nothing, he told himself. She hadn't even managed to supply any useful information about Tony Lullaby and tattooed Dave, so what chance she would know about Bunderlin's secret twin? But whatever he might learn from Maureen, it would have to wait until another time for he did not relish the idea of being seen coming and going from her shop now that it so clearly advertised its trade.

That left only Scobie but Martin had no wish to make a tour of the bars in search of him. Nothing for it, then, but to wait and wonder, to listen to some music whilst trying to ignore the party downstairs, and to stare at the files and books scattered on his table and despair of even making a start on that paper, which he ought to have finished long ago.

There were others, of course there were others. There was Veryan – whatever became of her? There were the old teachers from Barton Lane Primary School. And there was his dad, in a world of his own in the nursing home. All of which was to say that there was nobody. Except Jean, of course, his older sister in Kearsley. She was overdue a visit.

Suddenly the music stopped. A door banged down below and Martin heard voices from the street. He looked out as Maureen's party were climbing into a taxi, leaving the place as quiet as a busy high street ever gets. It would be noisy again a little later but in the meantime he would enjoy the respite. He was about to pour himself a large glass of wine when there was a hammering at his door. He ignored it at first thinking that it was probably a latecomer to the party. But it carried on and as it began to sound more insistent Samson joined in, first with a single perfunctory bark from somewhere behind the cushions on the settee, and then, nose pressed hard against the gap at the bottom of the door, a continuous canine shouting that nothing would persuade him to quieten. Martin looked down from the window but whoever was there was right inside the door recess and couldn't be seen. Reluctantly, he went downstairs.

It was Scobie Sharples. 'Oh, thank God you're there, squire,' he said. 'Thought you'd buggered off out.'

'What do you want?'

'You've got to come with me.'

'No chance. Where to anyway? '

'Mr Bundy wants you. I've got the van. Don't worry, I'm not pissed. Not had a bleeding chance yet.'

'Tell him I'm not going anywhere. If he wants to see me it will have to wait.'

'No, you don't understand, squire. He's asking for you. In the hospital. They took him in at tea time. So you'd better come.'

'Oh. What's wrong with him? What's happened?'

'Buggered if I know. Just sort of keeled over. Had to go with him, see, 'cause he's not given me anything yet. Well, it was lucky I did 'cause he told me to come and get you.'

Martin got into the green van and Scobie drove erratically to the General Hospital and pulled up in an ambulance bay at the side entrance. 'Ward seven, it is. I'm not going in. Got to get this van back. You'll have to find your own way home.'

'That's fine, Scobie. Thanks,' he replied. 'Oh, look, drop by some time over the weekend and you can maybe answer a couple of questions for me.'

'No, wait, wait,' Scobie called as Martin was about to shut the door. 'Mr Bundy never did give me my cash in hand, like. So, if you'd oblige...'

'What?'

'Still owes me for the day. It'd be easiest if you give it me, squire. Save troubling him.'

'Oh very well then.' He pulled a fiver from his pocket and handed it to him.

'Mr Bundy usually gives me a bit more than that. Well, I mean today, like. Got to be a couple of notes today.'

He gave him another fiver.

'Thanks, squire. You're a gentleman. Mr Bundy said you'd... well, you know.'

As he drove off, Martin went to find ward seven.

Seventeen

Bunderlin was in a small side room just outside the main part of the ward when Martin arrived. The curtains were pulled round the bed so he waited in the corridor. People came and went. The end of visiting time crept closer, and Martin wondered whether to go and find someone who might be able to tell him what the problem was. Just then a nurse came from behind the curtains and stopped when she saw Martin. 'Are you waiting to see Peter Bunderlin?'

'Yes. Can you tell me how he is? What's wrong with him?'

'The doctor will be finished in a minute. Then he can tell you himself. Are you Martin?' She took a bunch of keys from her pocket. 'He said to give you these. Something about filling up some feeders. I take it you know what he means.'

'Haven't a clue.'

The doctor pulled back the curtains. 'So I'll see you again in the morning,' she was saying. 'Now, here's someone to see you, I think.'

Bunderlin was lying flat, his bulk almost overhanging the bed and he was looking very drowsy. He raised a hand in a gesture that waved away his visitor's questions. Martin sat in the chair beside the bed but Bunderlin became agitated as he did so.

'No, no. You must be away. My keys. They're in the drawer. No, the other woman has them.'

Martin held up the bunch of keys. 'I've got them. Do you need something?'

'You must go. The feeder's empty. Not the front door. Go to the back. And take some pieces of cheese. Ulla. She'll like you if you give her cheese.'

'OK,' said Martin, wondering what he was being asked to do. 'But how are you? What happened to you?'

'Should've filled it up. A new bag. There's a new bag. You'll see.'

'Right, well, I'll do what I can. Now, is there anything I can bring in for you? Clean pyjamas? Towel? Anything else.'

'The feeder, only the feeder. And the bowls. Now go.'

The more Martin hesitated, the more agitated Bunderlin became so, without waiting any longer, he left. On the way out of the ward, he stopped at the nurses' station and asked what was wrong with Bunderlin. 'We'll have a better idea in the morning,' she replied. 'You can ask him again tomorrow.'

It took Martin nearly an hour to walk home. First, he slipped into the flat to make sure that Samson was all right and to collect some cheese, presumably to coax some creature into letting him do whatever needed to be done, and then he drove to Barton Lane. He arrived at the house with the boarded-up top storey as it was starting to get dark.

For a few minutes he sat in the car looking at the place that crystallised Bunderlin's strange world. Remembering the house from years ago, Martin had guessed that an animal of some sort shared it with Bunderlin and needed to be fed. A goat, perhaps? No, that would be far too agile for anyone as disabled as Bunderlin had become. A pig? Yes, maybe a pig.

He had his answer when he went round the side of the house and noisily opened the tall heavy gate into the back garden. Inside the house a dog began to bark. This was crazy. Why did he agree to it? He ought to go away again and enlist the help of... Of whom? At ten o'clock on a Friday evening? He had thought at first that it sounded like a fairly big dog but now the racket it was making suggested it was probably small. But then, of course, Martin reflected, small dogs can be the most troublesome.

He picked his way past the clutter piled at the back of the house and peered through the kitchen window. A black and white Jack Russell was running back and forth and barking furiously. And in the gloom he could make out what looked like a bearded collie sitting askew in the corner thrashing its tail on the floor. Ah well, Martin thought, nothing for it but to let them out. He began trying different keys but the first few served only to get the larger, scruffy dog to join in the chaos. At last he found the right one, flung the door open and stood aside. The larger dog sped into the garden and the Jack Russell began attacking Martin's ankles and the bottoms of his trousers. He grabbed hold of it by the collar and held it at arm's length whilst trying to unwrap the cheese which, he now realised, it was probably very useful to have with him.

He released the dog and began to break off lumps of cheese, but the dog was more interested in taking lumps out of Martin. Eventually it began to calm down but remained very wary until at last Martin was able to step inside the kitchen.

He found the switch and turned on the light to reveal a revolting mass of dirty crockery, empty tins, bottles, food wrappings, filthy rags and towels all over the place. Just behind the door, and spread out as it opened, was a large pile of dog shit. He found an old spade by the door and cleared up the mess but more than that was far too big a job to tackle. He could only make sure the dogs were exercised, fed and watered.

The feeder which he was supposed to be looking for turned out to consist of a large plastic swing top bin with a big hole near the bottom. It stood in a washing-up bowl to be filled with dry dog food which it released into the bowl as the dogs ate it. There was an unopened bag of the food by the sink and Martin emptied it into the bin. For water, however, there was no similarly ingenious arrangement, only several old pans and bowls dotted around the place. He made sure they were all full.

By this time the dogs were nowhere to be seen. He would have looked for them but the garden defeated him for it was stacked high with discarded furniture, at least two scrap cars, assorted junk, a cement mixer and an old bath. He tried calling to the dogs but there was no response. Nothing for it but to wait until they saw fit to return.

He waited and waited and it grew quite dark but still there was no sign of them. Leaving the kitchen door open, he went into the lane, now leading to a small new housing development, but he could see nothing. Nor was there any sign of them in the darkness across the much reduced school playing field. Returning to the house, he went into the kitchen. The bearded collie had returned and was curled up on some old blankets under the table. How long should he wait for the Jack Russell? What should he do if it didn't return? Just leave it to its own devices and come back first thing in the morning? That wouldn't be right, but what else could he do?

Before he had to make up his mind, however, the dog returned. Briefly, it attacked Martin's ankles and then hurried over to one of the water bowls. Martin turned out the light, locked up and went home to exercise his own dog before settling in for the night.

He woke the following morning as the dawn was just beginning to break. It was quite clear now what he should do. Bunderlin could certainly not be discharged from hospital without drastic changes in his domestic arrangements, so Martin would have to find someone on the ward with whom he might discuss the matter. He would then alert Social Services and the RSPCA to the problem. Except, of course, that he would do no such thing. He would go round first thing and let the dogs out—making sure that they could not get out of the garden this time. Then he'd have a go at clearing up in that appalling kitchen, and in the afternoon he would go to the hospital and see how the daft old bugger was getting on.

After breakfast he loaded a bucket, some bleach, a scrubbing brush and Samson into the car. Before he could set off, his phone rang. It was Emma. 'Hi, Dad. It's me. Can you pick me up at Manchester Piccadilly in about an hour?'

Two hours later they pulled up outside Bunderlin's house. 'I should wait here if I were you. If you don't want to lose your breakfast.'

'No way. I must see this place, if it's as bad as you reckon.'

'Well don't say I didn't warn you. And look out for the Jack Russell when I open the door. She'll tear your ankles apart.'

They checked for gaps in the fence and plugged them as best they could. Satisfied that the dogs could not escape, Martin let them out. The bearded collie ran straight out and tried to find his way into the lane and the Jack Russell followed after only a brief assault on Martin. When he saw that they had given up trying to get loose, Martin went into the kitchen. Emma was staring at the cooker in disbelief.

'So what were you planning to do, for heaven's sake? Give it a quick wipe over and do the washing up?'

'I've got to do something. Can't leave it like this.'

'And this is the guy you sent down for life? Who's out to get his own back.'

'Well, I'm pretty sure now that he's quite harmless.'

'As murderers are.'

'No, really. He thinks of me as his friend. That's the only reason he tracked me down.'

'Dad, you're priceless. You should just call Environmental Health and let them sort it all out. What's the rest of the place like, anyway?' Despite Martin's protest, she went off to look around and left Martin wondering what he could usefully do that would make any difference.

After a few minutes, Emma returned. 'Hey, Dad, you should come here and take a look at this.'

'Really, I don't think we ought to be poking around.'

'No, you've got to see this. Really really got to.'

He followed her into the room where all those years ago he had first set eyes on Bunderlin. All the same clocks were still hanging on the walls. If the old boxes were still there, they were hidden under many years' accumulation of yet more. But on the table in front of the window there was a lady's red handbag, a box file and some notebooks and a small space where Bunderlin evidently sat to work upon his collection. On that cleared space there rested three wallets of photographs, two of which looked fairly new whilst the third was quite old. Emma picked up one of the newer ones and handed it to Martin. 'Take a look at that.'

Eighteen

'Really,' Martin said as he began to prepare some lunch, 'there's nothing there that I didn't know already. It's the sort of guy that he is. He... well, he keeps tabs on folks. Always did. It's just the particular sort of obsessive behaviour that he...'

'For goodness' sake, Dad,' Emma protested. 'So he's obsessive, he's a stalker. He nobbles the dog, he just lets himself in here when he feels like it. He's a convicted murderer and you gave evidence against him. And somehow or other he's managed to get you installed in this flat. And that notebook with our address in it and all those times and dates. That really is creepy. Mega creepy. Then there's the handbag. With half dozen different girls' passports in it, for heaven's sake. What's he doing with that? What's he involved with? Don't you think you ought to speak to the police? Or what about his probation officer? He must have a probation officer you could talk to.'

'No.' Martin was definite. 'I'll ask him about it, of course. And I'll find out what I can. But whatever is going on, I can't imagine that Bunderlin is involved.'

'But the stuff's there, in his house. Of course he's involved.'

'Or someone is taking advantage of him. So I'm not going to do anything that'll get him sent back to prison. He's on licence, remember.'

'Well I hope you know what you're doing.'

Emma was right to be concerned, of course. Even without the complication of the handbag, the notebook and the photographs that she had found on Bunderlin's table were unsettling, alarming even. It was not simply that he was still up to his old tricks. Judging by the apparent order in that goon's archive of a living room, he was so very methodical about it. And there was the packet of photographs from years ago, from before the fire. Photographs of the factory gates at Merrion Dyestuffs and the block of flats where Martin used to live. All apparently innocuous, but why were they on his table now, all these years later? Martin shuddered but tried to shrug it off.

'Yes, well, right now what I'm going to do is have some lunch. And then I'm going up to the hospital to see how he is. Here, do us a favour. Do some salad to go with these sandwiches.'

'Right. Anyway, I'm sure you'll do whatever you want. After all, you know the guy better than I do, but I still think you're mad to trust him.'

He gave Emma his spare key because she wanted to take Samson for a walk before going to Julia's, then he drove to the hospital. Bunderlin had been moved into the main ward and was sitting beside his bed when Martin arrived. 'You're looking better than you were yesterday. How are you?'

'Poked, prodded, pierced and pronounced healthy enough. My dogs, did you feed my dogs?'

'Yes. Don't worry about them. I'll make sure they're OK.'

'Good. Don't forget Scobie. He likes to help so just ask him. And I usually give him a fiver. A fiver a favour.'

'Yes, well, we'll see about that. Now, do you know how long you are likely to be in here?'

'Another day or so. You've got to stop these witches taking over.'

'What on earth do you mean?'

'It's the little one. The Girl Guide in a black jumper. Wants me to have meals on wheels.'

'And what's wrong with that?'

'Cheese on toast, yes. Beans on toast, yes. Pilchards on toast, yes. But pilchards on wheels, no. It's not natural and I won't have it.'

'They'll not let you home till they're sure you're going to be properly looked after.'

'I told them you and Scobie can do that.'

'For heavens' sake, what can I do? The new term starts in a few days. Besides, if they saw the state of your kitchen, they'd... They wouldn't let you anywhere near it. And they'll want to know that you can cope with the stairs.'

'Stairs, steps, stepping stones and wicked stepmothers. I haven't used the stairs for years. It's a bungalow now. A two-storey, twelve-stair bungalow.'

When he returned to the flat the outer door was open. He hurried to the top of the stairs and as he put his key into the lock, he heard voices from inside. Let it be Maureen from downstairs, he thought, or Sally, or... but not those two thugs. He went in to find snuffling Gerry Mason, on his own this time, trying hard to be menacing but failing to rise above the pathetic. Initial panic, and guilt that he had not forewarned Emma of the possibility of an encounter with this inconvenient idiot or his partner, began to give way to cautious relief. Emma, who was sitting calmly on the sofa, always found it hard to understand that other people might dislike her favourite dog. Samson was at her feet, his eyes fixed on the visitor. Gerry had backed as far away from the dog as possible and was standing in the corner beside the window, sneezing into a grubby handkerchief and doing his feeble best to explain the purpose of his visit.

'OK, mister,' he said, 'Dave wants his account settled by next weekend.'

'It's nothing to do with me.'

'It's Tony Lullaby or...' He gave way to a fit of sneezing and Samson pricked his ears and growled very softly. When Emma reached down to calm him, he rolled onto his back, front paws stiffly in the air and back legs spread-eagled. This move alarmed Gerry, as though he imagined the dog was taking up a position from which to launch an attack.

'Try not to sneeze,' said Emma with a straight face. 'It frightens him. He's a black belt canine kamikaze expert.'

'Just... just keep it there. I'm going. I promise you, I'm going.' He began to edge his way towards the door but then gave in to more sneezing. Samson sprang to his feet and snuffling Gerry let out a little cry of alarm. 'No! Hold on to it. I don't want to hurt you. Just get Dave his money and stuff and we'll leave you alone.'

'But I'm telling you it's nothing to do with me. I'm just a chap who happens to live above Maureen's shop—for the moment. I know nothing at all about this Tony fellow or his business with your friend.'

'That's what you say. But Dave knows different. So you'd better tell him where he can find Tony Lullaby. Or else come up with the goods yourself.'

'Not me. How much is it, anyway, that he owed your friend?'

'Twenty grand.'

'Twenty grand? Look, get this straight and get it across to your tattooed friend – it's nothing to do with me.'

'Well I'll tell him that's what you say. But, take my advice, mister, nobody messes with Dave.' By this time Gerry had inched his way to the door. Martin followed him to the top of the stairs and watched as he hurried away.

'Dad, you get worse all the time,' said Emma when he came back into the living room. 'That man's a banana. How many more of them are you gathering?'

'Don't ask.'

As he told her the full story, Emma sat open-mouthed, shaking her head. 'But why has this Dave guy taken so long to come looking for Tony? I mean, the fire in the shop, how long ago was it? Thirty years?'

'No, thirty years ago Bunderlin started a fire in a barber's shop. The guy who died was Webster and Bunderlin got a life sentence. He came out on licence, I don't know, five years ago, fifteen years ago. I've no idea when. Then, fairly recently, there's another fire and this Lullaby chap died.'

'So who started that one?'

'Haven't a clue. I don't know that anyone was ever blamed or suspected for it.'

'And you've not put two and two together?'

'I'm not even thinking about it. It's purely coincidental. Nothing to do with Bunderlin.'

'Well, it sounds very spooky to me.'

'I've just realised something,' said Martin. 'I think I can see what's been going on. Just now young Gerry said his friend wants his money and stuff. And stuff. When they first showed up, it was their share of the payout from some deal or other. And the return of some documents. So now we know what those documents are.'

'Bloody hell, Dad. This is getting really heavy.'

'Yes, but it wasn't Bunderlin who led them to me. It was Maureen downstairs. They must have seen me in the pub with her and assumed I had moved in on this character Lullaby's territory.'

'So the handbag belongs to the sex shop woman who just, oops, left it behind at Bunderlin's place one day. As you do when you happen to forget that you're carrying a pile of stolen passports around.'

'Basically, yes. Something like that.'

'Dad, you're bonkers. There's no hope for you. When is your house ready to move into?'

'Not for another six weeks at least.'

'You've got to be out of here way before then. But now, I'm off to Mum's. I'll see you on Monday and I'll want to know that you're doing something about this whole crazy farce.'

The following morning as Martin was about to let Samson into the car to take him to Rylands Park, Scobie Sharples turned up. 'Hello there, squire.'

'Oh, hello. Glad you've come. There was something I wanted to ask you about.' He opened the tailgate and Samson jumped into the back of the car, climbed over the seats and sat behind the steering wheel.

'Yeah, right,' said Scobie. 'Mr Bundy normally gives me a bit of, well, a man's got to eat and drink, right?'

'And you normally do various jobs for him, I gather?'

'Sometimes.'

'OK. There's something I need you to do for him. But first, tell me what you know about Tony Lullaby.'

'What? Who? Me? No, you've got it wrong, squire. Don't know nothing about Tony Lullaby. No, never heard of him. Well, no, I heard of him. Everybody's heard of him. But I don't know nothing, so I can't tell you nothing. So if that's all you want, I'll just fuck off. And I'll tell you this—you want to be careful going round asking about Tony Lullaby. The less you know, the better.'

'OK. All right. But don't hurry away. I thought you wanted to earn some money.'

'Oh, well, now you're talking, squire.'

'I need you to clean up Mr Bundy's kitchen.'

'What? No way. He's not told you that, has he? No, he wouldn't like it. Can't touch any of that stuff.'

'For heaven's sake, Scobie, I only mean the mess in the kitchen. You must have seen it. There's piles of rubbish and everything is thick with grease. Looks like it's never been cleaned since his mother died. So have you got a couple of hours?'

'I suppose so.'

'OK, I'll go and get some stuff for you. Then I'll drop you off and get you started.'

Later in the afternoon, Martin drove back to Barton Lane. Scobie was in the garden picking over the junk piled against the garage. 'Finished already?'

'Done what I can, squire. Done what I can.'

He went inside. The kitchen had been transformed from staggeringly unbelievable to merely disgusting and Scobie, who was grinning proudly at the results of his efforts, was filthy. 'Must be worth a few notes, squire.' Martin gave him fifteen pounds and offered to drive him home.

'You're a gentleman, squire. But no, I'll just take a walk to the bus station and get some dinner.'

'Better get cleaned up first.'

'It'll blow off, squire. Don't you worry. It'll blow off.'

'Well, all right. But before you go, tell me something. I know you don't want to talk about Tony Lullaby, so I'll not press you. But what about a couple of characters called Dave Brierley and Gerry Mason? Dave's about my age, tattooed. Gerry's in his twenties maybe. Probably used to be friends of Tony Lullaby.'

'Are you stupid, or what?' said Scobie. 'Don't have nothing to do with those two. They're bad news. Definitely bad news.'

'Dave got it into his head that I know where Tony is, so he's after some money that he reckons he's owed.'

'Then you're in deep shit, squire. Take my word for it.'

'No, I've put them right. At least, I think I have. I've explained that I never had any connection with whatever Tony was up to. But I'd like to know what it was all about.'

'No, you wouldn't, squire. And you've not explained nothing to Dave. Got no brain, see. Can't take it in.'

'So I suppose I'd better be careful then.'

'Real careful, squire. Real careful,' said Scobie as he set off walking in the direction of the bus station.

Nineteen

The new term was less than three days old and Martin was already growing a little weary of handing out advice to a seemingly endless stream of freshers who really ought to have had clearer ideas by this time about the courses they wished to register for. He was at the window with his back to the open door watching the comings and goings in the precinct below. There was a knock at his door. A confident knock this time. Not like the timid, tap tap-tapping of so many of the sheepish new undergraduates who had been coming to his room all day. It sounded like the knock of someone out to make an early impression.

'Come in,' he called, turning round. It was Emma. 'Oh, still here? I thought you would have gone by now.'

'Tomorrow. Sally's mum's going to drive us. Now, sit down, I've got something for you.'

'Sounds intriguing.'

'Well it's only what you ought to have been doing yourself,' said Emma unfolding a photocopied newspaper report. 'Actually there's not much in this, so it's probably not worth having.'

'But...?'

'But, Sally's sister's friend's dad is a copper so we asked him what he can remember about this Tony Lullaby. And it turns out your local Mafia godfather was a pram salesman.'

'A what?'

'Sold prams, cots and pushchairs for a living. Anthony Greaves, he was. Couldn't get a job because nobody was daft enough to employ him – too many gaps in his record. Six months here, a couple of years there for possession, car theft, burglary and the like. So in the end his doting mummy gave him a job in her shop. Do you remember Lullaby's, the pram shop on Eastgate?'

'Vaguely.'

'Well that was it. Burned down two years ago this winter and poor little Anthony was inside at the time.'

'Any idea what had happened?'

'The police suspected at first that it was an insurance scam because the shop was slowly trickling into the potty at the time. They thought someone might have been tampering with a gas heater but they never proved anything, so the coroner gave an open verdict and the insurance company eventually paid up. And now Mummy Greaves has a nice new baby shop and Maureen Tong has a nice new adult shop and everybody's happy.'

'Except tattooed Dave and snuffling Gerry.'

'Well, there you are. That's what I know. And I reckon that if you were to tell the police about those two poking around, it might just be enough for them to take another look at the case. Could get them off your back.'

'Yes, well, maybe when we know why Bunderlin has those passports.'

'For heaven's sake, Dad! Don't just sit around thinking about it. Tell him you know about them. Find out why he's got them.'

'Yes, I will.'

A few minutes later he watched as Emma crossed the precinct and went into the coffee bar near the library entrance. He began to feel a little guilty. She was concerned for him, very concerned, and his own easy going manner, his readiness to believe that the difficult situations would just evaporate, only heightened her sense of impending danger. Very well, he would do something about it. He would ring his building contractor and find out what was preventing him from finishing the work on his house on schedule. He would insist on completion within a fortnight and he would ring right away. Well, first thing next day as it was already getting rather late. His mobile phone began to ring.

It was Bunderlin. 'Martin, dear chap, they've given me my release papers. I need you to come for me.'

'Right, well, you'll have to hang on a bit longer because I can't get away until the end of the afternoon. So have your dinner there and I'll come for you about seven o'clock.'

'I've got to be home before then. I need you to come now.'

'Can't. You'll have to wait. See you at seven.' In fact, he could have gone right away. Registration would be finishing by now so there was no further need for him to be available in the Department. He would go to the library snack bar in case Emma was still around and maybe have a drink and a sandwich to save having to prepare a meal when he got home. As he was about to leave his room a young man appeared in the doorway.

'Dr Latham? Hi, I've just come over from the Union office.' He handed Martin a large envelope. 'We're running a special edition of *Phoenix* for freshers' week and intend to include this. We'll be printing tonight so if you want to do a reply could you drop it into the office before six? Cheers.' Without waiting for any response he turned and hurried away. Martin dropped the envelope onto his desk. He wasn't going to think about writing anything for the campus newspaper at this time in the afternoon.

Slowly and with great difficulty, Bunderlin shuffled his way round to the back of the house and Martin, following, realised that it was not going to be easy to walk away from this exasperating giant. They went into the house and the dogs, prancing and whirling about him, appeared to sense that their master was frail and needed to be treated with caution. Bunderlin sat by the table and the Jack Russell jumped onto his knee and began to lick his face whilst the bearded collie jumped up first at one side then at the other to be fussed, almost singing as he did so. In her excitement the Jack Russell peed on his knee but Bunderlin seemed hardly to notice. Suddenly the dogs ran off through the open door and he struggled to his feet. He made his way across to the sink and began to rummage underneath. 'Tidy, tidy, tidy. Scrubbing scrubbing scrubbing. For what? Four watts, is a very dim bulb. *When I consider how my light is spent in this dark world...*' He found a bottle of Riesling and then began to search for a corkscrew and glasses. 'Ah, no,' he said. 'Not here. No, not here. You get it, dear boy. It's under the table. Go on, under there. It's Ulla, she likes to chew the corks.'

Martin got down on his hands and knees and began to root amongst the dogs' bedding under the table. And there it was – an old corkscrew from which a cork has been almost chewed away. He dusted himself down, cleaned up the corkscrew as best he could and opened the bottle. He found a dirty glass by the sink, washed it but found nothing to wipe it on, and half filled it. He handed it to Bunderlin who looked at it with a puzzled expression. '*Come, fill the cup – fill the cup, fill the cup—and in the fire of spring the winter garment of repentance fling.*' He filled the glass to the brim and handed it to Martin. Then he picked up a mug from the table, wiped it on the corner of his jacket and filled it for himself. '*The bird of time has but a little way to fly—and lo, the bird is on the wing.*'

Martin took a sip of the wine and offered to go and sort out the bed but Bunderlin would not allow it. 'Nothing to do. All is ready, all is well.'

'If you say so. Now is there anything I can do before I leave you? Do you have a discharge letter I can take to your GP?'

He made no reply. Martin asked again if he wanted anything. 'Tell Scobie Sharples I need him.' Martin waited a moment, expecting him to add something. But he added nothing. Martin waited a little longer before opening the door to leave but still the big man remained silent. 'Oh well, good night.' Bunderlin raised his hand and let it drop to the arm of the chair. Questions about the red handbag and its contents would have to wait until another time.

Martin parked his car in the yard at the back of the block, locked up and walked round to the front. A figure was standing in the doorway and emerged into the light as he drew near. It was Dave Brierley. 'Well now, if it isn't Mister Smart Guy. My young friend came to see me the other day. Know what I mean?'

Martin took his keys from his pocket but thought that perhaps it might not be a good idea to open the door with this character close by. Should he continue along the street and come back when he'd shaken him off?

'Not a very clever little bleeder, young Gerry. Got it into his head that you'd told him you wasn't going to pay me. Well I thought, no, that isn't right. Nobody's that stupid. Know what I mean? So you just tell me young Gerry made a mistake, and then we can all sort of rest easy.'

'Your friend was quite right,' Martin replied. 'I'm nothing to do with Tony Lullaby, and I'm nothing to do with Maureen and her shop. So I'm afraid you'll have to look elsewhere.'

'And here was me thinking you're a clever sort of geezer. But you're not, are you? 'Cause clever geezers don't make stupid mistakes like that. Know what I mean? So let me ask you once again. Did my young friend make a mistake?'

'No.'

'OK, Mister Smart Guy, I get the picture. Now me, I'm a decent guy. Always try to do the right thing. Know what I mean? So here's what I'll do – I'll make you a deal. Either you pay me the full twenty, or you pay me five grand. That's a full seventy-five percent discount. Plus you give me back all my documents. Now is that fair, or what?'

'Look, whatever you and your friend Lullaby were involved in, it's nothing whatever to do with me. Not then and not now. So I can't help you.'

'I see. So what you're telling me is the lady's got all the stuff. So I'll just have to go and ask her again, won't I? And if she still can't remember anything I'll come back and tell you. And here's what I'll say.'

With that he punched Martin hard in the stomach and twice in the ribs. He bent over in pain and dropped to the ground. A voice hissed in his ear, 'Is that very clear, my friend?'

Twenty

He was still in pain the following morning when he drove to the university. His face was sore and bruised and his ribs ached. Having no lectures or classes until the following week and no special responsibility for new students this year, he would probably be able to spend the morning quietly in his room and leave at lunch time. He parked at the far end of the campus from the History Department hoping that the short walk might help to ease the stiffness. It didn't help much.

'Martin! Hey, Martin.' He stopped and turned around. It was Dorothy Willetts, the grandmotherly Professor of Philosophy with whom he shared a course in Ancient Greek Language and Literature. 'Goodness, you look like death warmed up. Whatever have you been doing?'

'Upsetting the wrong people. I'll tell you another time.'

'Well, do take care. Have you seen *Phoenix*? What's this ridiculous piece they're running? Do tell me they've got it all wrong.'

'I've no idea. Not seen it. Oh, wait a minute—someone did drop by late yesterday afternoon with something. But I didn't have time to look at it.'

'Pity. You probably should've done. Here, take my copy and I'll see you later.'

She hurried off towards the library and Martin carried on to the Department and went to his room, stopping at the coffee machine on the way but without calling in at the office as he would normally have done. He unfolded the copy of *Phoenix* that Dorothy Willetts had given him. There, on the front, was the piece she had referred to. Very short, but prominent:

History of Porn

Who is behind the new sex shop on Saint Mary's Street? International sex traders, local crime barons, racketeers? Wrong. It is none other than the University's very own Dr Martin Latham, Reader in Ancient History. Phoenix approached Dr Latham to ask for his comments but he has so far chosen to say nothing.

His first response was to laugh. The piece was just so ridiculous. But that soon gave way to anger and panic as he began to realise what sort of reaction there might be around the campus. He could see it already: pickets outside his lectures, hecklers within, students withdrawing from his courses in protest, campaigns for his removal. He snatched up the offending newspaper and was about to hurry away to the Union office when John Lucas, the Head of Department, appeared at his doorway. He was a small, middle-aged man, who always managed to find a bow tie of quite the wrong colour for the shirt he was wearing. Today's combination was blue and purple.

He stopped suddenly when he came into the room and stared at Martin's bruised face. 'Whatever is this nonsense you've got into, Martin?' he demanded, waving a copy of the paper.

'Just that,' Martin replied. 'Nonsense. They haven't bothered to check the facts. That shop is nothing to do with me. I just happen to be living temporarily in the adjoining flat.'

'You mean..? Let's get this straight. Are you telling me it's not your shop?'

'That's right. I rented a flat and someone else rented a shop from the same landlord. My front door happens to be beside the shop door.'

'And you're sure about this?'

'Yes, of course I'm sure, you... You didn't really think I'd get into that sort of thing, did you?'

'Well, you'd better sort it out, then. Right away. I mean, this could be really embarrassing for the whole department.' He turned and left the room but came back immediately. 'But how come you're living there? I mean, in Saint Mary's Street, for goodness' sake.'

'We sold the house. I've bought a cottage out at Borrinsmoor, but I can't move in until the new kitchen extension is built.'

'But Saint Mary's Street. Good God, man, it's a bit of a comedown, isn't it?'

'It's very interesting actually. An eye-opener.'

'Well, it's done something for your eyes. I can see that. For goodness' sake, man, go and... well, whatever. And sort that mess out.' He dropped his copy of *Phoenix* onto Martin's desk and walked away, muttering to himself.

Martin set off for the Union office, hurrying at first but immediately slowing right down as a sharp pain stabbed at his side. In the office a young man with long greasy hair was lounging behind the untidy desk. It was the same person who had brought the envelope to him late the previous afternoon. He sat upright when Martin walked in, as if expecting a confrontation. Calmly, Martin set the paper down in front of him and pointed to the offending article. 'You've got that wrong,' he said. 'Completely wrong. My neighbour's business is nothing at all to do with me. As you would have learned if you had taken the trouble to check your facts.'

'Not me. I'm just, well, I just sort of help out, like.'

'Well, you'd better just sort of help out, like, now. Because I want a retraction and an apology printed right away. This morning.'

'Can't do it. I mean, I can't. You need to talk to Jan. The editor. She's not around until this afternoon.'

'That's a pity, because that will be too late. See, I need that retraction printed well before then. I want all copies withdrawn from distribution now. So you'll have to dash around all your outlets and get them back. And then I want an A4 poster printed on a *Phoenix* masthead—I'll give you the wording in a minute— and I want to see it all over the campus by early afternoon. And if none of that is done I will be taking legal advice. Is that clear?'

'Well, it's clear, yes. But I'm not sure that I can do that myself.'

'Yes, you can. Your alternative is to land your paper and the editor in a pretty serious legal mess.'

'I suppose, if you put it that way...'

He would have gone to the Pennine Snack Bar as usual at lunch time and faced the inevitable questions about that wretched article, but the pain in his side made walking difficult. The confectioner's in the precinct was about as far as he could comfortably manage so he went there for a sandwich instead. In the window of the union office six or more of the posters which he had demanded were displayed. Indeed, he saw that they were displayed all over the precinct and along the walkway between there and History. Everywhere he looked, the *Phoenix* masthead was looking back at him with the banner headline, *Sorry, Dr Latham*. He smiled and then began to wonder which was the more embarrassing—this or the original article?

Later that afternoon he went home to collect Samson and then drove up to Borrinsmoor to see what progress was being made on his house. There was no sign of the builder. As he approached the front door, a green van pulled up behind his car and, assuming it was the builder returning from lunch, he left the door open and went through to the back of the house. There was little sign of anything having been done since his previous visit. A hole had been cut in the wall for a tumble dryer but the vent had not been fitted. Going out at the back, he saw that some steps had been built to take care of the two-foot drop outside the door. But that was all that had been done in two weeks. At this rate the job would be finished in about three years.

There were footsteps behind him. He turned, about to demand an explanation for the lack of progress, but it was Scobie Sharples. 'Afternoon, squire. Been following you all the way from the university. Mr Bundy is in hospital again.'

'But he only came home yesterday. What's wrong?'

'Search me. Nobody tells me anything. Lucky I'd gone round there. Been to the chippy for him, as a matter of fact. And there he is, flaked out on the kitchen floor. Anyway, I think you'd better go in and see him.'

'Yes, well, soon as I can.' As he climbed the doorsteps the pain in his side became intense and he caught his breath.

'You all right, squire?'

'Had a run in with our friend Dave last night. Cracked a rib, probably.'

'You're lucky if that's all he's done to you. Oh, here, nearly forgot. You'd best have these.' He handed Martin Bunderlin's keys. 'You'll need them to see to the dogs.'

Reluctantly, Martin took them from him and Scobie followed him out of the house. As Martin opened his car to let Samson out, he struggled to do so without causing too much pain in his side. 'Really done you in, hasn't he, squire?' said Scobie. 'You don't want to be messing with a geezer like that on your own, you know. Now, if you was to give the say-so, I could put him right for you.'

'You've changed your tune. You wouldn't even talk about him the other day.'

'Know how these guys tick, squire. See, your trouble is you don't understand. No offence, squire, but you're sort of clueless really.'

'So what do you suppose you can do that you wouldn't even think about before?.'

'You leave it with me, squire. Leave it with me.' He chuckled. 'A word in the right ear and it'll soon get back to Dave.'

Scobie drove towards town and Martin took Samson for a slow and cautious walk down the lane as far as the river and through the wood to Moorhouses before returning to his flat far too late in the afternoon to have any prospect of running into a builder.

He eased himself stiffly into the armchair and flicked through the TV channels looking for something undemanding to while away the evening and keep his self-pity at bay. His phone rang. It was Carol. Carol who? Of course, scatty Carol who wanted to work the Pennine magic on his cottage.

'So I thought if I could go up there with you I could have a good look around and get a feel of the place... Then we can go over to this absolutely wonderful place I know and see what we can find. Believe me, you'll be amazed at the things they have there.'

'But I'm not sure when I'm going to have the time to go looking round the dealers.'

'Look, don't worry about that. Are you free right now?'

'Well...'

'Look, why don't you pick me up and I can phone Gordon later on. He'll open up for me if he's got anything you might want, I know he will.'

He found himself, half an hour later, driving up to Carol's place in Heaton. She was at her front door before he was half way up the drive. 'Hello, Martin, it's great to see you. We'll just... Oh no, what's happened to you? Have you been in an accident?'

He cut the story short. 'I got mugged.'

'Oh no, you poor thing. Look, come in for a minute. I've got just the thing for you.' She hustled him into her living room every bit as efficiently as Dave Brierley had hustled him into his flat, and sat him in an armchair. 'You wait there. I'll be back in just a jiffy.'

'Here,' she said when she came back into the room. 'Hold this to your face for five minutes.' She handed him a cold flannel moistened with some exotic-smelling concoction. 'That will help to take the bruising away. Oh gosh, if only I'd been with you when it happened I could have stopped it swelling up and discolouring like that. You poor thing. Did they get away with anything?'

'Only my pride.'

'You poor thing.' She disappeared again and returned a little while later with a glass of what was probably only sparkling mineral water. 'Does that feel better?' she asked as she took away the flannel and handed him the drink.

'I'm sure it does,' he replied. At least he smelled prettier.

As they drove up to Borrinsmoor Carol tried to coax the story of Martin's mugging from him, but succeeded only in making him feel wretchedly aware of how unfriendly his monosyllabic replies must sound. And it really wasn't fair of him to be so irritated by her repeated interjections of, 'Oh, you poor thing.' She was only trying to be sympathetic.

As soon as they arrived, the cottage took over from Martin's bruises for Carol's attention. 'Oh, this is just wonderful!' She wanted to walk round to the back and take a look at the garden before going inside. 'Oh, this is super,' she said as Winter Hill came into view.

Inside, she went silently and systematically from one room to the next. From the living room to the old kitchen, to the extension and back to the living room. Upstairs and to the front bedroom. To the back room and to the bathroom. And back to the living room.

'It's...' she began, but paused. Her scatty manner had disappeared and Martin even fancied that she was beginning to appear quite professional. 'Can I say just one thing? Whatever you do, just don't try to turn it into a modern house.'

'No. That's not what I had in mind.'

'Good. That living room is lovely but the fireplace, well, they were all the rage, brick surrounds. But it's so false. Even a nineteen fifties tiled surround would look better. But what you really want is a proper old kitchen range.'

She was right, of course. But the contractor was taking so long that he had no stomach for any more major work. 'Don't worry about that,' said Carol. 'I know someone who could do it. So just tell me you want a gorgeous old kitchen range in there.'

'Well, I must admit it would look good.'

'Leave it with me. I'll see what I can find and let you know. Then we need to get your builder moving again.'

'If you can do that, I'll...' He was about to say, 'I'll give you a free hand to decorate the place as you think it should be done.' But he stopped himself in time because that would be rather silly. Instead, he added lamely, 'I'll be forever in your debt.'

Twenty-one

There was a note through his door when he got home long after all the shops had shut. 'Mart, Need to see you in the New Zealander tonight. It's OK, you-know-who doesn't go in there any more. Maureen.'

Yes, well, Martin thought, there's someone else who doesn't go in there either. Except, of course, that he did need to find out whether Dave Brierley had begun to put more pressure on her and it was probably better to call in the New Zealander rather than the sex shop and risk being seen by someone from the University. But it would have to wait until after he had been to the hospital and it would only be for five minutes.

Bunderlin was sleeping when Martin arrived so he sat by the bed and waited. Gradually the ward filled with visitors, mostly ignoring the notice at the entrance requesting no more than two visitors to a patient at a time. A stern-faced, middle-aged woman among the crowd around the next bed looked over her shoulder at Martin and seemed to be thinking that really he should get out of the way to make room for her. Each time he inched his chair away to create a little more space for himself, she moved to push him further. Bunderlin remained asleep.

Martin went to find someone he might ask about him. 'Are you a relative?' asked the nurse at the desk near the entrance.

'A friend. I don't think he has any family. I'm Martin Latham—I believe he asked for me to come in.'

The nurse checked his notes. 'Oh, right, Mr Latham. Yes, we've got you down as next of kin. Don't seem to have an address or phone number for you, though.' Then having taken the missing details, he said, 'So, what can I say about him? We think he may have had a stroke. We're running tests so we'll have a clearer picture when we get those results.'

'So how bad is he?'

'Hard to say. We should know in the next twenty-four hours.'

Martin returned to his bedside. The chair had been taken away so he balanced on the edge of the bed at the foot where there was a little room. The crowd on one side were discussing arrangements for a granddaughter's birthday party and the old man on the other side was giving his wife, and everyone else who wasn't completely deaf, a graphic description of the embarrassing effects of his bowel disorder. Bunderlin slept on.

It was getting towards the end of visiting time and Martin began to write a brief note to leave beside his water jug. As he did so, Bunderlin opened his eyes.

'Hello,' said Martin.

Bunderlin looked at him blankly.

'How are you feeling?'

He made no response. He tried to sit up but failed.

Martin moved a little closer.

Bunderlin moved a finger as if suggesting that he was trying to say something. After a lot of effort he managed a faint whisper so that Martin was not sure he had heard correctly.

'Words.'

'Words?'

Bunderlin rested from the hard work before trying again. 'Gone,' he seemed to add this time.

'Gone? What's gone?' Martin felt helpless. He ought to be able to help by working out what Bunderlin was trying to say. Words, gone?

'Are you trying to tell me that your words have gone?'

Was there a flicker of a smile on the big man's face? He made another attempt. 'Scones.'

'Scones?'

After a long pause, Bunderlin added, 'Keys.'

'I've got your keys. Don't worry about your dogs. I'll take care of them.'

'Scones,' he said again. 'Help.'

'Ah, Scobie, you mean? Yes, Scobie will help.'

Bunderlin relaxed and closed his eyes.

On his way home, Martin stopped at Bunderlin's house to let out the dogs and make sure they were fed. The kitchen, though transformed by Scobie's efforts of a few days before, was nevertheless still revolting and not even fit for the dogs, let alone for a disabled old man who would no longer be able to look after himself. It was, perhaps, just about tolerable for now, but it would not be right to leave things like this for any longer than absolutely necessary, no matter how long it might be before Bunderlin would be able to return. 'Oh, for goodness sake, Peter Bunderlin, why did I let you drag me into this?' Martin muttered aloud as he locked up.

He had made up his mind. He had to get out of the tangle he had been drawn into. He would call in at the estate agent's office and give notice to quit the tenancy. Living in his cottage whilst the builder was still working on his kitchen extension would be luxury in comparison with all the complications of the flat in St Mary's Street. He would contact the RSPCA to see about the dogs and then he would speak to someone in the hospital about arrangements for Bunderlin's return whenever that might be. And he would be able to do all that the next day because he had the whole afternoon free of appointments.

He felt relieved to have made that decision but as he got out of his car, the sudden pain in his side reminded him that he was not yet free of the mess. He really did need to go and find

Scobie because it would be impossible to care for the dogs on his own, even for a short while. And then there was Maureen. She had wanted a word with him and he ought to find out if she knew anything about that bag, and whether tattooed Dave was threatening her as well. Maybe he should add a visit to the police station to that list of tasks for the next day.

It was well after nine when he went into the New Zealander. The place was crowded and smoky and many of the customers appeared much the worse for drink. Better get it over with, he thought. He went through to the saloon bar where he had spotted Scobie the previous time and found him perched on a high stool at the end of the bar.

'Ah, there you are, squire,' he said as Martin approached. He downed the last of his beer and called to the barman for two pints of bitter and a scotch. 'Go to see Mr Bundy, did you?'

'Yes. I guess he's going to be in there for a while so I'll need your help with his dogs. Call round there a couple of times through the day and let them out. Can you do that? And I'll drop in each evening.'

The barman put the drinks down in front of them. 'Cheers, squire,' said Scobie. 'Decent of you.' Martin paid.

'Now, these dogs. Are you going to be able to help out? Look, take his keys and get a spare one cut for yourself. Then put them through my letterbox."

'Well, OK, then. But, tell you what—if you was to slip me a couple of notes it might help a bit.'

Staying around the town centre for much longer could begin to get expensive, Martin thought. 'Here, take this,' he said, handing him a tenner. 'And have you seen Maureen Tong in here tonight?'

'Maureen? Tony Lullaby's piece, the dirty book shop girl? Sure, she's round in the front bar, I think.'

Martin felt conscious of eyes watching him as he went to the other bar. He stood near the door and looked around but, not seeing her in there, he decided he would leave. Before he could move, however, she was at his side. 'Hi, Mart. Been waiting for you. Where the fuck have you been?'

'Do you want a drink?'

'Not here. We'll go to the Gypsy's Tent. It's usually pretty quiet in there.'

The Gypsy's Tent was a small, dismal pub tucked away in a narrow back street and, as Maureen had said, it was quiet. A tall, thin, young man behind the bar was reading a tabloid newspaper when they went in and did not look up until Martin asked to be served. At the far end of the long narrow room two men were playing pool. There was no one else in the pub.

'So tell me,' said Martin as he put the drinks on the table beside the juke box, 'is Dave Brierley still pestering you?'

'The fucking bastard. But I need to know that you're not going to go and tell the police.'

'Why not? It's the obvious thing to do, isn't it? After all, the man's dangerous.'

'Look, just don't tell the police, that's all. I can deal with him myself.'

'But how? I mean, he's asking for twenty thousand pounds and he's vicious. You don't want to be dealing with a guy like that, surely?'

'Don't want to. Too bloody right I don't want to. But there's no choice.'

'What about the other stuff he's after? Documents, or whatever. Have you any any idea what all that is?'

'No. It was him and Tony. It was nothing to do with me and I've got nothing that belongs to either of them.'

'So why not just go to the police and let them sort him out?'

'For fuck's sake, Martin. Are you stupid? He'll only go and fit me up for some of the stuff that him and Tony did. And I really could do without that. Only just got the shop open and all that. I don't want... well, I don't need the aggravation.'

'So how do you reckon you will deal with Brierley?'

'I've agreed to pay him. I'll pay him off a bit each month. Just enough to keep him quiet.'

'But twenty thousand. Doesn't that just put you back where you started with Tony Lullaby? Never seeing anything of what you're earning.'

'I know. But I've got no choice. Anyway, I knocked him down to five thousand.'

'And what else?'

'Nothing. That's it.'

'So he agreed to a huge reduction, just like that?'

'Well, no. Not quite. He thinks I've got some stuff that belonged to him and Tony. I haven't. Honest, I haven't, but I can string him along for a bit till I work out what to do next.'

She pulled a tissue from her handbag and began to dab at her eyes. 'I just wish someone would... You know what? Went into my kitchen tonight to get myself some tea. And I picked up this bread knife and I just thought, if only someone would stick that up Dave sodding Brierley we'd all be better off. 'Cause there's no bastard would shed a tear if he copped it.'

Later in the evening when Martin got back from taking Samson for his late night walk round the block, the conversation with Maureen was still going through his mind. He felt a little bit guilty for leaving her alone in the pub. In the short time that he had known her she had appeared hard, streetwise and cynical. Inevitable, perhaps, after her long involvement in the darker side of town centre life. But this time he thought he saw a little of the nervous teenager who had ventured reluctantly into prostitution and stayed too long, just long enough to be drawn into the dehumanising and vicious world of Tony Lullaby. And she knew all about those passports, he was sure of it.

Someone began to hammer at the street door. Samson barked softly and slid down from the sofa where he'd settled himself down for the night. Martin was about to shut him into the flat before going down the stairs but then thought that it might be as well to let him come. He paused at the door. What if it was Brierley yet again? Perhaps he should go quietly back upstairs. The caller knocked again and Samson barked. Holding his collar, Martin cautiously opened the door. It was Scobie Sharples with a loose paper parcel in his hand. Martin led the way upstairs.

'You got anything to drink, squire?' said Scobie as he unwrapped his parcel and began to tuck into fish and chips.

'Tea, coffee, milk.'

'Forget it. Look, I thought I'd better tell you this, 'cause you'd like to know, see. No, tell you what, I will have a cup of tea. Three sugars.'

Martin went to put the kettle on. 'So what was it you thought I'd like to know?'

'Ah yes. Good news, squire. Good news. Dave is off your back.'

'How can I be sure of that?'

'Good and proper, squire, believe me. He'll not be around no more. Good and proper, that's what.'

'So what did you do? What did you tell him? Had you got something he wanted?'

'Me? Got something for him? No way, squire, no way. I just put the word around and it got back to him. But it's your lucky day, squire, cause something else cropped up. Anyway, take it from me, you're in the clear.'

Twenty-two

'Gosh, this all sounds terribly exciting,' said Dorothy Willetts. 'And do you really think this Sharples fellow will have managed to smooth things over for you?'

'We'll see. He might have done, but somehow I doubt it. Realistically, I have to acknowledge that he probably won't make very much difference.'

They were having lunch in the Pennine Snack Bar following a morning spent sorting out seminar groups and various handouts for the Ancient Greek course. Dorothy had been insistent that Martin tell her all about how he came to fall foul of a vicious criminal and how he had managed to give the wrong impression about the St Mary's Street sex shop. 'You really do make my life at the moment seem very humdrum.' In fact, he had given only an edited version of what had been going on over the past few weeks.

'Well, right now I'd give quite a lot for a bit of humdrum. I'll be moving into my new place in a couple of days. I'm off to the estate agent now to wind things up at the flat.'

His mobile phone began to ring. It was the hospital. 'Dr Latham? It's about your uncle...'

'But I don't...'

'Peter Bunderlin. I'm afraid he's not responding to treatment and we thought you would want to come and be with him.'

Bunderlin was in a side room when Martin arrived. Although he was connected to an array of monitors, had a drip in his arm and an oxygen mask over his nose and mouth, he looked peaceful. 'What is the outlook for him?' Martin asked the nurse who had brought him into the room.

'It's hard to say. His blood pressure and his pulse are all over the place.'

Martin stayed with him. Samson would be all right until late afternoon or early evening. Perhaps by that time Bunderlin would at least be stable and he could slip out then for an hour or two. Find Scobie and get him to see to the dogs. What if...? No, by evening he would be stable and Martin would be able to go home, get a night's sleep and sort out his lecture notes and rearrange some appointments if necessary.

Bunderlin remained perfectly still. He would bring a book with him when he came back in the evening. Time dragged by so slowly otherwise. Every quarter of an hour or so the nurse came in and checked the monitors. Martin waited. There were various posters and notices around the room but before long he had exhausted the possibilities for making anagrams from them. He glanced at his watch. Five o'clock. Another hour, then he would slip home. He went to the drinks machine near the entrance and got a coffee.

A few minutes before six o'clock there was a flurry of activity. Something had changed. One of the monitor displays was different. But what was the difference? Was it the bleeping or the flashing? He couldn't tell. He couldn't remember what it was doing before. Immediately, two nurses were in the room calmly checking their patient and all the equipment. Martin moved out of the way. After a few moments one of the nurses left the room. She came back very quickly with a doctor who examined Bunderlin briefly. Then the older nurse came to Martin. 'I'm sorry,' she said. 'He died.'

He called at Bunderlin's house on his way home and let the dogs out. If their excitement on being let out and the piles of shit in the kitchen were any indication, then Scobie had probably not been there through the day. Martin cleared up and then sat at the table as he waited for the dogs to return. What now? he wondered. Maybe he should try to introduce them to Samson and perhaps all three would get along together at Borrinsmoor. No, of course not, he realised at once. That was a silly idea. It was not just that he could almost hear Emma protesting – 'For heaven's sake, Dad, don't be an idiot.' He couldn't even have Samson on his own at Borrinsmoor yet because there would still be builders coming and going at all times of day. At least he hoped there would be. Damn. Why hadn't he thought of that problem before? So it would have to be the RSPCA for Bunderlin's dogs and his sister Jean for Samson. Or maybe she could be persuaded to take Ulla and Klaus as well.

He filled up the feeder and the water bowls and went through to the room where Emma had found the photographs and the handbag. So far as he could tell, nothing had been disturbed. Taking in the piles and piles of boxes he could see a hint of order, and more than just a hint, amongst the overwhelming impression of chaos. These boxes were all arranged tidily and numbered. He shook his head, not envying whoever would have the task sorting it all out. He went into the front room. That, too, was stacked high with boxes and bundles of newspapers. The two piles on either side were separated by just sufficient space to get to the huge armchair in the centre, which must have served Bunderlin as a bed. On one side of the room, one of the long case clocks that he remembered from years ago was looking out over the top of the pile. Its companion on the opposite side of the room, if it was still there, was hidden.

As he came out of the room he glanced up the stairs. That too was filled up with boxes and more boxes. Near the top a makeshift shelf had been put in place and on top of it were a large tea chest and several suitcases. The shelf sagged under their weight. How long must it have been since anyone went upstairs?

By this time the dogs had returned and were tucking in to a feed. As Martin began to turn out the lights ready to lock up, he wondered what Bunderlin used for a bathroom. Another walk through the house confirmed that only the two rooms downstairs and the kitchen were accessible. He locked up and glanced around the scrap-yard of a garden. Adjoining the house was a brick-built lean-to. He pushed the door open expecting it to be filled up with more boxes. But it was not. It was a very dirty but perfectly functional wash house with a shallow stone sink, an old cast iron, wooden-rollered mangle draped with grey and faded towels, and a zinc bath. In the corner was a lavatory without a seat and, beside it, a large industrial circular saw.

When he arrived home the lights were on in Maureen's shop and he thought that perhaps he should call in and tell her the news. But he chose not to. It could wait until later. He sat down with a mug of coffee and as his thoughts drifted back over the years that he had known Bunderlin his eyes filled with tears. Samson climbed onto the sofa beside him and rested his chin on his knee.

Before long someone began to knock at his door and he went down to be greeted by Maureen who looked a little shocked, even distressed. 'Have you heard?'

'Yes. Do you want to come up for a coffee?' How on earth could she know about it already?

'Need something a bit stronger than coffee. But, go on, it'll do.'

She locked her door and followed him up to the flat. 'It scares me,' she said. 'Really does scare me. It's so, well, spooky.'

He poured a mug of coffee and handed it to her. 'Cheers, Mart. Still, it means the pressure's off.'

'The pressure's off? I don't follow you. Are we both talking about the same thing?'

'Oh, for fuck's sake, Mart, there's not something else as well, is there? I'm talking about Dave Brierley. You know—that fucking bastard who trashed my shop the other day.'

'Oh. So what's happened?'

'He's dead. Hit and run late last night outside the back of the Beach Club. Some kid joyriding.'

It took a moment for this to sink in. Is this what Scobie was talking about when he said something else had cropped up? But why would he not say so? 'Right. And that's what frightens you?' He wasn't sure that he understood what she was saying, but thinking about it scared him a bit as well.

'Too right it does. I mean, it's like last time. I say how I wish Tony was topped and then next day he's fried in his shop. And then last night. Me telling you all that about wishing someone could take the knife to him and that's it. Next day, well same bleeding day actually, he's in an accident. Some accident.'

'Do they know how it happened? Have they picked up the driver?'

'No. It's some kid. Just scarpered. So they'll go and harass all the kids they know. And if they find whoever did it they should give him a medal.' She finished her coffee. 'Better go now. And you're not going to talk to the police, are you? I mean, there's no point now anyway. Hey, was there something else? You said there was something else happened.'

'Yes. It's Bunderlin. Mr Bundy. He died in hospital a couple of hours ago.'

'Oh shit. Poor old geezer. He was nice. Completely potty, but he was nice.' After a moment she added, 'He got the landlord here to let me rent the shop.'

'He was the landlord. It's his shop.'

'You sure about that? I didn't know that. I thought it was the office down the street. That's where I pay the rent to.'

'They're just the agents.'

'Bloody hell. So what happens now? Will I be able to keep the shop?'

Twenty-three

The following day being Friday, Martin did not need to be at the university. He took the opportunity instead to go with Samson for a long early walk through Rylands Park and let the fresh air clear his mind of the thoughts that had been troubling him through the night. It was Scobie he was worried about. Martin couldn't help wondering whether he really could have been stupid enough to stage an accident to get tattooed Dave Brierley out of the way. He had, after all, offered to sort him out and only a few hours later Dave had met with a nasty accident. And Scobie reports, job done.

Well, that was not quite how it was. Scobie had 'put the word around' and that might have been enough to solve the problem but then 'something else had cropped up' and Dave won't be around any more. That was it. Martin took a deep breath. Was Scobie driving that...? No, surely not. He'd not asked for a couple of notes as he always seemed to do. Didn't Martin know him well enough by now to know that he couldn't do a favour without suggesting it was worth a couple of notes? What a crazy contract killing that would have been.

He walked along the path beside the miniature golf course and Samson emerged from a gap in the hedge a little further ahead. Had he been looking for Bunderlin, to scrounge some apple from him? They carried on together towards the car park beside the old library and Martin's phone began to ring. It was the hospital enquiring discreetly whether he was proceeding with arrangements for Bunderlin's funeral. He wasn't going to pick this one up, so he suggested that they contact the estate agent who might know of the whereabouts of any relatives. He was about to say that he did have access to the house and might therefore be able to help, but then he thought better of it and kept quiet. It probably confused them, of course, because they had him down as next-of-kin. But all he could really do was make sure that the dogs were taken care of and then hand over the keys.

He called at the house on the way home to see to the dogs but found that Scobie was already there. 'Morning there, squire. Daft little buggers, these. Eat, shit, chase the cats and then sleep all day. Daft little buggers. You going in to see Mr Bundy today?'

'No. I'm afraid I've got a bit of bad news. He died last night.'

'Well dear, oh dear. Dear, oh fucking dear. Poor old sod. Seen it coming, I did, squire. As a matter of fact, I thought he'd already croaked when I brought him his fish and chips the other day. He was a saint. Did you know that, squire? It was him who done for that fucking barber that time. A saint he was.'

'We're going to have to get these dogs moved out. I was thinking...'

'You just leave that to me. I know who'll have them.'

'Who?'

'Leave it to me,' he replied. 'I'll get them in the van now.' He opened the gate and let the dogs into the lane. Immediately they went running towards the school field and Scobie opened up his van.

'Look, hadn't you better check first? We need to be sure that...'

'Don't fret, squire. Just leave it to me.'

'Well, all right then. But one other thing—Brierley's accident. Do the police know who was driving the car?'

'No. My guess is they'll not bother. Save themselves the trouble. Tell you what I think, though. I reckon it was Dave's stupid little side-kick.'

'Why do you think that?'

'Cause that's the word going round. But I'm saying nowt else.'

Martin shook his head. The Lostock old lags club was beyond his understanding. He took back the spare key, locked up and drove away once Scobie had got the dogs into his van.

Almost as soon as he sat down with a cup of tea, his phone rang. It was Carol. 'Martin, great news. I've found this really super kitchen range. You'll just love it. Are you free?'

'What? Now, you mean?'

'We could be up there in half an hour. And there's lots of other stuff you'll want to see as well.'

'I'm afraid I have an appointment shortly. Won't be finished till late afternoon, I should think.'

'Not to worry. Tell you what – why don't you pick me up when you've finished. Will five o'clock be all right?'

'Well, I suppose so. Will this place, wherever it is, still be open then?'

'He'll show us round any time we like. So I'll see you at five. Bye.'

Dynamic and efficient, or just plain pushy? He switched off his phone and finished his drink.

The estate agent's outer office was bright and modern with comfortable seating amongst the display boards showing houses and shops for sale and to rent. Martin had already spoken to the man at the desk and was now waiting to see Jonathan Feeney, one of the partners. Eventually a middle-aged man in a brown tweed suit and a faded red shirt came into the reception area and approached. He looked at Martin over the top of his black-rimmed spectacles. 'Mr Latham?' His deep crackly voice seemed to accuse Martin of being Mr Latham. 'Come with me.'

He led the way into a tiny office crammed with filing cabinets and a leather-topped desk that deserved better surroundings. In front of the desk was a small plastic chair, which Martin sat in without waiting to be invited. Feeney took the grand old swivel armchair behind it. He made himself comfortable and began to trim a cigar. Then, carefully placing the cigar on the blotter in front of him, he said, 'They phoned this morning, the hospital. Sad news, sad news. *Sic transit gloria mundi*. Now, Mr Latham. Oh, Doctor it is. Yes, forgive me. Dr Latham, have you brought your documents?'

'Er, no. I think you must have misunderstood. I simply wanted to let you know about Peter Bunderlin's death in case you might have, well, might have been his legal agent or whatever. And I've already spoken to your lettings folk about the tenancy of the flat at number 57 St Mary's Street. I wish to relinquish that.'

'No need. That will just sort itself out. In a manner of speaking. But I should check your documents first. Driving licence? Passport?'

'I have my driving licence here.' He took it from his wallet and pushed it across the desk. 'But why do you need this? I think we must be talking at cross purposes here.'

'No, no. That's fine. Now, where did I put that file? Ah, here we are.' He picked up a folder from the floor and opened it. 'I, Peter Bunderlin... and all that, and all that. Yes, and there's... Just give me a minute, Dr Latham.' He picked up the cigar and put it in his mouth but did not light it. He put it down again. 'Yes, that's it. All very simple and straightforward. I shall need a grant of probate, of course, before we can... But I can put you in the picture. No harm in that. As the sole beneficiary it all comes to you. House situate at one hundred and two Barton Lane and contents thereof together with contents and outbuildings contained within the curtilage of the said hereditament, shop and flat situate at fifty-seven Saint Mary's Street. It's all worded properly, of course, Dr Latham. I'm just translating as we go along. Contents of the flat except that which is the property of the sitting tenant, that being your own good self, the flat being the upper storey, and fittings and fixtures of the shop. Basically means it's all yours unless it's already yours. Or Miss Tong's. There's a portfolio of shares as well. I'll draw up a schedule for you. One condition. The lease on the shop in the name of Miss Maureen Tong can't be terminated without penalty for five years from, well, from when we actually make the transfers, I suppose. No, I tell a lie, five years from when we drew this up. So there we are. Now, you asked my receptionist if we know who will be arranging the funeral. That's you, Dr Latham.'

He didn't have time to sit and take it all in before driving to Carol's place. And then, swept along on her enthusiasm for his absolutely gorgeous cottage, and her friend Gordon's wonderful business, he couldn't concentrate upon anything. 'So I know you're just going to love this place when you see it. The range is just perfect. I said as soon as I saw it, my friend Martin will go crazy when he sees this, it's just so right.'

He did his best to follow her directions and eventually arrived at a builders' merchant's yard on the southern edge of the town. Between the main yard and what looked like an old farmhouse was a smaller place where various reclaimed architectural items were stored. Carol led the way to the side door of the house and rang the bell. 'Down here!' called a voice from behind a large wooden outbuilding.

Martin followed Carol down the path beside the outbuilding and into a covered area when an assortment of stoves, boilers and fireplaces was housed. 'Hi there, Gordon,' Carol called to the tall thin man who was rearranging his stock. 'This is my friend Martin. When I told him about the kitchen range he said he just had to come and see it.'

'You poke around, Carol, love. I'll be here when you want me.'

'Right. Over here, then, Martin.'

He followed her further into the labyrinth.

'There,' she said triumphantly when they came to the end of the long row of fireplaces. 'Isn't that just super?'

It was a black iron range with an oven and hot cabinet on one side of the fire grate and a hob on the other. Just like the one they used to have in their council house when he was very young. It was probably ideal for his cottage and after carefully looking it over and standing back to visualise it in his living room, and glancing around to see what else the merchant had in stock, he said it was good and he would like to have it.

'Leave it with me. I can get the whole job done for you in about a week. Oh, and that reminds me—I had a word with your builder. He promised me he'll finish your kitchen within a couple of weeks.'

They spent a little while longer browsing among the stock but Martin had no wish to prolong the work on his cottage any longer than necessary. But he did agree that it would be a good idea to replace the assortment of cheap plastic door handles with a matching set of something in keeping with the character of the place. And, yes, stripping the doors and skirting boards, and sanding and sealing the floorboards was probably, as Carol put it, just crying out to be done.

He drove Carol back home, trying all the time to respond appropriately to her bubbling recital of all the wonderful possibilities of his cottage. It wasn't really that she irritated him. He was simply preoccupied with his thoughts about Bunderlin and his growing feeling of guilt about his impatience with the daft old bugger who only ever wanted to be his friend.

As he dropped Carol at her door, he found himself inviting her for a meal at the weekend. 'That would be lovely,' she said. 'Tell you what—I know this really super restaurant, and I do mean super, you'll absolutely love it. It's right in the centre of Manchester, really tucked out of sight so it's not very well known yet because they only opened a few weeks ago, but they are really going places. I'll book us a table.'

He watched her walk up to her front door. She opened it, switched on the light and turned to wave to him. A silly little wave of the fingers from beside a girly excited grin. He drove home to spend the evening with a bottle of Riesling and maybe shed a tear for Bunderlin.

Twenty-four

Jean Meadowcroft was down near the bottom of her long garden. He could see her wide-brimmed cotton hat bobbing along behind the fruit bushes. Three of the dogs were chasing each other around the untidy lawn nearer the house. Samson and Bunderlin's two, for Scobie's good intentions had come to nothing, were getting along well enough but Jean's own cocker spaniel remained wary. It watched and barked from behind the door of the tool shed, occasionally dashing out to join them very briefly and then scurrying back to safety. The two goats, in their separate small paddock, ignored this canine mayhem and so did the Shetland pony.

'Batty, that one, if you ask me,' said a voice.

Martin looked round as a man passing by paused to make an observation. 'Sorry?'

'That one down there,' he said, pointing to Jean with his walking stick. 'The goat woman. Completely bonkers.'

'Not half as bad as her neighbours,' Martin snapped back. But he knew Jean would just smile.

'Should be locked up, if you ask me.'

'Good job nobody's asking you.'

The neighbour humphed and walked away. Martin went through the gate and down to the far end of the garden. Jean looked up as he approached. 'Hello there, our kid. Checking on your brood?'

'Well, seeing how you're getting along with them. Are they settling in?'

'Sure. They're fine. There were four dogs last night and there's still four today. So, fine. No problem. Do you want to go in and make a pot of tea while I just finish off pruning these currant bushes?'

She came into the slightly untidy kitchen as Martin was pouring the tea. 'Know what he called you, the chap who passed by just as I got here?'

'Daft old bat, I should imagine.'

'The goat woman.'

She laughed. 'That was Mrs Bundy, wasn't it?'

'Yes. I never did ask you what you knew about them. It never mattered before, of course.'

'You knew them as well as any of us. Except Mam, of course. Pity we never got her to talk about them.'

'They were already in the house when you started at Barton Lane, weren't they?'

'Yes. Old Bundy had just come back from being interned on the Isle of Man. Not that I knew what that meant. I suppose I would have thought they'd been on holiday.'

'What I'm really curious about, though, is, er, did Bunderlin have a brother, a twin maybe? Or were there younger brothers who were twins?'

'I'm pretty certain there were no brothers. I'm sure I'd have known if there were. Why? What's this about twins?'

'Just a remark he made. "Always think of the twin," he said, or something like that. And I wondered if maybe when he was convicted he was covering up for someone else. I mean, he hardly put up any sort of defence. And then wasn't there someone that Mam used to call the Bundy Boy?'

'That was Peter. Definitely Peter was the Bundy Boy.'

'Oh well, that'll be it, then. It's just that I'd begun to wonder if there could have been another one just like him but even dafter. You know—kept hidden away from the world.'

'You're barking up the wrong tree there, our kid. Mam would have known if there'd been another Bundy kid. She used to send Peter a birthday card every year. In fact, when he was going up to secondary school she was all for giving him a prayer book.'

'A what? What on earth for?'

'That was Dad's reaction as well. Said, what would Peter Bundy ever want with a prayer book? So she gave him some other little book instead.'

'Do you remember the cuckoo clock Mrs Bundy gave me? Didn't you have one like it?'

'That's right. They gave it to me when I went to college. They invited me down to the shop to choose it myself. I guess that would be the same shop where your lady friend sells her frilly knickers and naughty videos. Your shop now, of course.' She began to laugh. 'Martin, dear Martin, that's a hoot, isn't it. Imagine, my little kid brother inherits a sex shop. Have you been in there yet? Had a look around?'

'No. Not since she opened.'

'Well, you must. And then you must tell me all about it. In fact, tell you what, I'll come round and you can take me in and show me the place yourself. I want to see what she's like, this lady friend of yours.'

'She's not my lady friend,' said Martin firmly.

'No, of course not, dear. Tell me to be sensible. Stop it, Jean! Don't be silly! There we are. I've done it for you. Sensible again.'

Martin poured himself another mug of tea. 'Come back to your cuckoo clock. You said they gave it you when you went to college. Who gave it you? I mean, I always took it for granted that Mam and Dad gave it you.'

'No, it was the Bundies. You were not the first to strike up a friendship with the goat lady, our kid.'

'Obviously not. I suppose it's beginning to make a little bit of sense now. Only a bit, though. There was one other thing – I know that Old Bundy was still living long after Mrs Bundy had died. But he never owned the property, not even the shop. It was hers and it went straight to her son. So who was he, Old Bundy? Family, obviously, because he looked exactly like Bunderlin, but what was the relationship?'

'Can't help you there. I assumed they were married. Mind you, he must have been a lot older. I do know that she was only a teenager when they came to England. And Peter was born round about the same time.'

'Begins to sound intriguing. I expect the answer to it all is somewhere among the mountain of junk in the house.'

'Is it bad?'

'Packed to the ceilings. You can only just get into a tiny area downstairs. And upstairs is completely inaccessible.'

'Sounds fascinating.'

When he was leaving, Jean walked with him to the car and, as he was about to drive away, she said, 'I've just had this really interesting idea. You say that upstairs is completely blocked off so that nobody can have been up there for years. So what if... I mean, just what if... Well, wouldn't it be exciting if you got up there and found Old Bundy's mummified body? Or even the mad bad brother. Imagine that!'

'For heaven's sake, Jean! Go and feed your goats.'

He arranged the funeral for Friday afternoon at the crematorium. Kathy Shawcross, one of the university chaplains, offered to conduct the service and said that if she did, it would have to be a Christian service. She could do no other without compromising her own position, but she would do it in such a way as to respect the integrity of Bunderlin as an unbeliever. Martin said he would think about it but, at a loss to understand what she meant, he tried elsewhere. Having no success, however, he asked Kathy to go ahead. He considered asking her to include a few stanzas from the *Rubaiyat* instead of the Psalms but chose instead to ask for a few minutes to give his own tribute. If Kathy didn't know what was coming, so much the better. The main thing, though, was to get the scattering of ashes right. And he was pretty sure that he knew how to handle that.

In the end it made little difference. Only Jean, Maureen and Scobie were there beside himself and Kathy. She read the prayers from her book and the twenty-third psalm and Martin wondered how many flights of word association that would have set off for the man in the enormous coffin on the catafalque. Martin took only five minutes and finished with:

> '*Myself when young did eagerly frequent*
> *doctor and saint, and heard great argument*
> *about it and about. But evermore*
> *came out by the same door as in I went.*
> *With them the seed of wisdom did I sow,*
> *and with my own hand laboured it to grow.*
> *And this was all the harvest that I reaped—*
> *I came like water, and like wind I go.*'

On the way out, Maureen said, 'Hey, Mart, you did good there. You should be a priest, did you know that?' Scobie agreed. Obviously, they had not understood a thing—but why expect them to? Jean just smiled.

The funeral director caught up with him as he made his way towards the car park. 'We've got a problem,' he said, out of breath. 'Well, not a problem, no. It's just that he's too big so they're not going to be able to get him into the cremator. So we'll have to take him to Manchester. They would take the handles off but he'd probably still be too wide. Put the burners out, I shouldn't wonder. So... Anyway, look, it's not your problem. We'll get it sorted.'

The funeral director walked away flustered with embarrassment but Martin laughed quietly. Bunderlin would have found a couplet from the *Rubaiyat* to fit the occasion.

Martin and Carol drove into Manchester and parked somewhere near the Cathedral. Carol led the way to a narrow side street and down a stone stairway to an unobtrusive restaurant in a basement below an accountant's office. Martin's first impression was that the subdued lighting side-stepped the need for the more careful application of colour wash on the stone walls which better lighting would require. The young man who led them to their table managed a sufficiently authentic hint of French accent but the girl who took their orders made no attempt to conceal her north Cheshire origins.

'Don't you think this is just wonderful?' said Carol as Angela, not Angelique, poured their wine without any trace of the flourish they might have expected from the young man who had met them at the door.

'It's good,' Martin replied, not really sure what he thought about the place.

Carol giggled slightly. She decided she would have the entrecôte steak with escargots for a starter.

'Then I think I shall follow your recommendation but I'll start with the soup.'

'Not the soup, Martin. Try the mushrooms. Believe me, you will really love the mushrooms. In fact, I will also have the mushrooms.'

Maybe it was just as well that he had not chosen the beef steak pie that had been so very tempting.

'Tell me about yourself, then,' he asked when they had ordered. 'How did you first get into interior design?'

'That, Martin is a long, long story. It first started before I married Alan. That's my ex. He was a junior partner in a firm of architects and he had these clients, a really wonderful couple, who were converting an old chapel into flats. With their own absolutely gorgeous apartment on two levels in the main part of the building. Anyway, Bernard and Marjorie, that's who they were, they got the impression that I worked for the partnership as well, on the design side...

'...and then when we divorced, we had to sell the house and I ended up in that horrible little semi in Heaton. But not for long I can tell you. No, I'm looking out for a place like yours, really. Now that is charm. But, gosh, here's me going on about me all the time. You should tell me something about yourself. So what have you been doing today?'

'Well, not a typical day. I was at a funeral.'

'Oh no. Oh gosh, I'm so sorry, I'm so insensitive. You poor thing. Was it someone close?'

'No, I wouldn't say close. I'd known him since I was small. He was...' He hesitated and Carol reached across and put her hand on his arm.

'I understand, Martin. You don't have to talk about it.' The trouble was, he did want to talk about Bunderlin, but not with Carol who had transformed herself into the Comforting Angel. She noticed straight away that tears had come to his eyes. 'Martin, you're so lovely, so sensitive. Look, why don't we take a walk across town and afterwards have a glass of wine in this lovely little wine bar that I know? It's called The Bowl of Night.'

Martin laughed. 'That would be very fitting.'

Twenty-five

Martin walked down the side street opposite the bus station and went along the potholed lane between the back of the shops and the railway line. He had to pick his way carefully between the puddles left by the recent rain, but still managed to end up with both shoes full of muddy water. At the bottom was a row of lock-up garages and then, on its own on a rough, overgrown patch, was a large wooden shed with security grilles over the windows. When he came a little closer he could see that, once again, there was no point in going any further for the shed was still padlocked, as it had been for three days now. This shed, with no running water, no sanitation, no heating, was Scobie Sharples's place, but Scobie had vanished.

He had disappeared right after the funeral and that worried Martin for it reawakened his suspicions about what had happened to tattooed Dave Brierley. Scobie was uncomfortably well-informed—or was he just guessing? Could he even have been there when it happened? Perhaps he'd been taken in for questioning, though there had been nothing in the local papers about the progress of any investigation into the accident.

As Martin turned to walk back to his car, the green Bedford appeared at the far end of the lane, so he returned to the shed and waited. When the van drew near, however, he saw that it was not Scobie at the wheel. It pulled up aggressively close, splashing Martin with dirty water, and the driver threw the door open, forcing him to jump out of the way. 'Who are you? What do you want?' snapped the tall, pony-tailed man as he climbed out of the van.

'I'm a friend of Scobie Sharples. Have you any idea where he is?'

'Don't give me that. Friend of Scobie, my arse. What are you? Social Security?'

'No, really. Just a friend.'

'Listen, pal, I don't know where Scobie is, and if I did know, I wouldn't tell you. So you can just push off out of here and don't come back.'

'But I see you're using his van,' Martin persisted.

The man's eyes narrowed. 'Like fuck it's his van. You've been watching him, haven't you? What's going on? Who are you?'

'Look, if you see him, will you tell him that Martin was looking for him?'

He walked back to his car and drove out to Borrinsmoor to let in Carol's pine stripping contractor who wanted to return and rehang the doors he had taken away for treatment. He was surprised to discover that already the old skirting boards had been stripped back to bare timber and the floor was sanded and sealed. And the kitchen range was installed. How long had all that taken? If Carol could work her Pennine magic on his building contractor and get the extension completed she would deserve... Well, she would earn his lasting gratitude.

For so long he had looked forward to moving out here. Ever since it became inevitable that he and Julia would split up he had dreamed of a place like this, with the town laid out in the valley below him and open country as far as the eye could see to the rear. But the reality was an anticlimax. A kitchen instead of an unfinished extension at the back of the house might have helped a bit, but maybe he would not have to put up with that inconvenience for too much longer. Worse, though, he missed Julia. He had not acknowledged it before, but it was true. Infuriating, lovely Julia who picked at all his faults as much as he picked at all of hers. But he missed her. Perhaps if they had lived in separate houses at opposite ends of the town they might have been able to stay married.

And he missed Emma. Only ever his own untidiness in the bathroom now, just his own clothes strewn across the floor. And nobody to shout constantly, 'For God's sake, you two, can't you tidy anything away?' No Samson either. He left a spare key in the milk bottle box by the front door, went to the pub down on the main road for a meal and then drove to Bunderlin's place.

He stood in the middle of the kitchen and scratched his head. Where do you start, how do you start, to bring a place like this into order? He went into the back room and to the table where Emma had found the photographs only a few days before. They remained exactly where she had left them but the box file and notebooks and the lady's handbag had been removed. His first thought was that someone must have taken them, but there was no sign of any break-in. And people do move things about, of course—so it would all be somewhere else in the house There was a tin box which he had not noticed previously, with its hinged lid open. Inside was one five-pound note.

Martin's eye was drawn to a collection of small books between bookends at the back of the cleared space. They looked like a set of volumes in a series but, on close inspection, turned out to be six copies of the same book. *Palgrave's Golden Treasury* of poems. He picked up one of them and opened it where the ribbon marker was placed. The *Rubaiyat*. He smiled and looked at the others. In each one it was the *Rubaiyat* but at a different page. Presumably, Bunderlin liked to have the entire poem open at one go.

Underneath the table was a pile of what appeared to be scrap books with a glue stick and a pair of scissors on top. A quick look inside one of the books revealed a collection of annotated newspaper cuttings, photographs, bus tickets and till receipts. Without inspecting them any closer, Martin made a mental note to take them with him.

He lifted down one of the boxes from the pile beside the table. The weight took him by surprise and sent a sharp pain through his side, which was still far from recovered after his encounter with tattooed Dave. He dropped the box and it burst open on the floor but offered no dramatic revelations. It was full of newspapers, all in bundles, tied up with string and packed neatly together. He left it where it had fallen and went into the front room.

In the middle of the room was a large recliner armchair with several grubby blankets thrown over it and beside it, on the floor, was a collection of abandoned crockery. There were more boxes as in the back room but most of the space was taken up with various small items of furniture piled almost to the ceiling. Behind the door, underneath three bicycles, were two large tea chests that appeared to be full of clocks and watches. Resting on top of them was a bundle of neatly handwritten ledgers.

At the foot of the stairs he looked up at the boxes and cases stacked there and almost heard again Jean saying, 'What if you found Old Bundy up there?' Despite the renewed pain in his side, he managed to move some of the things and pile them on top of the stuff at the side until he reached the makeshift shelf at the top where he was able to clamber over the cases, but not without sending one of them clattering downstairs where it came to rest against the front door.

He tried a light switch on the landing but the bulb failed immediately so he went down to borrow the one from the kitchen. The bathroom was full of brushes, various vacuum cleaners, buckets and containers. The original bath had been removed and its replacement, by now very many years old, was leaning against the wall, still in its protective wrappings.

In the front bedroom an iron-framed double bed was dismantled and its base and ends were propped against the uncurtained window. In the middle of the room was a huge pile of clothes that came to about the height of the old marble-topped washstand opposite the door. A large, dark brown wardrobe with a full-length mirror that had lost most of its silvering, was filled with shoes, umbrellas, hats and a pile of boxes. Martin lifted the boxes out and looked inside them. Most seemed to be filled with paper dressmaking patterns and knitting patterns. One was full of photographs. Black and white contact prints.

He pulled out a few of the prints and took them to the landing where he could see them better. Cattle grazing in a meadow. A blurred close up of a donkey. Goats browsing on a hedge at the side of a field. A farmyard with large, timber-framed buildings to the rear. He put the photographs back and carefully replaced the boxes in the wardrobe. Something worth taking a little trouble over later.

He pulled open the large drawer at the bottom of the wardrobe. It was full of assorted small junk—various teapots, bald tennis balls, loose cutlery, a box of buttons, scissors, two notebooks with marbled paper covers and a stitched spine. He opened one of them. It looked like a diary with a separate, dated entry on each of just a few pages. The first date was some time in nineteen thirty-five but he could not decipher the Suetterlin handwriting. These he would take with him to see if Jim O'Neill could find someone in his Department who might be willing to transcribe and translate them.

The smaller room, surprisingly, was uncluttered except for a single bed without a mattress, on which were piled a few pieces of furniture. A small chest of drawers that was empty, a table and disintegrating wicker chairs, and two hat stands. At the window were the remains of the curtains that had once hung there.

There was just one other room that he had not yet looked in. Unlike the rooms in the rest of the house, the door was closed and Martin once again heard Jean saying gleefully, 'What if...' 'Oh, shut up, our Jean,' he muttered and pushed the door open.

In the light from the landing he could see that it was a workshop. Along the wall underneath the window was a bench with a small lathe and a grindstone at one end and a neatly ordered tool rack at the other. In the middle was an empty clock case but no sign of the movement that belonged to it. In the centre of the room a bandsaw was bolted to the floor and beside it was a saw bench and a treadle-operated fretsaw. Near the door was a brush, a shovel and a large sack full of sawdust and shavings. He left the ghost of Old Bundy to his work and pulled the door shut behind himself.

He carefully negotiated the junk on the stairs and went out to the garden where his first inclination was to decide that everything dumped in there was just rubbish and could be cleared away without his close supervision. But underneath the chaos was a vague hint of some rationale that might offer an insight into the big man's mind. And the two cars—how had he got those into the garden? There was no entrance wide enough to bring them through. But the crazy picture of Bunderlin the giant manhandling those cars over the sturdy fence evaporated when Martin remembered that there had once been a small field adjoining the garden.

Before locking up and leaving he had a look in the garage. The tree trunk and the railway sleeper propping the doors in place came away without too much trouble but then one door swung open on its only remaining hinge and clearly was not going to close again very easily. Inside, a large car was covered with a tarpaulin and packed around with sacks, cases, various components of different lawn mowers, engines and gearboxes, and a couple of zinc baths. Martin lifted the front of the tarpaulin to see what was underneath. And there, sadly beyond any dream of restoration, but unmistakable from its radiator grill, was a Triumph Renown.

He did his best to prop the doors shut and then went back into the house to pick up the two notebooks and the scrapbooks. He was about to lock up and come away when he realised that the weekly free newspaper and the junk mail on the table had not been there on his previous visit. Had Scobie moved in?

Martin drove a short distance and pulled up just before the zigzag lines at the school entrance. He adjusted his rear view mirror to get a clear view of the front of the house and turned on his radio. He turned it off again right away. Nothing worth listening to. After a few minutes he found that trying to keep an eye on the house through the mirror was too tiring so he turned the car round and parked on the opposite side. Half an hour later a single-decker bus pulled up at the stop nearly opposite Bunderlin's gate. Martin watched as Scobie got off the bus with a package under his arm and went round the back of the house. He gave him five minutes and then followed.

Scobie was sitting at the table in the kitchen eating fish and chips from the paper wrapper. 'Hello there, squire,' he said cheerfully through a mouthful of chips.

'How did you get in here?' Martin asked.

Scobie gestured towards the door and stuffed some fish into his mouth. 'Can't use the front door. Been locked for years. Lost the key. If you ask me, he never did have one. I never seen him open that door.'

'So how many keys did you get cut the other day?'

'Just the one, squire. That's all you wanted, wasn't it? Anyway, I gave it you. Never needed it myself. Got my own.'

'So is this where you've been since… well, how long have you been coming here?'

'How do you mean, squire? Oh, like overnight and all that. No, it's only for a few days. See, Jackie Cartwright, that's the geezer at the paper shop, he's looking after some stuff. And there's no way I'm going anywhere near that lock-up till he's shifted it. Not fucking likely.'

'What sort of stuff is that, then?'

'Don't know and I don't want to know. And neither do you, squire. So I'm just dossing down in here for a few days. I mean, Mr Bundy won't mind, not now, God rest his soul. And it'll be ages before anyone does anything with this place, if you ask me. What do you reckon?'

'I'm going to get it all cleared out pretty soon.'

'You? But what about...? Oh, wait a minute, you mean he's passed it down to you? It's yours now?'

'Yes.'

Scobie grinned a broad open grin full of stained teeth and chewed fish. 'Well now, isn't that the very best bit of good luck. Jackie Cartwright, you can stick your fucking shed all the way up your fucking arse. You've made my day, squire. Made my day.'

Twenty-six

Scobie had been working at the house for more than a week and in all this time he had never once suggested that his efforts might be worth a few notes. Martin would see that he was properly rewarded, of course, but he had assumed that Scobie would ask for some payment each day so he began to wonder whether he had found a more lucrative way of supplementing his giro. Something connected, perhaps, with whatever was in Jackie Cartwright's shed? Or had tattooed Dave Brierley's convenient tragic end brought him a windfall? When Martin arrived at the house to find an old Sierra parked outside, his suspicions began to grow but he said nothing. Eventually Scobie volunteered the information that the car belonged to a friend and he was simply looking after it while the friend was in prison. Martin tried not to speculate on the wider possibilities or drawbacks of such an arrangement.

Having first cleared himself a space in the front room and furnished it with a mattress bearing ample record of its history, Scobie had then set about clearing the back room of all the newspapers and other junk. He had now begun to fill it up again with boxes of photographs and letters and all the clocks that he was recovering from the rest of the house. All the old clothes, shoes and disintegrating bedding were gone, and the large skip outside at the front had been replaced with another, which was now also nearly full.

When Martin arrived on Sunday morning Scobie was in the front room rearranging boxes to no immediately apparent purpose, so he went into the back room and began to look through those that had been piled up in there. The letters were a disappointment for there was nothing relating to the early years in the house. The collection began in the early 1950s, and there were no personal letters. Paid bills, official letters, circulars and junk mail. But nothing from Germany and nothing worth saving.

The photographs were more interesting. Just one small bundle, though, the bundle that had come first to hand when Martin was looking through the wardrobe, was from Germany. They appeared to depict a large house and farmyard and a lot of very mixed livestock. Only three showed any people. Three girls, all with long plaited fair hair, looked like sisters. Two of them were maybe about fourteen and the younger was perhaps ten or so. Martin thought that one of the older girls may have been Greta Bunderlin but he could not be sure which. The next photo took him by surprise. A man aged about thirty standing beside a tractor looked exactly like Peter. This, Martin guessed, was Franz, whom he had seen once very briefly. The third photograph was rather disturbing. It was a family group of more than a dozen people spanning, maybe, three generations. Apart from two who were small and slim, all the men displayed the same family characteristics. Exceptionally large, powerful men. And the face of one had been completely scratched out.

The rest of the photographs were unsettling in a very different way. The first two sets were of places round and about Lostock and he knew the scenes well enough to recognise that the pictures must have dated from some years ago. The vehicles in some of them suggested a time during the late sixties, and an arcade of shops, which had been demolished to make way for the new bus station, put one of the sets no later than 1970. There were several shots of a thin-featured, shabbily dressed man aged in his late twenties or early thirties and then some of a young woman taken from too far away and too badly composed to be easily recognisable, except for the last one in which she was looking directly to camera and appeared surprised and far from pleased to see that she was being photographed. He recognised Veryan at once.

As he was studying the picture, Scobie came into the room and dumped a heavy box onto the floor with a loud thud. Startled, Martin turned around and Scobie took the photograph he was holding.

'Bloody hell, squire, where did you find this?'

'You know her then?'

'Took that fucking ages ago, he did. Ages ago.'

'Do you know where she is now?'

'Oh, come on, squire, don't you start this as well. Don't ask me to go in that shop. Gives me the jitters, that does.'

'What shop?'

'That bleeding camera shop down Chorley Road. Just leave me out of this. Had enough of going in there with Mr Bundy's films. Hanging about trying to avoid Madam Lah-di-dah. I can do without that.'

'Don't worry,' said Martin. 'I'll not ask you to go there, but I might just pay her a visit myself. You say she works at the camera shop on Chorley Road?'

'Not all the time. There's someone else in there most days. I wouldn't bother with her if I was you, squire. Waste of time. Anyway, what do you want me to do with the grandfather clocks? In the skip, if you ask me. Bottom's all rotted away to buggery on both of them.'

He had driven past Bates Photographic frequently enough and he hadn't forgotten that it was the place where Bunderlin had had his photos printed. But it had never occurred to him until now that there was any significance in his choosing that shop rather than any other. Perhaps he should have realised. After all, hadn't the note referred to it, not by the name over the window, but as Ann Bates's shop, suggesting that Bunderlin might have known the owner? But even if Martin had guessed that much he could not have guessed also that Veryan worked there. Time, at last, to go there and perhaps gain a clue to what Bunderlin might have been up to—beside keeping tabs on Martin. Trying to engineer an encounter with Veryan, possibly, the daft old bugger. But what for?

The shop was empty apart from a dark-haired young man of about twenty who was rearranging stock in the cabinets behind the counter.

'Good morning, sir. Can I help you?'

He asked for a roll of film and glanced around while the assistant went to get it. He was still not sure whether to ask for Mrs Bates or Veryan, but he spotted a sign at the foot of a staircase pointing upwards to 'Veryan Studio.'

'Is, er, Veryan here?' he asked.

'Who? Oh, Veryan. No. It's not a person, just the name of the studio. Mrs Bates is up there now if you want to see her.'

The stairs led up to a comfortable and light reception area but there was nobody at the desk. He rang the bell. A woman came from a back room carrying a mug of coffee. She was about fifty, slim with blonde, greying hair and a slightly freckled face. Unmistakably the woman he had known all those years ago.

'Mrs Bates?'

'Yes. How can I help?'

'You don't remember me, do you? Well, of course not. Why should you?'

'Have you come to collect some photographs?'

'No. I'm afraid you never were very pleased to see me. So if I'm intruding I'll go. But I would like to ask you something first. About someone we both knew a long time ago.'

She looked cautious, wary of a stranger putting on an act of familiarity. And then she realised he was no stranger. 'Wait a minute,' she said. 'I should know you, shouldn't I? You're... Yes, of course! It was years ago, wasn't it? I've not seen you since you were in the Crown Court.'

'I missed you when it was over. Got into conversation with someone else and then you'd gone. Well, it wasn't the time or place...'

'No, indeed. Poor old Bird. Couldn't help thinking he got a rough deal. So what brings you back? Is he out yet? Picking up from where he left off, is he?'

'Well, he did, yes. I even found myself living in his flat, would you believe. Still there till next week.'

'The flat?' She began to laugh. 'Oh, gosh. That's priceless. The place in St Mary's Street, over the shop, you mean?'

'You know it, then?'

'Of course, I know it. I lived there. I was his first tenant. But how come..?'

When he arrived at Borrinsmoor three vehicles, including the contractor's van, were parked outside. He smiled ruefully at the thought that his own efforts to spur the work on had failed completely whereas the builders had sprung into action as soon as Carol appeared on the scene. It was that Pennine magic. Or maybe just the fact that his own efforts had amounted to no more than muttering and swearing to himself. He went into the new kitchen and was greeted immediately by Carol.

'Martin, this is all going so well. They'll be finished by Friday. Now, look, why don't I make us all a nice cup of tea and then we can think about planning a house-warming party for you. Gosh, think of that, Martin. In here at last and ready to show it off to all your friends.'

'You've done well. I'm pleased.' His first thought was not the house-warming party but whether or not he should bring Samson back from Jean's. But no, not really. He'd settled already into the mad menagerie and it would be unfair to take him away again.

'Now, why don't you do a list of all the people you want to invite, and I'll get the invitations done,' said Carol when she brought the tea into the living room. 'The question is, of course, do you want a proper dinner party or an open house, come-and-go-as-you-please sort of thing? I always think a dinner party is nice but if you did an open house you could invite far more and it could be much sooner. Next weekend, even. So what do you think?

But what he was thinking was that he wished Veryan—or Ann, is she now?—was unattached. Pity.

Twenty-seven

The house-warming was not a disaster but it was an embarrassment. Martin would have contented himself with drinks and snacks but Carol swept in and organised everything. She turned up towards the end of the morning with a carload of ingredients which she transformed into an impressive buffet. 'And don't worry about crockery. I know you won't have enough of your own, you men never do. So I have all that we need in the car. Do be a darling and bring it in.'

People began to arrive from the middle of the afternoon. A few drinks, a nosey around and a sampling of Carol's buffet—enough to show some appreciation for it but not enough to make any noticeable reduction in its extent. But, as Carol said, one has to make sure that latecomers have a hospitable table from which to select.

It was not the buffet, however, that prompted the most comments, knowing smiles and glances. 'Watch out,' said Jim O'Neill as he was leaving. 'She's got her eye on your kitchen.' Dorothy Willetts was a little more forthright. 'I'm sure she's very nice, Martin,' she said, 'but don't rush into anything. And for goodness sake, don't let people push you around.'

Mary Coulson, on the other hand, could scarcely conceal her delight with the apparent results of her own efforts at matchmaking. 'Do be kind to her, Martin. She deserves a break.'

Martin recalled the advice of Terry, his colleague from years ago at Merrion Dyestuffs. 'Best way to drop a bird who doesn't want to be dropped? Easy, take her to the pictures and sit in the front row picking your nose and farting.'

Martin woke the following morning almost wishing that he had a miserable hangover to obliterate the embarrassing recollections of the night before. But he remembered it all too clearly. Carol's easy assumption of the role of hostess. Her eagerness to show off the new kitchen and the renovation work. And her soliciting everyone's admiration for his meagre collection of watercolours.

There was a moment, after everybody had gone, when he suspected that for once he ought to take the lead. She was stretching on the settee next to him, not close but relaxed, her shoes kicked off and her feet tucked underneath her. And it would have been nice...

'So. End of a notable day.'

She smiled at him but said nothing.

'Well, I'll...'

I'll what? Get your coat? Put some soft music on? Turn the lights down? Drive you home? He stood up, walked to the window and looked out into the darkness. Was he beginning to feel attracted to this woman who irritated him so much, but who was really quite charming and even desirable? Did he want her to stay or to leave? He turned to her but the moment had gone.

She phoned early the following morning, keen to work her spell in St Mary's Street. Two hours later he picked her up from her home and they drove to the flat. 'You mustn't lose any time, Martin,' she said. 'Really make sure that you get the place absolutely tip-top because you want to attract the very best tenants you can.'

As she followed him up the dismal staircase to the flat, Martin fancied that he could already hear what she was going to say. They stepped inside.

'The very first thing... Well, two things actually. You really do have to do something with those stairs. It's terribly important that it looks inviting as soon as you open the door. And that shop. That, Martin, is absolutely dreadful. You've just got to renew the external paintwork. Make sure that it's utterly different from that shop. God, who in their right mind would want to live over a place like that? And then—you don't mind me saying this, do you? No, of course not. But you need to change your own image or people will just rip you off. Be more professional. Don't drape your sweater round your shoulders like you do.'

She'd got it all worked out and no amount of Pennine magic, or any other sort of magic, would turn the flat into anything other than what it was. A pretty dismal place firmly rooted at the bottom end of the housing market. And Martin had to distance himself from it all. He saw the opportunity to offer morning coffee in the town centre and then try to escape to Ann Bates's camera shop.

As he slammed the door and locked up, Maureen came out of the shop. 'Hi, Mart. Hoped I might catch you.' She stepped aside to let him into the shop. He glanced cautiously over his shoulder towards Carol who was hovering in the background.

'Oh, sorry. If you're... Well, look, it's just a quick word I wanted. See, I've got this chance of having Candy Biggles here for a promotion thing. Just wanted to check it'd be all right with you. Don't mean anything, sort of, you know... Just come and meet Candy in the shop. Then maybe an evening do. Invitations only, of course.'

'Who is Candy Biggles?' Maybe he shouldn't have asked.

'Come off it, Mart. You must know. She's only the number one porno actress. And I do mean number one.'

'Oh, I see. OK, well, you just go ahead with whatever you want. So long as you stick to the terms of your licence you shouldn't have any problem.'

'Thanks, Mart. I'll send you an invite.'

'What was that about?' Asked Carol a little frostily as she got into the car.

'It's a long story. A very long one,' Martin replied, thinking that maybe he had discovered something far more effective than the front row of the cinema.

Several days passed without a phone call from Carol but that did not trouble Martin, though it did occur to him that he ought, perhaps, to have a conversation with John Lucas in order to pre-empt any renewed speculation about his involvement with the sex shop. But he was more concerned to contact Ann Bates and regretted leaving things so open ended as a vague intention to call in at her shop some time. She was a very elusive woman. He did catch her at last one Friday afternoon in her studio and she said she could probably spare an hour over coffee. No sooner, however, had they sat down than her phone rang.

'Sorry about this, Martin,' she said, putting the phone away. 'Got to go. Trouble at home. Before I go, give me your number.'

He handed her a card.

'I'll phone you tonight. I've been looking forward to catching up with you.' She gathered up her things and hurried out leaving Martin to finish his coffee alone in the studio. Deflated, he drank up and took the cups down to Stuart in the shop on his way out. She phoned quite early that evening and invited him to her house for a meal and Martin found himself once again wondering whether there was still a Mr Bates.

Scobie had been in a bad mood for several days and it worried Martin because it was so much out of character. He wondered if it was anything to do with the dubious goings-on of his circle of associates or even, maybe, connected with the death of Dave Brierley. He still suspected that Scobie knew more about that than he had so far been prepared to tell.

It turned out to have nothing to do with crime, criminals or anything even remotely connected with the New Zealander and its company. Martin called at the house late on Friday morning on his way home from the university and found Scobie in the front room, which was now empty save for the old armchair, Scobie's mattress, and the two long-case clocks he had saved from the skip. Scobie, who was studying the racing pages of the *Sun*, looked up as he walked in. 'Feeling lucky today, squire, so pick yourself a winner. You've got about an hour to get your first bet on. Can't lose today.'

'I think I'll pass on that one.'

'Well, suit yourself. At least give me a couple of notes and I'll bring us some fish and chips.'

He handed him a fiver and wondered how much there had been in Bunderlin's tin box when Scobie moved in. 'Just get your own. I'm out for dinner tonight.'

'Going somewhere nice, squire?'

'Yes. Caught up with Ann Bates at last and she's invited me round to her place. I'm hoping she can fill me in with a little bit of what she knew about Mr Bundy. And like I told you, I knew her years ago, so we've got a bit of catching up to do.'

'For fuck's sake, squire, can't you leave anything alone? That was the one thing I couldn't work out with Mr Bundy. Decent guy like him. What did he want with her, the stuck-up cow? And now you're at it. Beats me, it does, I'm telling you.'

'Yes, well, it isn't anything to do with you, is it?'

'I fucking hope not. I fucking do. Besides, I reckon that me and dirty Maureen could tell you a lot more about Mr Bundy than ever Madam Lah-di-dah can. A lot more.'

Suddenly, Scobie had sunk back into his foul mood and Martin realised that it had begun when he told him about his visit to the shop. But he didn't probe. He just added one more question to his list.

Longford was the large detached house at the end of Wingate Avenue. Martin drove through the gates and parked at the front. As he locked up he noticed that although there was room to turn, it would be very awkward late at night after a couple of glasses of wine. He was about to get back in and turn around in readiness but Veryan, or Ann, having heard him approach, was already at the door.

She was wearing a close-fitting blue dress with a low neck. A garnet pendant rested just above her cleavage and for a moment he could not look away. She smiled. He followed her through to the back of the house and into a small sitting room with a view across the golf course and the town skyline in the distance. She poured him a glass of fruit juice.

'Well, this is...' He let the sentence hang in the air. 'You've done well for yourself.'

She smiled but said nothing.

'Do I call you Ann or Veryan?'

'Oh, gosh. It's Ann. Left all that nonsense behind long ago. Then married into a good honest monosyllable. Veryan's just one of my favourite places in Cornwall now. And my studio, of course. But tell me about yourself. What have you been up to since, how long ago is it?'

'Ages. Stayed at the university. Apart from a spell in East Anglia doing research. Came back as a research assistant and then got taken on as a lecturer.'

'So how is it you're in Bird's old flat?'

'It was just a stopgap. When Julia and I divorced I needed to find somewhere to stay while my new place was being refurbished. It's only just been finished—I moved in a few days ago. Anyway, as soon as I'd agreed to move I got a letter offering me the flat and saying that the landlord had agreed to waive the requirement for a security deposit. I assumed that meant Julia had been pulling strings and doing deals so that I wouldn't have any excuse to hang around waiting for my cottage to be finished. Anyway, it was rather too good to turn down so I grabbed the chance. And then, of course, I discovered that Bunderlin had been keeping track. Goodness knows how. I suppose when you were there Franz was still using the shop.'

'Old Frank, yes. I think he pretty well lived there among his clocks but he wasn't trading any more, as I recall. Must have been some relation to Bird. Looked just like an older version of him. So Bird, Bunderlin, is he still around?'

'Ah, no. He died quite recently. But that's not all.' He told her the story in brief. 'Anyway, I've got this amiable rogue helping me out. He was Bunderlin's, er, errand boy, you might call him, and he's latched on to me now. Knows far more than he's saying, so I'm keeping him on in the hope that eventually I might find out what's been going on. But not just that. I quite like the guy really. And somehow I get the impression that I've inherited him along with all the other stuff. And another oddball character as well. Maureen Tong.'

'So where does she come into the story? This is absolutely intriguing. I'll go and dish up then you can carry on with this crazy tale.'

She went into the kitchen and Martin wondered whether to follow. Before he could make any move the door opened and a frail white-haired old man in pyjamas came in. 'Who are you?' he demanded.

'I'm Martin.'

'Martin? Martin who? I don't know you. Where's Doris?'

'I don't know.'

'Doris! Where've you gone to now, stupid woman?'

Ann came back into the room and began to guide the old man to a chair. 'Come on, now, Geoffrey. Are you going to sit down?'

'Who are you?'

'I'm Ann.'

'No, you're not. You're not Ann. Where's Doris?' He sat down. Then he got up again. 'I'm going to bed.'

'Give me ten minutes,' Ann said to Martin. 'I'll be down again when he's settled.' She helped him as he shuffled out of the room, swearing at her and demanding to see Doris.

A little while later she returned. 'That's it. He's settled now. Should sleep for the rest of the evening, even till morning with a bit of luck. We go through this palaver every night. So, ready to eat?'

He followed her into the dining room where his eye was immediately drawn to a collection of black and white photographs of Lakeland scenes on one wall complemented by a set of water colours of the same scenes on the adjoining wall. Ann waited, quite proudly, Martin thought, as he took his time to look at them all. 'These are beautiful. Your work?'

'Geoffrey's

'The old guy just now...?'

'Yes. My husband. Alzheimer's. We'd been married three years when it started. And now... well, you saw how he is. Been like that five years.'

After a very brief awkward silence, Martin steered the conversation back to Geoffrey's photographs and paintings and that led to recollections of favourite places and it was not until after the meal, when Martin was starting his third large glass of Soave, that they returned to stories of Bunderlin.

'I was relieved in a way when he was convicted,' said Ann. 'Well no, that's not it. I was really screwed up actually. What I mean is that I was just thankful it wasn't Eric.'

'Eric?'

'My brother. Oh gosh, it's still painful to talk about it. To think I believed Eric could have done it. But he could, I know he could. He was so full of hate for Webster. I used to really look up to Eric. Five years older than me, he was, and always the best big brother a girl could have. So I got terribly upset when I began to hear him crying at night. I mean, fifteen years old and crying himself to sleep.' She paused and took a deep breath.' So I went to him in his room. Wouldn't tell me at first, but eventually he opened up. It was Webster. So horrible to him every time he went for a haircut. But what made it ten times worse was when he blurted it out to Dad. He wouldn't hear any wrong of that creep. He was never one of your spivs or Nancy boys. He was a corporal in Dad's regiment. There at the D-Day landings. Men like that are trustworthy, honourable men. Corporal Webster could teach the rest of you a thing or two. So Eric got a beating for telling nasty lies. He always used to say he would get his own back one day.'

'So I can see why you were worried.'

'He completely messed up at school. Left without any GCEs and never worked in a decent job. Drifted from one dismal bedsit to another and got in with the wrong crowd. We kept in touch for a while, at least I did, I tried to, but not Mum and Dad. Until, what, not long after the fire and Eric got a prison sentence for a string of car thefts. And that was when Dad completely disowned him. Wouldn't give him any credit for pleading guilty. Absolutely not. As soon as he said that word "Guilty", Dad stood up and walked out of the court. Eric was no longer the son of Major George Scobie Sharples.'

Twenty-eight

As Martin stood at his kitchen window the moors in the distance came into view intermittently, quickly disappearing again behind the low cloud and rain sweeping across the Western Pennines. For a brief moment the masts on Winter Hill stood out against the grey sky beyond. And in the next minute everything from the far hills to his garden fence had sunk into the mist. It had been like this for a week and though he always affected not to completely dislike such bad weather, today he genuinely did not mind for he did not have to go out. It was the start of the Christmas vacation but unlike every other vacation for the past several years, no outstanding work nagged for his attention.

His phone rang. It was Ann. 'Morning, Martin. Just thought I'd let you know I'm having a lazy morning.'

'Ah, what luxury. All go well yesterday?'

'Fine. We got him settled in eventually. I felt a bit guilty walking out and leaving him behind like that. I mean, knowing that he's never going to come home again. But I really couldn't cope with much more of it.'

She had acknowledged at last that she could no longer look after Geoffrey herself and that he needed to be in a nursing home. It was primarily for his own welfare, of course, and secondly for Ann's sake who had worn herself into the ground trying to combine the duties of nurse and business woman. Martin had felt a little guilty for immediately thinking how much easier it would be for them to find time to be friends. It wouldn't be right, after all, for Geoffrey was still her husband even though, as she said, she had really lost him five years before. He lived in a time and place of his own now with Doris, his first wife, who had died twenty years ago. Was she saying that she was a single woman again, Martin wondered.

'So what are you doing later today?'

'Nothing. Just being lazy.'

'You could come here and do that. It's the perfect place for it, you know.'

'I was hoping you might say that.'

Quickly he tidied up but not so thoroughly that the place looked unnatural. He just gathered the various scattered things into more orderly piles, wiped around and tidied up in the kitchen and in the bathroom and then, just in case, in the bedroom.

Part of the time he was as excited as a teenager at the thought that Ann was coming over for the day. And then he was cautious and wary and apprehensive. She was a married woman and it wasn't right to think this way about her. But he couldn't think any other way really, for he had been attracted to her from the very beginning when she came across to him in the Haymarket all those years ago and angrily snapped, 'Tell your friend to leave me alone.' He'd blown it then because he always managed to choose the wrong moment. And this was, once again, the wrong time. She was coming because she wanted to renew contact with her brother, and because she was interested to learn what had happened to Bunderlin in the years since she had known him. But the smiling eyes and, from time to time, the hand on his arm, had a different message. And she was more interested to hear about Martin than about Scobie or Bunderlin.

The memory of earlier, very definite, rejections whispered caution to Martin and when Ann sat on the sofa, he took the armchair. When she appeared to hesitate, wondering whether to stay for the evening, he simply waited for her to decide. 'I really ought to go,' she said at last. 'Pop in to see Geoffrey at their mealtime and then stay with him till bedtime.' And Martin, for whom dithering was a way of life, held back from undue haste.

Little remained to be done at the house except for a thorough clean and renewing the fence following the removal of Bunderlin's private scrap yard. Scobie quite cheerfully accepted the fact that he would soon have to move out, but he refused to listen when Martin offered to help. 'I'll just fuck off back to Jackie Cartwright's place,' he insisted. 'In fact, I'll do that now, Mr Professor. I'll bring the car round before you get that fucking fence back and I'll stick my bed in it.'

'Too late,' Martin replied. 'I threw that onto the skip this morning.'

'You done what? Fucking hell, squire, what did you do that for?'

'It was revolting. You need something better. Now, if you'll listen to me, I have a suggestion to make.'

'Go on, then.'

'Move into the flat.'

'Oh.' He made a show of reluctance as he gathered up his few possessions and bundled them into the car. By the time Martin let him into the flat, however, he was grinning broadly. 'The funny thing about this, you know, squire, is Madam Lah-di-dah lived here.'

'Yes, I know. And it's about time you agreed to see her. She's been very anxious about you.'

'Don't give us that crap. She couldn't give a monkey's tosser.'

'Well she's coming round this afternoon with some blankets and crockery and other stuff. That's how much she doesn't care.'

'You'd got all this organised, hadn't you? You and her. She put you up to it, did she? Oh sod it, I suppose she'll never be satisfied till she's given me the once over. Anyway, give me a couple of notes and I'll go to the chippy for us.'

Martin left Scobie to dine alone and then phoned Ann to let her know that he was installed and would probably be willing for her to call round with all the stuff she'd already sorted out for him. Then he drove to the university to prepare for the following day's seminars and to collect a pile of essays for marking.

Later that evening as he was reading through the umpteenth competent but unimaginative rehash of his lecture on the respective merits of Plato and Aristophanes as sources for the historical Socrates, he heard a car draw to a halt on the gravel outside. He went to the door as Ann was getting out of her car.

'Hi, Martin. Hope it's not too late in the day for a glass of this,' she said holding up a bottle of wine.

'Come in. I'll find some glasses.'

She followed him into the kitchen. 'It was weird this afternoon,' she said. 'Rather strained for a few minutes and then for a while it was almost as if the past thirty years didn't exist. But suddenly time was up and he very nearly pushed me out. Still, he agreed to let me go round and help him sort out his application for housing benefit. But that's enough of my silly old brother.'

As Martin poured her a glass of wine she put a finger on the rim. 'That's about as much as I should have if I'm to drive again later.' And then, with a smile and the hint of a laugh, she added, 'Oh go on, fill it up.'

Twenty-nine

The house was sold. Even before the sale board went up, the developer who owned the land to the rear made an unbeatable offer so that he could demolish it and improve the access to his site and hence gain planning approval for another twenty houses. There was a muted protest from some of the neighbours but most were apparently happy to see the end of what had for so long been an eyesore.

Scobie was more than satisfied with his move into the flat over the shop and the prospect of housing benefit to pay his rent. He was none too pleased, on the other hand, to think that the Squire had taken up with Madam La-di-dah and between them they were organising his once carefree life – even to the extent of making him throw out Bunderlin's cast-off jackets that he was so fond of wearing, and get himself fitted out with poncey new stuff from the charity shop.

'Madam La-di-dah!' said Ann. 'Why on earth does he call me that?'

'Because you married the posh git with the Jag and got yourself into the papers. At least that's what he said.'

'Oh dear. And to think that all this time he knew where I was and never came anywhere near. And I had no idea where he'd got to. I could have passed him in the street and not recognised him because it had been so long since last I'd seen him. That's a horrible thought.' Then, after a pensive moment, she added, 'How long had he known Bird?'

'I'm not sure. I assumed they met whilst in prison.'

Ann nodded. 'Hope so,' she said after a moment.

After lunch the weather seemed to brighten a little so they decided to wrap up and take a walk down to the river. 'Before we go,' Martin said, 'I have something for you. You might want to take it with you.' He brought a box from his study and handed it to her.

'For me? Thank you.' She felt the weight of it as if trying to guess what was inside.

'It's not really from me. Think of it as a gift from Bird.'

She opened the box and took out a camera. 'Oh wow. This is wonderful. Do you realise what this is? It's a very early Zeiss twin lens reflex. One of the very earliest, in fact. No, I'm not taking it out. I'll get it properly serviced first. Oh gosh, there's a film in it. So it was him. We had a customer, I never met him, Stuart did, who bought films for one of these. Apparently he used to get Stuart to load the film for him. Funny, he never said anything about him being particularly big. Just scruffy – which fits, I suppose.'

'That would be your brother, actually. He did all the running around for him at the end. Presumably Bird could at least load it himself, though he didn't have much of a clue about taking photos. Do you remember slapping down a wallet of photographs in front of me in the Haymarket many years ago?'

'Oh gosh, yes. Taken with this. Yes, of course I remember. And I remember seeing him with it. This lovely thing in those great big clumsy hands, like bunches of bananas. No wonder he was such a completely useless photographer.'

'I'm glad you like it. When I found it I thought it simply had to be for you.'

'You're sweet.' She kissed him lightly on the cheek. 'Thank you.'

Later, as they sheltered from the rain in the lee of Sykes's barn, Ann asked, 'Have you got anywhere with putting together all the bits and pieces of his life?'

'Not really. There's a couple of big gaps at the moment. There's his mother's journals, but I'll have those pretty soon because I've got one of the post grads in the German Department transcribing and translating them. The really big gap, though, is to do with the fire. He seems to have had scrap books for everything and kept every letter, bill and bus ticket that he ever had. But I can't find anything relating to the fire or that period. Except for a couple of wallets of photos. Some of you, some of me. I don't understand it.'

'Martin, for a bright chap you're very slow, aren't you? Hey look, I think the rain's eased off again. Let's press on and get a drink in the village.'

They set out along the unmade road that descended steeply into Moorhouses, the village a short distance from Borrinsmoor. If they hurried they would be in time to get a pot of tea before the café closed. 'I'll race you,' called Ann as she set off at a brisk pace leaving Martin struggling to keep up. They reached the café as Mrs Clark was about to close but she took pity and served them.

'Just now,' said Martin when he got his breath back. 'I thought you were about to tell me something I ought to have realised before. When I said I couldn't find anything to do with the time before the fire.'

'Well stop and think. You're a historian. You're supposed to know where to find the records you need.'

'Oh, of course. Evidence. It was all taken away. Shouldn't be too difficult to get access to it, though.'

'Easy. Well, I guess so. His solicitor must be entitled to re-examine it. I mean, if someone wanted to appeal, their lawyer would have to be able to go through it all. Look, I've had an idea. Why don't we make this our project? Let's you and me, well, try and put together his story.'

Thirty

As he drove down the long descent from Borrinsmoor, towards the motorway, Martin expected that he would emerge into better weather on the lower slopes of the moors. But there was no break in the mist and drizzle and the weather report confirmed that it covered the whole of the country and would probably do so until the end of the week. He braked sharply to avoid a blue Astra that cut in close without warning. Why did weather like this always bring out the worst in drivers?

The journey to Manchester took nearly twice as long as usual and Emma was waiting on the station approach when he arrived. 'What kept you? I'm soaked,' she said as she threw her rucksack into the back of the car.

He pulled away slowly and braked suddenly as the vehicle in front moved out. Emma lurched forward and nearly fell off the seat. 'Idiot!'

'It's OK,' Martin responded. 'He can do that, he's a taxi.'

'So what's this I've been hearing from Auntie Jean? Found yourself a new lady friend, she tells me. It's not the retired professional from the sex shop, is it?'

'Don't be daft. You can meet her this evening if you're staying at my place. If fact, you may have met her already. Ann Bates. Owns the photographic shop on Chorley Road.'

'So how did that happen? Do tell.'

'Knew her years ago. She was the one Bunderlin was interested in before he latched on to me. And it turns out her brother, whom she hadn't seen for donkeys' years, was his errand boy. Well, old lags together actually. Scobie hero-worshipped Bunderlin because of what he'd done to old Webster.'

'Who?'

'Webster. The barber whose shop Bunderlin set fire to.'

'No, the other one. What did you say his name was?'

'Scobie. Scobie Sharples.'

'But that's... You mean the scruffy thin guy with the baggy great jacket that he wears like an overcoat?'

'That's right. How do you know him?'

''Cause that's who Mum had sorting out the garden before we sold the house. He just turned up one day offering to do odd jobs.'

Things were beginning to fall into place. 'Chat quite a lot with him, did you?'

'Yes, suppose I did really. Quite a nice guy really, in a funny sort of way.'

'That explains a lot.'

Before going home, Martin drove to the university because Jim O'Neill had called the previous day to say that his post grad student had translated the notebooks. All very fascinating stuff, apparently, but not enough to do anything with in the German Department. Did he not realise that more than half of it was in English, Jim had said. But someone in History or even down in Women's Studies could well be interested.

'Women's Studies?' queried Emma. 'What's your hoarding old arsonist got to do with Women's Studies?'

'His mother. They were her journals. I'm hoping they might shed a bit of light on how she came to live in Lostock just before the war.'

When they got home, Martin began to prepare some lunch and Emma curled up in a chair with Mrs Bundy's journals. 'Hey, Dad,' she called, 'this is really interesting. You should read it.'

After a few minutes she brought the binder into the kitchen and continued to read as she followed Martin about, dropping hints and snippets as she did so. 'Oh gosh. Did you know... well, maybe not. Yet. But there's this woman she mentions and I think it must be, well, read it for yourself.'

'Do you not have to go and unpack?'

'Not if I'm going to Mum's tomorrow.' She perched on a tall stool near the window. 'Oh wow, it is! Because... Look, I don't know how you can bear to mess around in here and not sit down to read this.'

Eventually she put the binder to one side and came to the table to eat. After a few minutes she asked, 'Where's Dumpelwald? OK, somewhere near Koblenz, I suppose. But where exactly?'

'Don't know. Why the interest? What did you discover just now?'

'Well, you can read it for yourself. But I was just thinking. I could go to Germany after Christmas. Sally would come as well, I know she would, 'cause we were thinking about doing something. Won't want to at Easter, not with finals coming up. Oh, God, finals. Groan. So this would be a perfect chance. I mean, it shouldn't cost much. I'll ring Sally after lunch. In fact, I'll ring her now.' She took her plate out to the phone and sat at the foot of the stairs finishing her meal and chattering with her friend. By the time Martin had cleared the table and put the kettle on, Emma and Sally had made up their minds to spend a few days in Dumpelwald, wherever that might be, and Martin still didn't know what she had found so fascinating in Mrs Bundy's diary.

He settled down to read but by this time it was already two o'clock. He had got no further than the first page when they heard a car pull up outside. 'Who do you know who drives a big white Saab?' asked Emma. He put the journals down and went to let Ann in.

'What shall we do with Scobie?' It was Martin who voiced the question but they had both been wondering about it. For

Christmas was almost upon them and it would hardly be right to leave him on his own. Scobie, however, was still quite adamant that he did not wish to see Madam La-di-dah any more than was absolutely necessary.

It was Emma who solved the problem. She was going to have Christmas dinner with Julia and Barry but planned to borrow Julia's car and come over to Borrinsmoor for the evening. She would drop in at the flat on the way and bring Scobie with her. She was pretty sure that he would do as she suggested—'if he really is the guy who did all that garden work for Mum'—and if she didn't say that Ann would be there he wouldn't be any the wiser until the ice was broken.

'Emma, you're a dear,' said Ann. 'Now, Martin, do you think we've got time before Wednesday to spend a day in Jonathan Feeney's office?'

'Feeney? What for?'

'He's got all the items from the trial. Can't let it out of his office, though.'

'So it was Feeney who handled the defence? I thought he was just an estate agent. Might as well have been for the defence he managed to put up.'

'I thought so too until I spoke to him. He was a junior partner in his grandfather's law firm. Apparently Bird simply wasn't interested in defending himself properly. It seems he thought he should be able to tell the court his own version of events and everyone would believe him, and that would be all there was to it. Feeney and the barrister got a bit fed up with him.'

'Well maybe it all worked out OK in the end. Because what would have happened if they'd defended him properly? They'd have got him an indefinite stay in Broadmoor, no doubt.'

'You're assuming that he really did do it.'

'Well of course he did. Maybe he didn't intend Webster to get killed, but I'm sure he started the fire. We'll just have to see what's in the box. How about Friday?'

'This is getting really interesting,' said Emma. 'Can I come too?'

Ann seemed about to say, 'Why not?' but Martin said, 'No, I think three of us would just get in each other's way.'

'There's lots of stuff to sift through,' said Ann. 'Could be a help.'

'That's settled, then. I'll come with you. Did he tell you I'm going to Dumpelwald?'

'Where?'

'It's where his mother came from. Not Dad's mother, my gran. She was from Northwich. Bunderlin's mother. It's all there in the journals but Dad's not had time to look at it yet, so don't ask him about it, 'cause he hasn't got a clue. Anyway, I'm going there over New Year with Sally. She's my friend from university. Well, actually she lives near Kearsley not far from my Auntie Jean. That's Dad's sister. So we reckoned we might just be able to find some family members still there. Mind you, that could be a bit, er, you-know-what. Well, you probably don't actually, but read the journals and you'll see what I mean.

Thirty-one

A couple of days after Boxing Day it began to snow and long before lunchtime the moors had disappeared. A deep drift was building up against the garden wall and the shed and Ann was reluctantly beginning to acknowledge that it would be quite impossible to visit Geoffrey in the nursing home that day. Less than half a mile away the roads would be driveable, but that half mile was rapidly becoming impenetrable. It was the perfect day for examining the contents of an archive box.

To Martin's and Ann's satisfaction, but to Emma's frustration, Jonathan Feeney had decided that he did not really have to insist that the box of evidence should remain on his premises. So Ann said she would pick it up and bring it round on Thursday. And Emma, missing the chance to sift through it all there and then, left for Germany. She and Sally had four days in which to find what they were looking for and return in time for the start of the new term.

With almost childlike eagerness Martin began to lay out the packets on the dining table. 'So which do we start with?' said Ann.

'Let's try the photographs.'

She picked up the first packet and began to hand them one by one to Martin. 'Oh God, these are awful. He should never have been allowed to use a camera.'

There were more than twenty blurred, poorly exposed and poorly composed photos of a man who was barely recognisable but whom Martin thought might have been the person he recalled Bunderlin watching in the Haymarket. On the back of each was the name Webster with a date and a time and place. There were more similar photos in the next packet but then Ann said, 'And now we seem to come to another interest.' She handed Martin a photograph of himself cycling out of the main entrance of Merrion Dyestuffs. There were lots more of him, and several of the block of flats where he used to live. But nothing in any of them gave any hint of Bunderlin's reasons for taking the photos.

There seemed to be little of any relevance in the rest of the pile. Old bills, circulars, official letters and papers with no bearing on the case at all. Stuff with no reason to be retained as evidence and precious little reason to be saved even by its original owner – like the mountain of papers that had later filled up the house.

One large envelope remained. Ann tipped out onto the table six notebooks and they both thought maybe these might shed a little light on Bunderlin's preoccupations. They were all filled with lists. Lists of places in and around the town with a time against each one and a date at the top. Summaries of his surveillance perhaps? He flicked through and spotted one that began with Merrion Dyestuffs, followed by a series of street names which he recognised at once as his own route home after work.

'How does that make you feel?' said Ann.

'It's a bit spooky really. I suppose there would have been some of these for you as well.' They were silent for a moment. 'I'll make a pot of coffee,' said Martin at last to break the spell. He went to put the kettle on.

'Hey, wait a minute. What's this?' She had found a folded piece of newspaper tucked inside one of the notebooks. Carefully she opened it out and laid it flat on the table. 'Ah, finally. The very last thing and I think it explains it all.'

Martin sat down again and read the cutting.

Barber guilty of cruelty. Gents hairdresser Samuel Webster, 52, of Clayton Lane, Lostock, was today found guilty of causing unnecessary suffering to two racing greyhounds. He was fined thirty pounds and banned from keeping dogs for two years. The court heard that Webster, an official at The Grange Stadium, had hanged the dogs in the yard at his shop. In his defence he maintained that this was an accepted way of dealing with dogs that were no longer fit to race.

They sat together without saying anything for several minutes. Then Ann gave a sort of laugh, a shuddering sort of laugh to release tension. When Martin looked into her eyes, he saw that she had been crying. So had he. They embraced and let themselves cry properly.

'It's a relief in a way,' Martin said.

'Yes. I suppose really I didn't want to think we might turn up something quite dreadful about him. Yes, I know, he was guilty of a terrible crime. But I can't help thinking that underneath it all he was a good guy really.'

'Sure. A daft old bugger. A dangerous old bugger. Gets a life sentence because he was so angry about dogs being hurt.'

'Oh, wait a minute,' said Ann after a few moments. 'The date on this clipping—it's long after the photos start.'

'Ah. He could have known the case was pending, of course.'

'Maybe. But suddenly it feels a bit unsatisfactory again. Still nothing to indicate what started him off. Do you think maybe…? I didn't want to say this, didn't want to think it. But do you suppose Eric might have been involved after all?'

It was possible but unlikely, Martin thought, though he couldn't say why. 'I'd guess he was following up rumours about what Webster was up to with the dogs. He was a friend of every animal around, after all.'

Just then there was a hammering at the door, muffled by the snow, and Martin went to answer it. Whether by skill or foolhardiness, Scobie had battled his way to the cottage. 'You need to come right away, squire. The Tong lady wants you. Her with the pretty picture books and the leather knickers.' He turned and began to pick his way back to his car, as if assuming that Martin would raise no question or objection.

'I'll come when I've got time. And certainly not in this weather. What does she want, anyway?'

'A bit of advice, I should think. Kind of legal.'

'I can't give legal advice.'

'That's what I said. Told her. If you want to know when King Harold had his eye put out, I said, the squire's your man. Anything else, and he's useless. No offence, squire, but that's right isn't it? You know fuck all about the dodgy side of things. Why should you? But I said I'd fetch you, useless or not.'

'Could be something to do with the tenancy of course,' said Martin. 'But what's wrong with the phone, for goodness' sake? Tell her to phone me. Otherwise I'll come when the roads are clear. I'm not turning out while it's like this.'

'I think you should come now. It's nowt to do with the shop. It's Tony Lullaby. They're digging him up. Well, not him, of course. But the police must have thought it was time they checked who it was they buried.'

Bewildered and slightly panicked, Martin still insisted that he could not simply drop everything and rush off to the shop. He asked Scobie to come inside for some coffee but he was in too much of a hurry. 'OK, but tell me what you mean, they're digging him up?'

'Well, digging him up. Yesterday it was, so they'll be finished by now.'

'You mean he's been exhumed?'

'Exhumed, resumed, if that means digging him up, yes he's been exhumed.'

'You're beginning to sound a bit like Mr Bundy.'

'Ah now, Mr Bundy. He would have known what to do. Clever man, that. Not like you and me. He'd got brains.'

'But I don't follow this. Why have they...?'

'I told you. They want to know who it is. That's got to be it.'

'But why now?'

'OK, I'll tell you what I think. I put the word about. About Tony Lullaby's old lady fucking off to see her boy in sunny Spain —that's how I got him off your back, squire. Anyway, as soon as it gets back to Dave off he goes to Mother Lullaby—must've done —and says, look I know your little Tony's in Costa del Wheresit so just tell me where, give me an address. And Mother Lullaby thinks, this isn't nice, some bugger knows what we've been up to. So she has Dave bumped off and can't say I blame her for that. Trouble is, when the police start snooping around, all roads lead back to the pram shop. Beats me why they want to pin it on anybody if you ask me. Why can't they just say, thank fuck for that, like the rest of us?'

'So Tony Lullaby wasn't killed in the fire? And you knew all along?'

'That's right.'

'And is Maureen involved in any of this?'

'Made out she didn't even know it wasn't Tony that died till I told her this morning. Anyway she's in a state about it so maybe she really didn't know till now. I told her, just sit tight. Tony's not going to come back 'cause then his little scam will fall apart. And he gets done for murder.'

'But if it's not him in the grave, they'll soon find out. Probably know already.'

'No way, squire. No way. They'll just decide it really is Tony and put him back.'

'Not if it's someone else. I mean, there's DNA testing. That's pretty conclusive. If they have a record of Tony's DNA.'

'Precisely, squire. Precisely. They do have, must have, cause he was done for all sorts of how's-your-father.'

'Well, there you are then. They'll find out right away that the DNA from the body doesn't match their record.'

'No they won't. So long as Mother Lullaby keeps her mouth shut. I mean, she might be a bit surprised when they tell her it really is Tony in the box, but she's not going to say, no it isn't it's some other sod. Specially not the other sod it really is, if you get my drift.'

'Not in the slightest. You've completely lost me. Why won't a DNA test show that it's someone else and not Tony?'

'Because, Mister Professor, it's his twin brother. That means the same genes, the same shirt and the same pair of trousers.'

In that moment Martin recalled an earlier scrap of conversation with Bunderlin and, up to a point, he thought that at last he understood it. But only up to a point, for there was once again a hint of the big man's crazy word association in what Scobie was saying. Time will tell, he thought. But, at least, he realised now that Bunderlin's reference to a twin, shortly before he died, was probably nothing to do with the fire in Webster's shop. It was this much more recent one.

'So are you coming, then, or what?' said Scobie impatiently.

'Not in this weather. Tell Maureen I'll see her within the next couple of days.'

'Suit yourself. I'll go and tell her you're snowed in.' Waving aside Martin's offer of a mug of coffee, he turned on his heel and headed towards his car. As he did so, he slipped in the snow and fell heavily. 'Oh well,' he said as he picked himself up, 'maybe I will have a cuppa after all. Madam Lah-di-dah's not here, is she?'

'Yes. Does that make a difference?'

'No, I suppose not. But you're a bugger, you are, squire. Did you know that? A bugger, a bit of a lad, if you ask me.'

He perched on a tall stool in the kitchen and kept casting glances out of the window as if watching for an imminent thaw to begin. Ann came into the room and Scobie tried to look unflustered. 'Hello, Eric,' she said. 'Nice to see you.'

'Yes, well, I was just passing a message on to the squire. I'll be on my way now. Dirty Maureen's bound to be getting into a panic 'cause I told her I'd be back right away.'

'Problems?' inquired Ann.

'No, nothing really. Nothing at all.'

But the imminent thaw that Scobie had been looking for had turned into a blizzard and he had to accept that he would be unable to drive for quite some time.

Emma phoned later in the afternoon to say that she and Sally had arrived in Koblenz. They had hired a car and were intending to make their way to Dumpelwald the following day. Scobie, who was still anxiously watching for the imminent thaw, picked up the mention of Koblenz. 'What's she buggered off there for, squire?'

'She thought she might find out something about the place Mr Bundy's mother came from.'

'Well as long as she doesn't expect to find Old Frankie, 'cause she won't.'

'What do you mean? How do you know about...?'

'Frankie, the old guy. He's the one who brought Mother B to England in the first place. Bit of a tough guy, if you ask me. On the run, I should think, 'cause he would never let Mr Bundy or his old queen tell anyone back in Deutschland where they'd fucked off to, but the old queen just kept sending letters anyway and never told Frankie. Till, of course, the sister comes over to England. Then when Mr Bundy went to the big hotel by the brewery the old guy takes a trip to Deutschland. Trouble was, of course, no sooner does he get out there than he shuffled his mortals and never came back.'

Martin listened in fascination. 'How did you know all this?'

''Cause Mr Bundy told me, of course. How the fuck do you think I know? Yes, poor old sod. There he is, banged up for that bastard Webster and the padre sends for him to say, Oh by the way, if you're thinking of asking for your dear old Uncle Frankie to visit, forget it, he's brown bread.'

Martin had realised all along, of course, that Scobie was dubiously well informed about the dealings of the Lostock underworld, but he had not expected that he would know a great deal about Bunderlin's story. Despite their long association the big man would not have taken Scobie into his confidence. It wasn't in his nature and, besides, Scobie was surely no more than just a hanger-on. Wasn't he?

It was the middle of the afternoon before there was any hint of a change in the weather. Scobie was still fretfully watching the sky and Martin and Ann were wondering what to do with him. It had stopped snowing but the drifts were high at the back of the house. A loud rumbling broke into the muffled silence and a cascade of snow fell past the kitchen window. Martin went to the window for a closer look, Ann put the kettle on, and Scobie came through from the living room. 'That's it now, squire,' he said. 'Started to melt. It'll all be gone by tonight so I'll just fuck off. You coming or what?'

Despite the improved driving conditions, Martin was no more keen than before to drive into town on an errand he did not really believe was necessary, but he promised to contact Maureen within a day or two. Scobie left, muttering to himself. Less than five minutes later he was hammering on the door again. 'You got any WD40, jump leads, stuff like that?'

Scobie's battery, however, had finally died and no amount of first aid was going to guarantee him a chance of getting home. 'Come on,' said Martin, 'I'll take you. You can get a new battery tomorrow.'

Without too much trouble Martin nudged his car through the snow and onto the road. 'Can't think what you want to live in a place like this for. You're going to be snowed in every winter. Course, you're a bit of a rum bugger so I suppose you like it.'

Martin ignored him and let him carry on chunnering about the weather. 'Your lass snowed in yet, out there in Deutschland?'

'No. It's fine where they are.'

'We would have gone there, you know. Me and Mr Bundy. But they wouldn't let him, the bastards.'

'And he would have taken you with him?'

'Sure he would. Went with him on holiday once. Did you know that, squire?'

The thought of Scobie and Bunderlin taking a holiday together was beyond Martin's imagining. 'Where did you go?'

Scobie chuckled. 'You name it, we went there. Train to Norwich, then London, then Plymouth, I think it was – somewhere down south at least – and then all the fucking way up to Fort William. Slept on trains, stations, car parks. Fucking knackered I was by the time we got back. Mind you, squire, he was a clever bloke. Up and down on the trains like that for nearly a week and at the end of it he could list off every station we'd been through. And he made up this long poem he used to recite. Now then, how did it go? *Before the something said goodbye...* Wish I could remember.'

'What about, *Before the Roman came to Rye, and out to Severn strode, the rolling English drunkard made the rolling English road.*'

'That's it, squire! That's spot on. So you went with him as well, did you? Take you all over the place, did he?'

They drove past the bus station, behind the town hall and approached St Mary's Street. 'Tell you what, squire, you drop me near Jackie Cartwright's shop and I'll go and get a battery from him now.'

'From the newsagent? A car battery?'

'Sure. He's always got two or three cars he's looking after. Takes the batteries out, you see, so that no bugger can drive them off. So you can usually get whatever you want from Jackie. As a matter of fact, I should really change my car 'cause the tax has run out.'

'I'm not sure that I want to know too much about this scheme.'

'Works pretty good, squire. I mean, if you're inside you need to know that no bugger's messing with your car and it'll still be there when you come out.'

Thirty-two

Nervously, like a schoolboy venturing where he ought not, Martin slipped into Maureen's shop after a quick look up and down the street to check that there was nobody around who might recognise him. It was the first time he had been inside since it had opened and the sight that confronted him confirmed his fears. Beyond the bead curtain just inside the door were shelves of magazines and videos on display that left the top shelves of newsagents looking tame indeed in comparison. Around the counter were displayed outrageous underwear, whips, leather and plastic belts and harnesses and 'real feel' imitation genitalia. And along the wall behind the counter were posters depicting scenes of sexual inventiveness that rivalled ancient Rome at its most decadent – and far surpassed it for graphic quality. Maureen, sitting by her till, was engrossed in a puzzle book. She looked up casually when he walked in.

'Oh hi, Mart. Nice to see you.'

'Well, I thought I'd better drop by. Scobie told me about...'

'Him, he's a barmy little get. Trying to put the wind up me, he was.'

'So you're OK about what's going on?'

'This malarkey about them digging Tony up and all that? It's him all right. Maybe I shouldn't have put it about that it might not be but, well, that seemed like a good idea at the time.'

'So what about this tale Scobie's telling?'

'Twin brother? Bollocks. Don't know where he got that idea from.'

'You're sure there's no twin?'

'Should be. I grew up with the fucking bastard. Well, near enough. He was about five years older than me and they lived next door to us. So I should know if there's any more of him. Anyway, even if he did put some other sod in the fire, he's not going to come back now unless the police bring him. Either way, he's out of it. Fancy a coffee?'

He wanted to say no and get out of the shop as quickly as possible, but he didn't.

'You wait there. I'll put the kettle on.'

She went into the back room. A few minutes passed and Martin began to feel apprehensive and panicky in case anyone came into the shop. What would he do if someone should ask for advice about what to buy? Or do customers in this sort of place just keep quiet and hide their faces behind upturned collars? Hurry up, Maureen, he thought. It shouldn't take this long to make coffee.

Someone did come in, but not before Maureen had returned. Martin looked up when he heard the door open and the bead curtain rustle and he was surprised to see a very ordinary looking woman of about sixty. 'Here, Maureen, love, do us a favour, will you?' she said. 'Change me a couple of fifties. Two in one day, I ask you. Got a nerve, some folk. Giving a fifty in a bread shop. Cleaned me out of fivers.' As she handed Maureen the two notes she looked Martin up and down and managed to ask, 'So who are you, then?' without saying a word.

'This is Martin,' Maureen responded. 'He's the landlord here.'

'Oh right. Set me up in a shop like this, could you?'

'Sorry. I'm not... Well, this is the only shop I have.'

'Only kidding. No, I'll be sticking with bread and cakes. Each to his own, that's what I say. I wouldn't know where to start. Still, I don't suppose you'd get very far with a bread shop.'

'I don't suppose I would,' Martin replied.

'Look, I'm sorry to go on about this,' said Martin after the woman had left, 'but why have the police reopened the investigation into Tony Lullaby's fire?'

'They haven't. It's not happening, none of it. It's all daft Scobie getting the wrong end of the stick. I'll admit he had me going for a bit but I went and checked.'

'You checked?'

'Sure. Took a walk past the cemetery. OK, they were digging in there. Got that little excavator thing, you know. But it's a cemetery, for God's sake. They were only digging a new grave. Or getting an old one ready to put another coffin in. And it was miles away from Tony. Well, fifty yards. Anyway, they don't do exhuming in broad daylight—even I know that much. Comes up with some bloody stupid tales, does Scobie.'

'Right. And now he's managed to connect Mrs Greaves with Dave Brierley's accident.'

'I wouldn't put it past her, actually. I mean if Scobie did persuade the bastard that Tony's buggered off to Spain, he really would start to turn the screws on her as well, same as he was doing to me. And she's not the sweetest of little old ladies. Not by a fucking long way.'

'I get it. The wrong word in the wrong ear...' said Martin, realising that perhaps he'd had a hand in this himself when he accepted Scobie's offer to sort out Dave Brierley.

As Martin walked back to his car he wondered what other apocryphal tales Scobie might put about to sow confusion and panic. He was about to head off towards Borrinsmoor when his phone rang. It was Ann. 'Eric phoned just now. Said can you go and pick him up because he's got a new battery and needs to fit it right away. He'll be waiting at the back of Cartwright's shop.'

It was almost dark when Martin negotiated the potholes along the lane behind the shops. Scobie was waiting near the lock-up that used to be his home.

'Thanks, squire,' he said as he lifted the battery into the boot. 'Should have time to get this in and bring the old one back. Need to get it done tonight.'

'Can't it wait till morning?'

'No way. The old one needs to be... Well, put it this way— it'll have to go on charge tonight or else some poor sod won't get to work in the morning.'

Martin refrained from probing further.

'Got this back for you, by the way,' said Scobie, handing Martin a plastic shopping bag containing a battered box file and a couple of scrapbooks. 'Thought maybe you might want it. It's some of Mr Bundy's papers. Just the stuff he was using when he went into hospital. Took it off for safe keeping, I did, but then, of course, Jackie locked me out. Still, better late than never. That's right, isn't it, squire? Better late than never. Oh, wait a minute.' He reached into the plastic bag and pulled out something bundled in newspaper. 'You'll not want this. I'll get it back where it belongs.'

Martin was fairly sure he knew what was in the bundle. 'It's not a handbag, by any chance, is it?'

'I don't know and you don't want to know either.'

'And the contents of this bag which we don't know about, they won't get back to their wrongful owner because he has recently deceased. Is that it?'

'Don't know, squire. Don't know. And for fuck's sake don't tell Madam Lah-di-dah any of this. It's all over now so there's no other poor sods going to get hurt.'

They returned to Borrinsmoor and Martin held the torch while Scobie fitted the borrowed battery. 'Come in for a bite to eat,' he said when it was finished. 'There's something I want to ask you about.'

'Here we go again, squire. You and your questions. I see her Ladyship's still here,' he said, pointing to Ann's car. 'Tell you what —I'll fuck off back to Jackie's place and get this battery on charge.

And I'll come over tomorrow when Madam Lah-di-dah's gone to see her old man. Give me a couple of notes and I'll bring us some fish and chips.'

Martin let him go. He was still keen to find out how much Scobie knew about his mentor, but it could wait until another time. A quick look through the box file and the scrapbooks and then a quiet evening with Ann were much more to his liking just now.

'It looks like there were several others beside yourself,' said Ann as he loaded the dishwasher.

'Others?'

'Yes. These notebooks seem to be a record of everyone he was keeping track of.'

He set the machine going and went over to have a look. There were seven similar notebooks, each bearing an address on the first page followed by a series of dates, below which were written what appeared to be times and destinations. And tucked into the back of each were a few really bad photographs of, presumably, the person he was following. The notebook with the longest list and the most photographs was the one bearing Martin's old address.

'So I suppose I should try to contact these folk and discreetly ask what they knew about Bird.'

'Might be an idea.'

'I'll see what light Scobie can shed first, though. What about the rest of the stuff?'

'Might have helped if the girls had seen it before they set off.'

'How?'

'There's a couple of letters from Lotte. They're from a long time back but she'd obviously left Dumpelwald. Could have given them a better place to start.'

'I guess Emma will phone tonight. They've got two more days before they have to head home.'

'And then there's this,' said Ann. She passed him a piece of paper that was falling apart along the folds. Carefully he opened it and laid it flat on the table. They read it together but said nothing for a few minutes.

'So he knew all along exactly who I was,' said Martin at last. 'I suppose it means I really do have to carry on and work out the story behind his crazy collection.'

They thought the ice had been broken when Scobie moved into the flat and at Christmas when Emma had brought him back for a meal, and on a couple of occasions since then when he'd shown no obvious signs of being ill at ease with his sister. But he still went through the ritual of avoiding her. He came back as promised the next day but his battered old Sierra had been sitting at the roadside a little way uphill from the cottage for nearly half an hour without him getting out of it. And then, when Ann drove off at last on her way to the nursing home, he came to the door.

'Got held up, squire,' he said as he thrust a paper package at Martin. 'Better stick these in the microwave. Warm them up a bit.' Scobie's usual fare was really no less appetising than usual, it couldn't be, though the batter and half the chips were securely glued to the paper wrapping. Martin carefully separated food from paper and reheated it, thinking, as he did so, that perhaps he ought to have prepared something else instead. But Scobie tucked in with relish. 'Good old plain English food, squire. Beats all this foreign stuff, any day.'

Martin steered the conversation away from the superiority of fish and chips over all else, and towards the bundle of notebooks. 'I take it that this one, for example,' he said handing Scobie the one with his own address on the first page, 'was when you were following me.'

'Right first time, squire. Spot on.'

'So what about the others? Who were all these other people he had you keeping an eye on?'

'Weren't no other people, squire. Only you. That was enough, I can tell you.'

'But there's six other addresses here. You must have been watching someone else as well. And these photographs. Why were you interested in all of these?'

'No, Mr Professor. You've got it all wrong. Completely wrong. They're all geezers called fucking Latham. Got them out of the phone book. I'm glad your name wasn't Smith, I can tell you that.'

'I get it. You get one or two photos then report back to Mr Bundy and he tells you whether you've got the right one or not. Is that it?'

'Spot on, squire. Spot on.'

'So how many addresses did you, well, check up on before you got to me?'

'Fucking hundreds, squire. No, to tell the truth it was only half a dozen, something like that. Well, there they are. Notebook for every one.'

'And did any of those people ever realise you were watching them?'

'No. Kept out of the way, squire.'

'Till you got to me. What about these?'

He passed Scobie the photos of Emma and Julia taken in the garden.

'I like taking pictures, see. Well, I'd cleared all those fucking bushes and rubbish out of the back so I thought it might look good in a photo. Anyway, I needed to get a bit friendly cause Mr Bundy wanted me to find out as much as I could.'

'So you were asking my wife and daughter about me behind my back?'

'That's it, squire. Spot on. And the first thing your missus tells me is she's throwing you out. But don't fret, she didn't tell me what you'd been up to. None of my business. Told her I didn't want to know. Just sort of casually asked where you might be going. So if that's all you wanted to know, I'll fuck off before her ladyship gets back.'

'No, stay a bit longer. What I don't understand is why all the hide-and-seek business. Why couldn't you just come out with it and ask if I'm the Martin Latham who used to know Peter Bunderlin?'

'Cause of the fishwife, squire. Cause of the fishwife.'

'Who?'

'Mrs Fish. His probation officer. Interfering little busybody told him not to look for you. So we did it on the QT. She did eventually tell him he'd be all right. But he was nervous, squire. Real nervous. See, all those years back the police didn't like him having all his little notebooks. So that was where I came in.'

'But even when he knew you'd found the right guy, it was still ages before he came out of the woodwork.'

'He was poorly, you see, squire. Poorly. Couldn't get out much so I just used to take him down to the park with his dogs. And you know something? If you'd followed your dog instead of just letting him run off like he does, you'd have met Mr Bundy a lot sooner. A lot sooner.'

As he was leaving, Scobie said almost casually, 'By the way, Dirty Maureen wants to see you. She's in a two and eight cause I gave her some stuff she didn't want. Thinks you might know what to do with it, stupid cow.'

'So what is the stuff you gave her?'

'I don't know and if you'll take my advice, you don't want to know neither.'

After a quick glance up and down the street, Martin slipped into the shop. 'Scobie tells me you have a problem.'

'Fucking right I've got a problem.' She came from behind the counter, slipped the lock on the door and put up the closed sign. 'Let's go through to the back.'

He followed her into the storeroom.

'Gerry Mason's been picked up, by the way. You see that in the paper?'

'No.'

'It was him what hit Dave Brierley. Meant to be picking him up and driving him home but he was so pissed he just drove into him. Then scarpered, of course. And the daft little sod's been driving around in Dave's Merc ever since with the front all smashed in and blood on the headlamp. Now is that stupid, or what?'

'So what's the problem for you?'

'Nowt to do with that.' She walked over to a cupboard at the far end of the room and took out the same red handbag that Scobie had the previous day. and which Martin recalled seeing in Bunderlin's back room.

'It's this,' Maureen said. 'I need to get rid of it. And I need to make sure nobody else knows anything about it.

'Are you going to tell me what it is?'

'It's best you don't know. Honest, Mart.

'I've heard that a lot lately. But what if I already know?'

'Bloody hell, Mart! How would you know?'

'Because it was on Mr Bundy's table.'

'Oh.' She got up and went to put the kettle on. 'Gave it Mr Bundy to look after, I did. Right before the fire. Anyway Scobie's only gone and brought the bloody thing back. At least that means no fucker else has got it.'

'So why did you have it?'

'Tony made me take it because he was shit scared he was going to get picked up. But then he toasted himself on his gas fire before I could give it back. So what the fuck do I do with the stuff now?'

'Why are you asking me?'

''Cause daft Scobie reckoned you might have seen it at Mr Bundy's place.'

So was that it? Not advice, just the reassurance that Martin hadn't stumbled upon too much and wasn't going to rock the boat. He wouldn't, of course, becasuse he was pretty sure that whatever the details of Tony Lullaby's devious scheme, only he and Dave Brierley were involved. Nobody really needed to know anything about it, Martin thought and he smiled, shaking his head slightly, as he realised that he was beginning to see things from a Lostock old lag's perspective.

'Know what?' said Maureen after a moment's thought. 'I'm going to burn those, er, those things. Those kids, they had a loan for a school trip then handed over their passports 'cause they can't repay. Don't have to now. Never did, really. They scammed Dave Brierley's own scam so sod it. It's all over now.'

Thirty-three

A second and a third reading through the newspaper cuttings suggested no deeply significant reason for the inclusion of many of them. Martin had expected that most, if not all, would relate to episodes he already knew a little about. Like the explanations at the end of a detective novel, they would amount to the final pieces in the jigsaw puzzle of the story. And so they did, very many of them, along with the letters. But many more were pieces of different stories. Stories of Lostock's petty criminals—including Scobie. A solitary MP's forlorn campaign to save Rylands Hall. A product recall involving a faulty gas heater. A Barton Lane school teacher's inclusion in the Honours List. Local election results. A huge number of reports, probably all that Bunderlin had ever spotted, containing some reference to animals—from Sharston Brewery's reluctant decision to pension off their dray horses to readers' letters complaining about rats. And three different reports concerning the fire at Lullaby's baby shop.

He was taken aback to discover that slotted in amongst all these, and placed according to date of publication and nothing else, were the only two letters he had himself written to newspapers, both regretting the demise of Classics in schools. From the personal columns of the county newspaper there was the announcement of the engagement of Miss Ann Scobie Sharples to Mr Geoffrey Bates and Martin was a little surprised to notice that this was only ten years ago. It was one of the earliest of the cuttings.

'So what does all that lot tell us?' said Ann.

'They stretch back about ten years. Like all the other stuff he'd piled into the house, apart from the odds and ends. So I guess that must be when he came out of prison. And probably in all that time he's taken an interest in both you and me. And, of course, every petty criminal he got to know when he was inside.'

Emma phoned shortly before their flight home. They had got no further than Dumpelwald and Martin supposed that meant they would not have been able to find out very much at all of any interest. He had the brief story from them in the coffee bar at the airport.

Their enquiries for Bauernhof Bunderlin had produced only blank faces until they asked a fairly elderly man and met with a string of untranslatable abuse. Driving around the town and the outskirts revealed nothing and they had resigned themselves to failure when an old lady approached them in the market square. She was the wife of the man who had been so hostile the previous day but when she heard of two English girls asking about the Bunderlin family, she guessed that they must have some connection with Greta and Franz.

The family, though once respected, came to be hated, especially because of Gunther Bunderlin's enthusiastic involvement in the Nazi party. He had been arrested, never to return, after the war and the rest of the family simply disappeared without leaving any clue as to where they had gone. But Franz was different. Franz was a hero. Franz had taken his young cousin to safety and rumour had it that he had been back to the big house on the night when his brother Joachim died. 'Some people said Franz was a bad man. No, Franz was good. I know,' the old lady had said. And when Emma had said that her Dad had known Greta, the old lady's eyes filled with tears. And then she had gone and Emma had a photograph of her walking away through the market.

'So how about you? Have you pieced it all together yet?'

'Just about, but I have this nagging feeling there's something we still haven't spotted. There are probably one or two clues in the photographs. If they're all there. We haven't really looked at them properly yet.'

'Right,' said Emma. 'That's is a job for me. I bet you've hardly looked at them. Remember that first lot? You would have just tossed them away.'

They dropped Sally at her parents' place in Farnworth and then carried on to Borrinsmoor where Ann's car was parked at the side of the cottage. Emma went straight inside and left Martin to bring her baggage. By the time Martin came into the living room she and Ann already had the packets of photos on the coffee table. Emma set them in order.

'Here we go then. First picture—one scruffy little dog. Tell me about it.'

'It's Kenneth—his fox terrier. I had him for a while and then Jean took him when she moved to Kearsley.'

'And this?'

'It's the shop when Franz was still using it.'

There were a lot of photos taken in and around the town centre. 'And this is the frustrating bit,' said Martin. 'Because amongst all these completely unrecognisable people there might be someone significant.' They peered closely but could see nothing of interest. Ann suggested that it might help if she took the negatives and enlarged them, so Emma spent a long time sorting those out.

Eventually they came to the collection that included photographs of Ann. 'This one's me. You might not think so, but it is.'

'Next,' said Emma placing another picture of Ann on the table. 'Me again.'

'And again. So why did he take these? Did he fancy you? Was that it?'

'I don't think that was it. It never really occurred to me to wonder why he did it. He was just a crazy guy and he was beginning to annoy me a bit.'

'I bet he was. What a weirdo. And now we come to someone else. Oh, wait a minute.' Emma looked closely at the picture for a few moments. 'I could have a guess at this one myself.' She showed it first to Martin. 'You recognise him?'

It was a thin young man of about thirty or so. Martin had seen these pictures before but not thought a great deal about them. And he was still sure that he didn't know who it was. Unless, perhaps, it was the man who had once silently scrounged the price of a drink from Bunderlin in the Swan. Emma handed the photo to Ann.

'Oh my God!' said Ann. 'You know what this means, don't you?'

'There's more,' said Emma and handed her six more, which she studied in silence.

Ann pulled off a piece of kitchen towel and dabbed at her eyes. 'Here, take a look,' she said and handed them to Martin.

He looked at them one by one. On his own he would not have recognised him except as the man in the Swan.

'It's Eric,' said Ann. 'Stupid, silly old, dear old Bird. He went looking for my brother. He knew him before he went to prison. Oh God, that's too much. Why didn't he tell me, for heaven's sake?'

Part Three

Thirty-four

Peter Bunderlin's story.

There was a new dog in the park. A greyhound. Dark brindle, almost black. Kenneth saw it as soon as its owner unclipped its lead so he ran over, barking wildly. The greyhound sped off with Kenneth in pursuit for no more than twenty yards before giving up and going over to sniff at the hedge. 'You should keep that dog on a lead,' called the man who'd come in with the greyhound. 'Bloody nuisance, it is.' Peter Bunderlin ignored him.

A few moments later the greyhound came running back and Kenneth had another go. The man started shouting again but Bunderlin didn't hear what he was saying. He just carried on walking in the direction of the rose gardens.

From his favourite seat in the shady corner underneath the verandah he could watch as people came and went and some of his friends came looking for him. He took three apples from his pocket, unfolded his penknife, and cut them into small pieces which he set out on the seat. Minutes later a brown and white spaniel came and sat in front of him. He made it wait for a few moments and then took a piece of apple and held it out to the dog. It stood up at once and snatched greedily at the titbit. Then it sat down again and waited for a second piece. After the third piece Bunderlin held out his empty hand. The dog sniffed it and ran away.

Bunderlin sat there for half an hour. Three dogs came for their morning tit-bits and one man walked past—the greenhouse keeper with an empty sack slung over his shoulder. Bunderlin stood up, stretched to ease the stiffness and went over to the café, leaving three pieces of apple on the seat for Roxy, the Dalmatian, who hadn't showed up yet.

The greyhound with the bad-tempered owner was there again the next day. As it ran past, with Kenneth barking furiously, Bunderlin began to whistle. The silent whistle that dogs could understand. The greyhound hardly noticed at first. But on the way back he veered over towards Bunderlin, stopped momentarily, and ran back to his owner. Bunderlin smiled. The dog would be his friend.

On the fourth day he came and stood at Bunderlin's feet. It wasn't easy to give him a piece of apple through his muzzle and before he had succeeded the bad-tempered man had run up to them. He slapped the dog sharply across its shoulders and sent it running away. 'What the bloody hell do you think you're doing?' he snapped angrily and breathlessly at Bunderlin. 'If you've nobbled Collier Boy, you'll bloody well pay for it. Believe me, you won't nobble another.'

Silly man, Bunderlin thought. He took an apple from his pocket and offered it to the man. 'Collier Boy wants an apple. Take the cage off his face and give him this.'

'You're barmy. You're fucking barmy. Just stay away from my dog or I'll...' But he didn't say what he would do. Never mind, Bunderlin thought, by now the dog is probably ready to start coming to him underneath the verandah. The silly man stumped off along the path beside the miniature golf course, calling to Collier Boy as he went. Bunderlin went back home to carry on sorting out all his Mama's things.

The following morning he arranged her things in a pile in the garden The notebooks—not all of them—he placed carefully like a house of cards in the centre. Round them and round them and over them and over them went her clothes with all the letters and papers between them and over them and under them. And finally he criss-crossed the pile with her hair ribbons. Then he went into the house for his special poetry book and the box of matches.

He waited until the fire was burning properly and then found the place he had marked in his book. He began to read out the poem which the priest wouldn't allow him to read at the funeral. *Remember me when I am gone away...* When the fire had finished he raked together the ashes and shovelled them into a bucket. Then he went into the kitchen, poured himself a glass of wine and read and reread her last letter. 'My dear Peter, Very soon I will have to say goodbye...'

He was still there late in the afternoon, gently sobbing, when Franz came home. He felt his uncle's hand on his shoulder. *'Meine liebste* Gretchen. *Nur ein Madchen,'* the old man whispered.

The following morning Kenneth and Bunderlin went as usual to the park but, instead of watching the dog run for a while, Bunderlin went directly to the rose gardens. He stood just inside the gateway and waited. At last Collier Boy came along the passage beside the library followed closely by the silly man. Bunderlin watched as the dog raced up and down the length of the playing fields. And when he came within a hundred yards or so of the gardens, Bunderlin began the silent whistling. The dog heard him and stopped briefly. He whistled again and the dog looked in his direction. But the silly man called to him and he ran off. Bunderlin carried on to his seat in the corner underneath the verandah.

As he expected, Collier Boy came looking for him. Bunderlin stood in the gateway to the gardens, looking this way and that.

He whistled and the dog came trotting up to him. He unfastened his muzzle and offered him a piece of apple. He took it in his mouth but spat it out straight away. Bunderlin searched his pockets and found two dog biscuits and a caramel toffee which were far more to Collier Boy's liking. Then he showed the dog an empty hand and replaced his muzzle. Suddenly he ran off and Bunderlin leaned back and smiled. He had another new friend. But he did not like the silly man and he didn't think Collier Boy liked him much either.

Collier Boy came at the same time the following day and the day after that. But then he stopped coming. Bunderlin stood by the gate to watch but he didn't come. Well, that was all right. He had not stopped being his friend—the silly man had stopped bringing him. It meant there were two friends he had to look for. Martin, like Mama said he should, and now Collier Boy as well.

He soon found Collier Boy because little Mary, who comes with Roxy the Dalmatian, told him when he asked her. She'd seen him with his owner heading towards the meadows. 'Too many distractions here, I shouldn't wonder. And you should watch it, you know, Mr Bundy. Making friends with all the dogs like you do. They don't like that sort of thing, these greyhound people. Not right in their heads, if you ask me. What's dogs for, but being friends? That's what I say, Mr Bundy. Now if you really want to see him you should get yourself down to the dog track, the Grange. Not good enough no more for the big tracks but he'll race another season at the Grange. That's what I reckon, anyway.'

So he went to the dog track on Thursday evening. There were lots of people going in but not like the crowds packing in to Burnden Park. He went through the turnstile and followed the group in front. But instead of going into the stand, because the seats were far too small for him, he carried on in front of the tiered seats and stood by the fence at the track side where some others had gathered. The programme said there were nine races that night and Collier Boy was running in the third.

It was over the far side where the races started from and already they were pushing some dogs into the traps. Someone kept up a stream of talk over the loudspeakers but it echoed round and around the stand and came out garbled. Suddenly the first race started. The gates flew up and six dogs sped out. They were still all together in a tight bunch when they came past where Bunderlin was standing and everyone was shouting and screaming and sounding very silly. Then the voice over the loudspeakers seemed to say something about a photograph. A few moments later it sounded as though the voice was saying which dog had won and suddenly lots of folk were hurrying off to the men on little wooden platform things. In the next race the dogs were much more strung out when they came past and the dash to the platforms began before the announcement on the loudspeaker.

At last it was time for Collier Boy's race. They started just the same as before but when they came to where Bunderlin was standing Collier Boy was about ten yards behind all the others. He looked splendid, running easily at the tail end where he could be seen properly. Wonderful dog.

'Fucking useless,' said one of the men standing nearby. 'My granny's poodle could do better than that.'

''My granny could do better than that,' echoed his friend.

'Good dog in his day,' said someone else. 'But that's got to be the end. Shame really, but there you go. That's racing.'

He never saw Collier Boy again. He was never in any of the races after that and when Bunderlin asked someone, one of the men with the big binoculars hanging round their necks, he said, 'He'll not race no more, that one, mate. Gone to live with the pussy cats and poodles, I shouldn't wonder.' So that was it.

Bunderlin had other things to do. Franz wanted him to help get the flat over the shop clean and tidy and painted because Miss Sharples was going to come and live there. Miss Sharples was nice. On the day when she came with all her things Bunderlin was there hanging some curtains so he let her in when she got to the top of the stairs. 'Oh wow,' she said and laughed a little bit. 'Another giant.' Then her face went red and she put her hand up to her mouth and said, 'Oops, sorry.' She was nice.

He wanted to help her unpack her things but she said no thanks, she'd like to take her time doing it all on her own. And then she said, 'But pop in tomorrow and have a cup of tea with me.'

'*Come fill the cup,*' he said. '*the Bird of Time has but a little way.*'

'Oh right. And you're the Bird, I take it.'

'Bird of paradise, bird of prey, Bird's custard, birds in the wilderness. *Here we sits like birds in the wilderness.* Yes, I'm Bird.'

Miss Sharples laughed. 'Bird, you're priceless.'

'Now I have to go and look for my friend.'

'So who's your friend?'

'Collier Boy. He's a dog.'

'Oh right. Like you're a bird?' She was laughing again.

'He was a racer. But now he's gone to live with the pussy cats and poodles, so I have to go and look for him.'

'You can look for my brother while you're at it. I think he's with the pussy cats and poodles as well.'

'What is his name? Watt is his name. No, his name is Sharples.'

'His name is Eric.'

'I'll find him for you.' Miss Sharples was nice and he wanted to help her because she was sad about her brother.

Thirty-five

One day quite soon after she had moved into the flat, Miss Sharples came and joined Bunderlin in the park. He was sitting in the corner under the verandah when she came past and spotted him. 'Hey, I found you,' she called. 'Do you mind if I join you?' She sat down next to him and said she wasn't actually looking for him, she didn't mean that. She told him about going to the library and liking to take a short cut through the gardens and how she was getting the flat really nice now. Bunderlin said nothing.

'So what are you doing?'

'*What was he doing, the great god Pan, down in the reeds by the river?*'

'Oh, wait a minute, wait a minute. I should know it. Yes, something about splashing and paddling. And making Pan-pipes. You're priceless, you are.'

'Come with me. I'll buy you a cup of tea,' he said eventually.

She went with him to the café facing the rose gardens and as they approached, Kenneth came running across from the far side. He ran to the café door and sat there waiting but when Bunderlin opened it and he and Miss Sharples went inside, Kenneth stayed outside waiting.

Bunderlin went to the counter and called out, 'Could we have a pot of tea and some scones out here, please?' And then they sat at a table by the window. Kenneth saw them and came to sit by the window. When the girl in the black skirt and the white apron brought out the tea and scones he stood up and began to wag his tail.

Bunderlin poured the tea very clumsily into the cups and the saucers and onto the table. Miss Sharples carefully emptied her saucer into her cup and then did the same with Bunderlin's. 'There we are,' she said. 'Saucered and blowed and ready to drink.' And then she began to tell him about the photography business she was going to start and how she wanted to do weddings and maybe one day she would do the dress-making as well but that would have to wait because she didn't have a good enough sewing machine yet. Bunderlin said nothing.

After a while he stood up and gathered all the scones into his pocket. 'I have to go now,' he said. Miss Sharples followed him out of the café and they set off in the direction of the library with Kenneth jumping up between them catching scones. 'Meet me in the Wheatsheaf tonight,' he said.

'Can't. Tonight's my meditation night. You should try it, you know. Suhija Meditation Centre on Eastgate. Know what they do, some of them, when they've finished the prelims and they're accepted as pupils? They take a new name. So I'm going to be Veryan. And I'll tell you what, you can be Bird. Like you said the other day. Remember? Anyway, you've got to stop calling me Miss Sharples because that sounds so stuffy. Call me Veryan from now on.'

The next day he carried his mama's sewing machine down from the little front bedroom where she used to sew, and put it into the car. And the big box with all the coloured silks and cottons and buttons and zippers and scissors and everything else. And he took them to the flat and gave them to Veryan because she was nice and she would like them and use them just like his mama did.

'Bird, do you really mean it? It's for me? It's wonderful.'

'Meet me tonight in the Wheatsheaf.'

She smiled. 'OK, I might just do that.'

Then he went to start looking for Eric and Martin. First of all, he went to the Post Office where they had the telephone directories so that he could copy into one of his notebooks all the numbers for people called Sharples. There were a lot of them. The phones in the Post Office were easier to use because they were underneath big hoods, not in the red boxes. He stood a bag of coins on the little shelf and started with the first number. 'Does Eric Sharples live there?'

'No,' said the voice at the other end.

He crossed that number out and tried the next. 'Does Eric Sharples live there?'

When he had tried twelve numbers, seven of which he had crossed out and five of which were left to try again because nobody had answered, and fifteen more were left that he hadn't tried yet, he realised that Veryan would already have done this. All those people would wonder why they had had two calls from different people asking for Eric Sharples. So he thought that Eric probably lived somewhere a long way away or else he didn't have his own phone just like he and Franz didn't have their own phone. So he went back to the shelf where the directories were and listed all the numbers for people called Latham into another of his new notebooks.

This worked much better. There were not as many Lathams as Sharpleses. Two of them said that there was someone called Martin but he was out. One of them said Martin had moved into a new flat on Firswood Lane. And another one said he was Martin.

'So what do you want?' the voice asked while Bunderlin was writing in his notebook.

'Are you the same Martin who used to come to our house?'

'No idea, mate. Who are you?'

'Did you bring a cat for my mama?'

'Did I what? What is this?'

'A cat. A ginger one with a broken leg.'

'Not me. When?'

'1955.'

The line went dead. It probably wasn't the real Martin because if it was he should have remembered about the cat so he put a big question mark next to that address in his notebook so that he would remember to speak to the man again if none of the others were the real Martin.

Veryan came to the Wheatsheaf that evening as she said she would, but she did not stay very long because she said she was going to meet some friends from the meditation centre. She bought Bird a glass of wine and told him that she had already tried the sewing machine. 'It's really good,' she said. 'Very good indeed. So at the weekend I'm going to get some material and a pattern and I'll make myself a blouse. And you'll be able to see the results of your kindness.'

Kind hearts and coronets. Kind hearts are more than coronets.

Veryan laughed. 'How do people keep up with you?'

'Where did your brother go?'

'Oh gosh. Like I said – how do people keep up with you? He went to prison and then he didn't want to see me any more. So now I'm not sure where he is. But tell me about this friend of yours. Martin, is it?'

'He's kind to cats.'

'Right, well I hope you find him. Now I'm going to have to hurry along. Bye.'

Later that evening he had a good idea. He went to the New Zealander because that was where a lot of people who had been in prison went to drink, probably so that they could find their friends. It was quite crowded really so he began asking people if they knew where Eric Sharples was. Nearly everybody said, no, but some said, who wants to know? And when he said that he did, they still said, no. But then somebody, a young man with tattoos all over his arms, said, 'You mean daft Scobie. You'll not find him in here, mate, 'cause he's brassic. Try the back of the market hall or the Sally Army hostel.'

There were three young men behind the market hall sharing a bottle of wine and a cigarette, but when he asked for daft Scobie they just said, 'Piss off.' And the man at the Sally Army said he just comes and goes but right then he was goodness knows where. At least he knew where to wait for him. The trouble was, of course, that not knowing what he looked like, he had to keep asking. He asked some people for Eric Sharples and other people he asked for daft Scobie. But just like in the New Zealander, people kept saying, no, or who wants to know, or piss off. So he had a good idea. Instead of asking people, he got his mama's old camera, the one which Aunt Lotte had brought from Germany, and started taking photographs, but he soon found he had to keep out of sight when he was doing that because people would come up to him and say, 'Who do you think you are?' Or, 'Piss off, you big fat git.' But if he got a lot of photographs, daft Scobie would be sure to be among them. And then he could show them to Veryan.

And he needed to have some pictures of Veryan to show to daft Scobie, or Eric, or whatever his name was. Veryan didn't like having her photo taken, though, which was strange because she was going to be a photographer herself. But it didn't really matter because he soon became quite good at taking pictures without people noticing what he was doing.

What he really liked was having a drink in the Wheatsheaf with Veryan because she was nice. Sometimes he would go to the flat and ask her to be at the Wheatsheaf later in the evening and sometimes she would be there. Just for a few minutes usually, but she would be there. But when it was her meditation evening she wouldn't come to the Wheatsheaf. So one time he decided to go to the meditation centre. He waited at the end of the road till he knew that she had gone in and then he got out of the car and went up and rang the doorbell. The man let him go in and wait in the big room but when all the ladies came back into the room and he asked Veryan to come to the Wheatsheaf she said that she couldn't and that he shouldn't really come here. Unless he wanted to do meditation, of course. So he went and sat in his car but when she came out much later in the evening, she was with her friends and they got into a minibus and he didn't know where they went. So he just carried on looking for daft Scobie – and Martin, of course.

A few days later he was very lucky. He was sitting on a bench near the bus station from where he could see across to the back of the market hall. Kenneth was wandering round rooting through the rubbish which the seagulls had pulled out of the litter bins. Then someone came over from near the market. A small thin man he was, running with a lopsided skipping sort of run, and he came up to Bunderlin. 'What the fuck do you think you're doing? You been watching for me. I know. My mates said. Who the fuck are you, anyway? Bleeding Goliath?'

Bunderlin said nothing. He looked around to check that Kenneth had not wandered away. Then he said, *'Am I a dog that thou comest to me with staves?'*

'You're fucking barmy.'

'You're daft Scobie.'

'What's that to you?'

'Veryan wants to see you.'

'Who the fuck's Veryan?'

'Your sister.'

'Well that's where you're wrong, squire. Dead wrong. 'Cause I don't have no sister called Veryan.'

'Miss Sharples.'

'Bloody hell, you mean our Ann?'

'The very one. The very Ann. Veryan.'

'Tell her to fuck off.'

'She'll be sad.'

He stood up and began to walk towards the fish and chip shop. Kenneth ran up to him and walked at his side. So did Scobie. 'So how come you know our Ann? How come she asks you to come looking for me? Eh? Tell me that.'

Bunderlin said nothing. Scobie followed him into the shop. 'Morning, Mr Bundy,' said the woman at the fryer.

'Mr Bundy? That's your name, then, is it? Mr Bundy?'

The woman wrapped up his fish and chips. Without a word Bunderlin handed the package to Scobie and gestured for another. Scobie and Kenneth followed as Bunderlin led the way back to the far side of the bus station.

'So how come you know our Ann?' Scobie asked again.

Bunderlin said nothing.

'I'm not going to see her. No way. Got things to do before I see our Ann again. So don't say anything about me. Not anything, understand?'

'Meet me tonight in the Wheatsheaf. Eight o'clock,' said Bunderlin. And then he walked across to the waste ground where he had left his car.

When he called at the flat Veryan wasn't in so he went to the Town Hall and into the Housing Department where she worked. He told the man at the desk that he wanted to see Veryan but he didn't know who he meant. So he told them it was Miss Sharples he wanted and how she had a new name now but she was still Miss Sharples, not like getting married and being Mrs Somebody-else. It wasn't that sort of new name.

After a few minutes Veryan came out of one of the doors along the corridor. 'Bird! What are you doing here? What do you want?'

'Meet me tonight in the Wheatsheaf.'

'No. I can't. Look, Bird, you mustn't come here. I'm working. I'm busy. You'll get me into trouble.'

He didn't want that, of course, so he left. It was nearly five o'clock so he drove to Firswood Lane and parked near the new block of flats at the end. Soon people began to arrive home from work and he managed to take photographs of most of them. There was a young man who came on a bicycle and went in through the middle door. Franz would be able to tell him if it was the real Martin, except that maybe he wouldn't because he only got the back of his head in the photo. But he would come back the next day and follow him to find out where he worked and maybe get some better photos on the way.

Scobie came to the Wheatsheaf that evening but he said that if Veryan came he would just fuck off. But she had said that she wouldn't be able to come and she didn't. Well, that was all right because the things Scobie needed to do first would take time. He didn't tell Bunderlin what any of it was but he did say don't tell Veryan anything about where he was or what he was doing. So Bunderlin said he wouldn't.

Bunderlin got an early start the following day. He waited near the Firswood Lane flats and when the young man he thought might be the real Martin set off on his bicycle, he followed him. He couldn't get any good photos because whenever he stopped and got the camera ready Martin, if it was him, was a long way off and he could only see his back anyway. But he saw where he worked and which way he rode so tomorrow he would be able to wait in the right places and maybe get some good pictures to show Franz. So, feeling quite pleased that he was doing just what he promised his Mama he would do, he drove to the park to play with Kenneth and meet his friends. Collier Boy wasn't there, of course.

Thirty-six

Franz said he did not know if the young man on the bicycle was the real Martin or not because he had never seen him when he brought the cat to the house. But he sometimes rode his bicycle to a house near the cricket ground and Franz said that was where his mama's friend Dorothy used to live. And sometimes he went to look at cars so Bunderlin tried to get the Triumph going so that he could give it to him. But Franz said it was kaput. It needed a new gearbox before it would be able to go again.

Before he could find out where to get a new gearbox, he wanted to help Scobie with whatever it was that he needed to finish so that he would be ready to see Veryan. When he asked him what it was that he needed to do, he said, 'Oh for fuck's sake, Mr Bundy, you're not going to keep on about our Ann, are you? And don't say anything to her about where I am. She doesn't need to know.'

'No need to know, two knees to kneel. But what are you doing?'

'Oh, you mean when I said I'd got things to do first? It's Webster. That's what it is. The barber. I want everyone to know about him. And I want to shut his shop down. That's what.'

But that was all that Scobie would say. So Bunderlin got one of his little notebooks and he wrote 'Webster' at the top of the first page. And then he watched him, and took some photographs, and was very careful about the times and the days and Scobie was sure to find it all very useful.

When he had got a lot of lists and photographs he showed them to Scobie. He laughed and said, 'Fucking hell, Mr Bundy, you're quite some guy, aren't you? Quite some guy.' Then he told him what he was doing. Every few days he pushed a note through Webster's letterbox just saying, 'Pervert.' Nothing else. And then he'd painted the word on his window and a couple of times he'd pissed through his letterbox, which was good. And he wasn't afraid of Webster going to the police about it because he would know why it was going on and he wouldn't want anybody else to know. And even if he did and Scobie had to go to court about it, that would be fine because then he could tell everyone, even the newspapers, all about the dirty old get, and it would be worth it for that. So Bunderlin carried on making the lists and taking the photographs.

But it was now June and it would soon be his mama's birthday so he had to speak to Martin. He was still looking at cars but he didn't buy one. Probably none of them were good enough so he thought maybe he should tell him about the Triumph. Then a strange thing happened. One evening when Webster was having a drink in the Swan, a young man came up to him and started to argue. Then he hit him and threw beer in his face. The landlord rushed over and told them to stop fighting and he told Webster not to come back, which was a strange thing because he wasn't the one who had started the fight. That was when he started to go to the Haymarket which was where Martin and his friends went to play pool. And sometimes Veryan went to the Haymarket as well with her friends from the meditation centre so that was nice.

Shortly after the fight in the Swan and round about the time that he started to talk to Martin, Bunderlin was reading the papers like he always did and cutting out the bits that he needed to keep. There was a report about Webster. It said he had been fined for killing greyhounds. That must have been why the young man had hit him and why Scobie wanted his shop to be closed. Bunderlin didn't like to think about Webster killing dogs especially when he wondered whether Collier Boy might have been one of them. It made him sad and angry and he cried like when his mama died. So he decided to ride on the trains for a few days.

When he came back he took Martin to the lake and he read the poem that the silly priest didn't like. And afterwards he took him to the meditation centre so that he could bring Veryan to the Swan where she would meet Eric. Veryan was so busy that she never had time to come anywhere and sometimes she said she didn't want Bunderlin going in to the Town Hall or the meditation centre so he thought that if Martin went instead they might start to be friends and she would want to come with him. But she didn't.

Now that he had found Martin and they had read the poem properly, it was time to go and get the box back from the churchyard. So that's what he did because it shouldn't really be there at all and he took it to show Martin. So Martin understood and now he was his friend. So all that Bunderlin had left to do was to get Scobie and Veryan to be friends like a sister and a brother should be. Maybe that wouldn't happen until Scobie's special job was finished.

He spent a few days doing some more lists and photographs of Webster for Scobie and then he went to ride on the trains for a while. And when he came back he knew it wasn't just Scobie who needed the barber shop to close. He had to do it for the greyhounds as well. It was silly to say that they went to live with the pussy cats and the poodles if they were going to the barber shop.

So when he filled up his car, he filled up his spare can as well and took it round to the shop. He went to the back and found that the gate to the back yard wasn't locked. There was a big shed in the yard, which was probably what he should burn down. But he tried the back door to the shop and it was unlocked, so he went in and poured petrol over everything in there, which would be very much better than the shed. Then he came outside and lit a cigarette, which made him cough a bit because he didn't smoke. He threw the cigarette into the room, pulled the door shut and hurried away to Martin's flat.

He was glad about what he had done because no more greyhounds would have to come there, but he was sad that he couldn't have done it long ago before Collier Boy stopped racing.

Later, he came to watch the fire engines and so did Martin. Then, when Martin went to the Haymarket, probably to play pool, Bunderlin went to the Swan to find Scobie and tell him what had happened.

'Bloody hell, Mr Bundy. What did you go and do that for? Don't get me wrong but, bloody hell, you could go down for that. I don't want you to go down, Mr Bundy. You're the only friend I've got. The only friend.'

'Go to Veryan.'

'To fuck with Veryan or whatever she calls herself. You know what, Mr Bundy? If you go down for this I'm going to come and find you. I'm not going to let you spend fuck knows how long in bleeding Strangeways without a friend. Not for that bastard Webster. You're my mate, Mr Bundy. My mate.'

Thirty-seven

It wasn't very nice in prison. The prison officers shouted a lot and there weren't any dogs or cats or any animals at all. But they let him keep the photograph of Kenneth that Martin sent him, so that was nice. The other prisoners called him Goliath and so did some of the officers. Scobie came like he said he would but he hadn't been to see Veryan and he didn't really want to talk about her. He only stayed for a few months but some time later he came back and he still hadn't been to see Veryan. But he stayed for a lot longer the second time so that was nice.

And then it was time for Bunderlin to go home. He stepped out through the small door in the big gate, walked forward a few paces and stopped. The prison officer who closed the door behind him may have said something but he didn't hear. He waited a few moments, looked around, and then set off at a brisk pace in the direction of the big bus station. He rode on one bus and then another bus. He walked through the big archway by the Town Hall, across the square, along St Mary's Street and past the shop. The shop, the shop. Empty now.

At last he stood at the front gate of the house next to the school and looked up at the boarded windows. He walked round the back, banging on the boards, the gate, the drainpipe as he went. No dogs, no pigs, no goats, no donkey, no cats, no Franz. No

Mama. New houses, houses, houses. No field at the back, so no more goats. Only half a garden now. Half a garden. Half a yard, half a yard, half a yard onward.

He found his old key among the things in the plastic bag which the prison officer had given back to him and went into the darkness inside the house. Twenty minutes later he was attacking the boards at the windows with a rusty crowbar and an old claw hammer. He made a big pile of rubbish in the middle of the garden, ready to burn it all on the same spot where he had cremated his mama's books and papers years ago. Not all of them. Some he forgot, some he missed and some he had to keep forever. Forever and ever, for every endeavour, amen.

At the front door there was a large mound of envelopes which had grown over the years and probably prevented, at last, any further deliveries of mail. As he stood looking at it, visualising how it had all come tumbling through the letterbox, he smiled. There was work to be done and he would need to find Mama Greta's paperknife with the mother-of-pearl handle.

The wooden box with the painted lid was where he had left it on the stairs years ago. When he took it into the back room a mouse scuttled across the table and disappeared behind it. Bunderlin stopped and for a few moments looked intently into the darkness where the mouse had gone, but it did not return. Carefully he laid out the contents of the box on the table. Paperknife in the middle ready for use. The photographs of the sisters and Franz he put in front of his little pile of poetry books. The camera that Aunt Lotte had given Mama Greta he put on top of the books. And the few letters he laid in a line along the front of the table. But the last one, the precious one that was beginning to fall apart, he unfolded and read again.

'My dear Peter,

Very soon I will have to say goodbye. The doctors cannot do anything more for me. Franz is an old man now and you know how hard it is for him to walk. So you will have to look after him, just like you look after Kenneth. Please do not think Franz was a bad man. He was so good and kind and gentle. Joachim would not have died if he had not tried to stop Franz helping us. So you must think of Franz as your papa, not Joachim. When I am not here to be your friend you must find another friend. Please try to find Martin. He is Dorothy Latham's boy and you remember how kind she was to us when other people were so unfriendly. Martin brought Prowler to live with us and he liked to come and help me feed the goats and pigs. Maybe you will remember him. I know he will be a good friend for you…'

He stopped reading, folded the letter and put it back into the box. Then, after sitting silently for several minutes, he was back on his feet and hurrying to and fro between the front door and the back room as he set to work on the huge mound of post. Boxes, boxes. Before he could complete his task he needed boxes. And pens, and notebooks, and scissors and glue, and a car, and a bottle of wine. *A flask of wine, a loaf of bread and thou.*

He got up and went out. As he hurried past the school, heading towards the town, the pain in his leg started again and he slowed down. Tomorrow and tomorrow and tomorrow. Valerie Fish would help. She might know where Martin is. He limped across the road and made his way to Parkside Crescent where the corner shop that used to be Spencer's the grocers was now a small supermarket. The wine, the bread, muesli. Over to the far side to get all the newspapers. And boxes. There, in the corner between the exit and the checkout was a large pile of boxes and yes, he could help himself, said the girl at the till. He went back and got a large ball of string. And then he set to work sorting out the boxes, flattening them and putting them into an orderly pile which he bound round and round and round with string so that he could drag them behind him as he limped triumphantly home.

He left the pile of boxes beside the door and went into the house as quietly as he could. Leaving the bread and the wine in the kitchen he opened the packet of muesli and took it into the back room. The mouse was there again on the table. Startled once more, it ran away but maybe not quite so quickly this time. Slowly, Bunderlin approached the table and sat in his chair. He poured out a small pile of muesli where the animal had been and leaned back to watch and wait.

Dusk came but the mouse did not return. Bunderlin went to get his boxes and started reassembling them ready to start work as soon as he returned from seeing Valerie Fish in the morning.

'No, Peter, you mustn't!' said Valerie Fish. 'You are not to go looking for Martin Latham. He was a prosecution witness at your trial, for goodness sake. You know very well if you start doing silly things like that I will have to send you back to prison. Give yourself a chance, Peter.'

Give a chance, take a chance, keep quiet. He leaned back in the chair and watched as the young probation officer tried to explain their system of regular appointments or whatever it was she thought he needed to know about. She was nicer than the prison staff because she sometimes smiled. And she didn't get cross when he didn't want to talk. But he could tell that she was getting a little bit flustered because she kept brushing her brown hair off her face and saying the same things twice. And he thought that now and again she was saying something like, 'Do you understand?' Then she stopped talking. She just watched and waited and at eleven o'clock she said it was time for him to go. She was nice.

When he got home he could see that the mouse had been at the muesli and he felt pleased about that. He was about to tip out a little more when he had a good idea. He punched a hole in the bottom of the packet and stood it on the window sill so that the mouse could come and go as it pleased. And then he began the long task of opening his mail and sorting it into bundles to store away in the boxes. The newspapers would have to wait until the post was finished.

The mice soon began to get used to sharing their house with someone else. One of them – he thought it was the same one he had seen when first he came home – was bold enough to feed at the muesli packet whilst Bunderlin was working at his table. But he didn't give it a name because he wasn't completely sure that he could tell which was which when he saw several of them together. If he found a dog to come and live with him he would have to make sure that he could protect the mice.

He lost track of how long it took to sort out the post. But he got it all done in the end. All the letters opened and sorted into proper order. Tied up in neat bundles and stored away in the boxes. Important bits cut from the newspapers and pasted into scrapbooks, and the rest just bundled up. And then there was all the stuff from before. The stuff that the policemen had thrown around so carelessly when they were trying to find out about Webster. In the end he got it all as tidy as it should be. Valerie Fish didn't seem to understand but so long as he said that he wasn't looking for Martin or getting drunk in the Wheatsheaf, she didn't really mind.

One Friday morning, after he'd been to see Valerie Fish, he called in at Mr Feeney's office. The shop and the flat had been empty for several months since the knitting machine woman had left. 'You should've authorised us to go ahead with a new let, Peter. It's no good at all, this one-at-a-time contract, you know. You should hand it over to us properly to deal with. See Mrs Richardson. She deals with the estate agency and the lettings agency side of the business. You should either sell it or let Mrs Richardson manage it properly. She could get you new tenants in there quick as a flash and then it would be earning money for you again.'

Coming out of Mr Feeney's office he bumped into his good old friend Scobie Sharples. 'Mr Bundy! It's you! You're out!'
      'When all the world is old, lad,
      And all the trees are brown;

And all the sport is stale, lad,
And all the wheels run down;
Creep home and take your place there,
The spent and maimed among:
God grant you find a face there,
You loved when all was young.

Out and about, out for the count, out like a light. Yes I'm out.'

'Fucking hell, Mr Bundy, it's good to see you. Just going for a bite to eat, were you, Mr Bundy?'

'Where is Ann? Veryan, Very Ann. Verily I say unto you.'

'How the fuck should I know? Not round here.'

'But you must know.'

'Haven't a clue, Mr Bundy, so don't start all that again. You don't want nothing to do with our Ann, the stuck-up cow. Always was too posh for the rest of us. Mind you, so was my old man. But you know what you can do with our Ann? You can send her to Buckingham Palace on a dustcart. Married that Bates fellow with the camera shops and if you ask me, they were at it long before his first wife died. So to fuck with our Ann.'

'I need to find my friends,' Bunderlin said and set out in the direction of the bus station. Scobie hurried along at his side.

'What friends are you talking about, Mr Bundy?'

'Ann. And Martin Latham. I must find him.'

'Leave that one to me. I'll put out one or two enquiries. I'll find this Latham geezer for you, Mr Bundy. But not our Ann, no way. We don't want no one else, Mr Bundy. Remember when it was you and me doing the garden? Remember that, do you? Doing the garden. Cabbages and taters and things like that. You going to grow things back in your own place? Got a good little garden, have you, Mr Bundy?'

When they reached the bus station, the bus that would have taken him to Barton Lane was pulling in but Scobie gently steered him in a different direction. 'It's over this way, Mr Bundy.' Around the corner, opposite the taxi rank was the same old dingy fish and chip shop that he used to use many years before. 'Believe me, or believe me not, you won't find a better chippy than this in the whole of Lostock.'

Scobie was still tagging along at his side later in the afternoon when Bunderlin decided that it was time to go home. He followed him back to the bus station and onto the bus. 'Not got a car yet, Mr Bundy? Just give the word and I'll get you fixed up. Jackie Cartwright does a good contract hire scam. Yes, that's what it is – contract hire. Or, of course, if it's a driver you want... Well, with you being so fucking big you'll have a bit of trouble getting behind the wheel. Tell, you what, Mr Bundy, leave it with me. Leave it with me.'

Bunderlin got off the bus at the school and Scobie followed. He hesitated when Bunderlin turned in through his gate, but only briefly. By the time he reached the back door, the little man was at his side again, chattering away. He paused as if waiting to be invited in, and shivered in the autumn chill, protected only by his threadbare jumper. Bunderlin went straight to his front room and called Scobie to follow him. He rummaged amongst a pile of old clothes on the floor beside his armchair. Picking up a tweed jacket, he handed it to Scobie. 'You'll need to roll the sleeves up a bit. Roll up, roll up. Roll out the barrel. Let's have a barrel of old clothes.' Bunderlin's cast-offs almost buried Scobie but he grinned and chuckled as he sorted out what he wanted. 'You're a saint, Mr Bundy. A real saint.'

'*For all the saints who from their labours rest.* Rest, dressed and Sunday best. Now I shall go and see to my animals. Come back in the morning.'

'Right you are, Mr Bundy. Right you are. What are we doing tomorrow?'

'I have to go to Scotland.'

Scobie looked alarmed. 'Ah now, Mr Bundy, when I said about driving I was thinking of more kind of local than that. Scotland, that's a fucking long way.'

'Ten minutes to ten o'clock tomorrow.'

'Well, right you are, then, Mr Bundy, if you insist. You're the boss.' He gathered up his bundle of clothes and went home.

Obediently, Scobie turned up the following morning. 'But look, Mr Bundy, it's like this... Well, I can get a car, but not till tomorrow. And I don't think I'm going to be able to... What I mean is it's got to be there and back in one day.'

Silently, Bunderlin locked his back door and strode off through the front gate and along the road. Scobie hurried to keep up. 'There's no car, Mr Bundy. Shall I come back with one tomorrow?'

Bunderlin strode on, ignoring Scobie's chunnering about the car, and turned down the passageway that led towards the station. By the time be got there he was limping and Scobie was able to keep up. 'Oh right, Mr Bundy! You're going by train! You should've told me. There was me thinking you needed me to drive you. Should've told me. So when's your train due?'

'Thirteen minutes past ten.'

As he spoke a humming came from the track and a squealing of wheels against the rails as the train rounded the bend on its approach to the station. 'Well, there you are then, Mr Bundy. I'll just fuck off.'

'No,' said Bunderlin. He watched carefully as the coaches rumbled past. And then, spotting the one he wanted, he said, 'That one! Come with me.' They hurried along the platform and Bunderlin wrenched open the door of the carriage he had decided upon. 'Go on. In you get,' he said to Scobie.

'What? Me, Mr Bundy? I've got to come with you?' He climbed into the carriage. 'Well, you're the boss.'

Twenty minutes later the train arrived at Manchester and everyone had to get off. 'That it, then, Mr Bundy? Is this where I fuck off?'

Bunderlin led the way onto the concourse and pointed to a huge map of the railway network in tiles on the high wall at the end. Pointing towards some spot on the upper part of the map, he said, 'That is where we are going.' And then he went to the ticket office and bought tickets for Norwich.

'Norwich, Mr Bundy? Thought you said we were going to Scotland.'

'And so we are. *Before the Roman came to Rye or out to Severn strode, the rolling English drunkard made the rolling English road.*'

For nearly the whole of a day Scobie kept up an unending stream of chattering. About the prison garden, and wasn't it great to work there. Better than the kitchen, of course, but they didn't leave you there so very long, did they, Mr Bundy? And there was the workshops. That was good, wasn't it, Mr Bundy, letting us use all them tools and things. And did you remember Mr Walmsley, the screw? Decent chap, really, Mr Walmsley. Got a pub down in Manchester somewhere now. And then there was... But Bunderlin let it all hang around in the air and Scobie was content to rehearse his own memories whilst Bunderlin caught hold of the occasional word here and there to play with. They'd had years of this variety of conversation in Strangeways.

At Norwich they had less than half an hour before needing to get back on the same train and return to Liverpool Street. From there it was a short distance to Paddington before settling down to a long ride to Plymouth. From time to time other passengers sat near them, but not if there were seats elsewhere. Mostly, people left them alone. By the time they approached Plymouth Scobie's chattering had dried up and he fell asleep, only to be wakened to leave the train and wait two hours on the cold station for the next one.

Dawn was breaking as they approached Paddington a second time. Bunderlin shook his drowsy companion. '*Awake for morning in the bowl of night, has flung the stone that puts the stars to flight,*' he called cheerfully. A young man across the aisle looked up, shook his head and gathered his things together. Scobie stretched. Meekly he followed his mentor as he hurried off towards the Euston train and their connection to Glasgow.

By late morning, as they were climbing to Beattock Summit, Scobie woke up and stretched. 'Where are we now, Mr Bundy? Are we in Glasgow yet?'

'Ever closer, ever closer. *Closer, my God, to thee.*'

'What are we going to do when we get there?'

'We have to go to Fort William. There won't be time to go up to Mallaig so we'll have a pot of tea on the station and then go home.'

Eventually, after three days journeying, their train finally trundled into Lostock Trinity Street and Scobie was yawning so hard that his eyes were streaming. 'Why did we do all that, Mr Bundy?' he asked

Bunderlin smiled.

> '*Before the Roman came to Rye, or out to Severn strode,*
> *The rolling English drunkard made the rolling English road.*
> *A reeling road, a rolling road that rambles round the shire.*
> *And after him the sexton ran, the parson and the squire.*
> *A merry road, a mazy road and such as we did tread*
> *The night we went to Birmingham by way of Beachy Head.*'

'Went to Birmingham, did we, Mr Bundy? Missed that, I did. Must've nodded off.'

Thirty-eight

Scobie stayed away for the next few days. Bunderlin spent the time watching for his mice, occasionally seeing one of them boldly dashing along the window ledge to the muesli packet. It would feed for just a few seconds and then hurry away to hide for many minutes. Sometimes it would be as much as an hour or even more before it would venture out again. But Bunderlin was patient.

As he watched and waited, he tried to make his plans. But for every plan he devised, Valerie Fish raised an objection. Don't look for Martin. Don't go to Germany. Don't make a bonfire. The woman at the RSPCA was just as bad. Why do you want a dog? You have to think very carefully about it. Is your home suitable? Have you had a dog before? He'd had dogs, cats, mice, donkeys, pigs, goats but the RSPCA woman couldn't understand what he meant and seemed to think he wouldn't know anything about looking after animals. He would have to fill in a form. And have someone visit his home. He walked out. He wanted a dog, not an RSPCA woman.

Then Scobie turned up. He came round to the back of the house and hammered at the kitchen door. 'You in there, Mr Bundy?' he shouted. 'I've done it, Mr Bundy. Got us a car.'

Bunderlin shuffled out from the mouse room and found Scobie in the kitchen doorway. 'Scobie, my friend. The very man I need. *Wee sleekit cowerin timorous* Scobie.'

'Come outside and take a look,' said Scobie. 'Got this car from Jackie Cartwright. So I can take you wherever you want. You just name it. Wherever you want. But not Scotland. Can't do fucking Scotland. No way.'

'Germany.'

'Nor Germany neither. Come on, Mr Bundy. You know what I mean. Wherever you like. The chippy, the pub, Burnden Park. Places like that. You name it.'

'You can go where I can't go. So I want you to find my friend for me.'

'Right you are, then, Mr Bundy. Bring him back here, shall I?'

'And I want a dog.'

'A dog? You want a dog? You want me to go out and find you a dog?'

'Yes.' Bunderlin suddenly felt happy and excited. Good old Scobie, faithful loyal Scobie. All the things that Bunderlin couldn't do himself, Scobie would do them. And Valerie Fish need not know anything at all about it.

The partnership started well enough. On Monday afternoon Scobie arrived at the house looking very pleased with himself and insisted that Bunderlin should come out to the car and see what he had brought. 'There you are, how about that. Take a look at them. What do you reckon?' he said proudly, peering into the back of the car through the misted up window. 'You can take whichever one you want, Mr Bundy. Oh, fucking hell, the little bleeders...'

On the back seat two puppies, a tiny white Jack Russell and a nondescript black mutt, were busily shredding the upholstery. After a moment's thought, however, Scobie decided it didn't really matter. With some old newspapers thrown over the seat Jackie wouldn't notice the damage. And once it had dried out it wouldn't smell quite so bad. Bunderlin hardly noticed what

Scobie was muttering about because he was too preoccupied with his new friends. He was aware of him hovering around and saying something about food, but he continued to ignore him.

'Tell you what, then, Mr Bundy,' Scobie tried once more. 'Give me a couple of notes and I'll nip off to the chippy for us.'

Scobie had only four weeks as Bunderlin's driver and got no further in his search for Martin Latham than surreptitiously watching a house whose sole occupant turned out to be a white-haired old lady who rarely ventured outside. Before he could move on to the next address on his list, however, he had to submit to the rituals of the Crown Court and go away for a long break. It was a very long one this time because he had previous.

Bunderlin didn't go to the trial but he cut out the reports in the newspapers and pasted them into his scrapbook. And then he settled down to watch his mice, play with Klaus and Ulla, and add to his rapidly growing collection of papers. Once a month, starting on the last Saturday of the month, he travelled the railways, always returning in time for his weekly meeting with Valerie Fish. After a while, however, he left off travelling because the dogs didn't really like it, especially not the London stations, though Bristol Parkway was OK for them and so was Crianlarich. But it was better if they all stayed at home and, besides, Bunderlin's legs were beginning to get much more painful.

Valerie Fish had advised him to avoid the Wheatsheaf so he did, but she never mentioned the New Zealander which had been Scobie's favourite pub ever since the Swan had been demolished. Bunderlin visited it for the first time after Scobie had gone away for his long holiday. It was full of people he recognised. Strangers. The familiar furtive faces of strangers from Strangeways. In the far corner, almost hidden by the smoke hanging in the air, were two he especially disliked. The thin-featured, dark-haired one, uncharacteristically smart for the New Zealander, was Tony Lullaby, who had still been inside when Bunderlin came out. With him was Dave Brierley the loan shark. Lullaby used to boast of his plans for a new business. He would go straight. Straight to the top as a travel agent, a tour operator. There was a lot of money in tour operating these days, and plenty of opportunity to trade in the white stuff. It just needed a reliable contact for the paperwork.

There was a woman with Brierley and Lullaby, sitting a little apart from them and looking sullenly into the room. Bunderlin stood at the bar and downed a pint of bitter in one draught. He ordered another. Nobody stopped to talk with him but several gave him a nod and a smile or 'Hi there, Mr Bundy.' And then when he ordered his next drink the barman wouldn't take any money. 'There's three more lined up for you after that one, Mr Bundy.'

The woman who had been with Brierley and Lullaby approached him. She was maybe in her late twenties, black-haired and heavily made up. 'You looking for a good time?' she asked.

'Time, time. Parsley, sage, rosemary and thyme.'

'Well, fuck you,' the woman replied and walked away.

She went back to her seat near the two conspirators in the corner but Lullaby sent her away again almost immediately. She approached Bunderlin once more. 'Come on then, big guy. You want me to show you a good time?'

He looked at her but said nothing.

'For fuck's sake. Do you want me, or what?' She looked nervously behind her in the direction of Tony Lullaby. Both he and Brierley were staring at her. 'Come on. Are you going to do business?' She was getting agitated and all the time glancing towards the corner.

'What is your business?'

'Don't be stupid. Are you coming, or what?'

'Show me the way, then.'

'Thank fuck for that.'

She grasped his arm and led him out of the bar. As they left, Bunderlin was vaguely aware of a lot of whistling and catcalling behind them.

She led the way to the taxi rank behind the Town Hall where they climbed into a cab and rode the short distance to a street of terraced houses off Eastgate. They went into the large house on the corner and immediately the woman went upstairs. Bunderlin waited at the bottom.

'What the fuck are you waiting for?' she called when she reached the top. 'Come on, can't you.'

He went slowly upstairs and followed her into a bedroom, growing more and more puzzled about what her business might be and why she should think that he might be interested. It didn't appear to have anything at all to do with animals or collecting. She opened a drawer in the dressing table and took something out. 'Here,' she said, handing him a tiny little packet of some sort, 'Put that on.'

Clearly, the woman was completely mad. Put it on? A little thing like that? And then she started to take all her clothes off and he wondered if maybe it was something to do with sex. But he couldn't be sure because he hadn't done it before, and he hadn't realised that this was how it happened.

Maureen—she told him her name when she was getting dressed again—was nice. She was gentle and kind and she smiled. And she helped him do it properly. Afterwards they went back to the pub but had to walk most of the way because there were not many taxis around that evening. The noise in the bar stopped as they walked in, leaving only the juke box playing. Bunderlin went to the bar to ask for the three pints which were still waiting for him. Maureen walked straight over to Tony Lullaby and slapped the money which Bunderlin had given her in front of him. She turned to Brierley, 'And you, you fucking bastard, that's twenty quid you owe.'

Thirty-nine

He did it with Maureen the following week and the week after that as well. Every Wednesday they went to the house around the corner from Eastgate but they didn't always take their clothes off. Sometimes Bunderlin liked to sit and let the words swirl around in his head and know that Maureen was there waiting. She was like Scobie, really. Always saying something, couldn't keep quiet. But she was nice. And whenever he gave her the money she would say, 'Is that it, then? Don't want to fuck?'

He didn't tell Valerie Fish very much about Maureen because, if he did, he would have to tell her about going to the New Zealander and she might not like that. And, though he couldn't be sure, she was probably not the sort of person who liked to talk very much about fucking. So he just said he'd got a girlfriend and then he told her about the dogs and he said he thought that some of the mice, but not all of them, had gone away. And sometimes she said, 'Yes, Peter, you told me that last week,' but sometimes she didn't. When he stopped talking and she had asked all her questions, she would look at the clock, make a note in her book and lean back in her chair until it was time for him to go. And every time she said, 'See you next week,' she smiled.

One day, after he had come from Valerie Fish's office and was walking towards the chippy, he saw Maureen. She came running across the bus station to him. 'Mr Bundy! Thank God, I've seen you. Please, you've got to help me.' She was breathless and agitated and all her make up was smudged. She looked frightened. 'Please, Mr Bundy, I need to find somewhere to go. Anywhere Tony Lullaby can't find me. I've got to get away from him or he'll... God knows what he'll do.'

'Come with me.' He led the way to the grubby little chip shop and, without asking Maureen what, if anything, she wanted, he bought fish and chips and then led the way across to the bus station. 'We'll eat these at home,' he said.

It was only a very short ride to Barton Lane but by the time they arrived, Maureen was much more relaxed. 'This your place then, Mr Bundy?' she said as he went in through the front gate. 'It's a bit, well, sort of...' She followed him round to the back and into the kitchen.

'Fucking hell, Mr Bundy, this is...' She looked around, taking in the many years' accumulation of clutter and filth.

He separated the two meals, handed Maureen one and began to unwrap his own. Unenthusiastically, she opened the package and began to pick at the not very warm fish and chips. Both dogs begged for titbits as Bunderlin tucked in to his lunch. Then Klaus went to Maureen and pawed her knee. Timidly, she offered him a chip which he took greedily, so she gave him more. And some fish. And with the help of the dog she managed to get through most of the unappetising meal.

'Look, I think I'd better be on my way now, Mr Bundy. I really do need to find some place I can stay, 'cause I daren't go back to Tony.'

'You can stay here.'

'No, honestly. I'll find somewhere. Probably have to go to the Sally Army hostel.'

He took a bottle of wine from amongst an assortment of bottles in the corner and poured her a cupful. She smiled thinly but clearly enjoyed it far more than the fish and chips.

She stood to leave. 'I really will have to go now. Cause if I'm going to have anywhere to stay I need to go and earn some money first.'

'No, wait,' Bunderlin replied. He went into the mouse room and returned a moment later. 'Have this,' he said, handing her some money.

She unrolled the notes. 'Fucking hell, Mr Bundy, do you mean it? There's a hundred quid here. Are you sure?'

'Come back if you need any more.'

She sat down again. 'Don't let Tony Lullaby know you helped me,' she said. 'Know what happened? It was that sod Dave Brierley grassed on me. I'd been doing a bit on the side at the Boulevard Hotel. Trying to get a bit by me. Trouble was, Dave saw me and told Tony. And Tony smacked me around a bit and took everything I'd got on me. Reckons I still owe him a grand for what I took from the punters at the Boulevard. It's my own fault 'cause I should've known he'd do that sooner or later. Did it last time he came out of prison. Took everything I'd been saving for my shop.'

'What shop?'

'Oh, it was a stupid idea really. Just thought it would be nice if I could open my own shop. Not much chance of that now.'

'If I'd known about it a few weeks ago, I could've helped you get a shop.'

'You what? Could you really? I might still think about it. Needs Tony out of the way, of course, but with the latest scam he's getting into with Dave Brierley he's going down for a very long time sooner or later. Know what he does, Dave Brierley? If any of his punters get behind with their payments, them with teenage daughters, he makes them hand over extra security. Passports, birth certificates, stuff like that – so long as it belongs to the kids. Says they'll get it back as soon as they've caught up with their payments. Like fuck they will. And in the meantime, of course, him and Tony are using it all to bring girls over. Anyone who's lucky enough to be a near match to one of the passports. Stupid little prats think they're going to be models or actresses so they fork out a grand apiece. And Tony picks up a nice packet for each one he hands over. Don't ask where to, cause I don't know, but they don't end up at the London Palladium, I can tell you that.'

She picked her way around the ragged blankets piled on the floor and paused before stepping outside. 'I shouldn't have told you any of that, Mr Bundy. The stupid bastards think I don't know what they're up to, so for God's sake don't say anything.' She didn't leave right away. Though she had appeared anxious to get out of that awful kitchen, she hesitated now. 'If you go to the New Zealander on Wednesday,' she added, 'don't let on that you've seen me.'

She was not in the New Zealander the following Wednesday but Lullaby and Brierley were in their usual corner. Bunderlin ignored them and stayed at the end of the bar near the cellar door. After a while, Lullaby came and stood beside him at the bar. 'What've you done with her, Bundy?' He didn't answer. 'Suit yourself,' said Lullaby. 'She can stay away for all I care. No use to me now and you can tell her that. No use because she's past it, the stupid cow.' He took his drinks back to the corner. Bunderlin stayed only an hour and then went home to his dogs.

It was a late afternoon more than three weeks afterwards when he saw her again. He was sorting out everything in the garden, oblivious of the December chill, trying to get it all more sensibly arranged. Machinery things he put with the cars beside the garage, other metal things against the back fence. Furniture and wood that could be used for making things he piled in front of the non-machinery metal things, and wood for the old night watchman's brazier which he didn't use any more he piled near the back door. He was about to start stacking the bricks and stones when Maureen turned up. Start stacking stones, stop stacking stones.

'Mr Bundy, am I glad to see you,' she said. 'Can I come in?'

As soon as she stepped into the kitchen, the dogs greeted her like an old friend and, though she was wary of them at first, she did pat and stroke them, though a little nervously. 'Bloody hell, Mr Bundy,' she said looking round the kitchen, 'are you never going to do anything to clean up in here?'

'A labour for Hercules. The fifth labour of Hercules – cleaning Old Bundy's kitchen.'

'Yes, well, her whoever, she'd better get a move on or you'll be getting bleeding typhoid or something.'

'Typhoid, rhomboid, trapezoid, haemorrhoid.'

'Yes, any of that lot, I shouldn't wonder. You got anything to drink?'

He took a bottle from the box on the table. 'Ah, sweet Maureen, *fill the cup that clears today of past regrets and future fears.*' He handed her a chipped mug full of wine.

'Future fears – you're right there, Mr Bundy. It's Tony. I'm scared he's going to do something really stupid.'

'Lullaby, hush-a-by, *hush-a-by baby on the tree top. When the wind blows the cradle will rock.*'

'It's fucking rocking all right now, I can tell you. Dave Brierley's been arrested and Tony's shit scared he's going to talk. He's pissed out of his skull already and still going at it, and when he gets like that, nobody's safe. Specially not me. And I can't go to the Sally Army again 'cause he'll only come and get me like he did last time.'

'A lass in a Sally Army bonnet
And a soldier with a cap upon his head
With a badge and a chequered band upon it
And a bible in the drawer beside the bed.'

'Oh, don't get all fucking stupid with me, Mr Bundy. I'm scared,' Maureen pleaded. 'I wish something bad would happen to the bastard, 'cause wherever I go, I know he's going to come and find me. Then God knows what he'll do. Last time, that time Brierley grassed on me, he said if I didn't work for him he'd make sure I couldn't work for nobody else neither.'

He went into the mouse room and returned with a few notes from the tin box that he kept all his money in. He handed the cash to Maureen. 'Go to a hotel for a few nights.'

'Bless you, Mr Bundy. You're a saint.' She stuffed the notes into her purse but, instead of putting it back into her bulging red handbag, she handed the bag to Bunderlin. 'Look after that for me, would you. I'll come for it when all this has blown over but whatever you do, don't let no fucker else get their mitts on it.'

That night there was a fire. It completely destroyed the store room at the back of Lullaby's baby shop in Eastgate before the fire brigade were able to bring it under control and stop it spreading to the adjoining properties. Bunderlin read about it in the evening paper the following day but didn't go for a look at it because he knew that Valerie Fish would not want him to do that. He just carried on as normal.

The next day Maureen came round again but she didn't want to take her handbag. 'He was in there, Mr Bundy,' she said. 'In the fire and serve him right, the bastard. Have you got any of that wine?'

Brierley was given a two-year sentence for handling stolen property and Tony Lullaby need not have panicked because their passports-for-hire business remained their secret, known only to themselves, various small time criminals from the New Zealander, and Maureen and Bunderlin. Maureen, once she had fully recovered from the beating Lullaby had given her, put all her efforts into earning enough capital to open her shop. She shed no tears for Lullaby but did admit to feeling just a little guilty at her gratitude for the fault on a ComfortTwin gas heater which, whether by accident, tampering or drunken incompetence, was identified at last as the main cause of her husband's demise.

Bunderlin ordered his life around collecting, playing with his dogs, his weekly visits to Valerie Fish and watching for Veryan who was now called Mrs Bates. And waiting for Scobie Sharples to come back and resume his search for Martin Latham.

From time to time Maureen came to the house by the school but she had a nice new handbag and never really wanted her old one back. Her visits frequently coincided with those occasions when the bank was unable to process withdrawals. Bunderlin could usually find something for her in his tin box in the mouse room.

She came close to starting her business about a year after Lullaby's fire. There was a shop available to rent on Chorley Lane and she would have signed the contract but the Council said they would not grant her a licence to trade from a shop in that part of town. 'And do you know how much they want for a licence?' she said. 'Two fucking thousand quid. So it's back to the Boulevard for yours truly.'

'Back to the Boulevard, back to the drawing board, back to the wall. Don't give up. I know of a shop that will come vacant before long. They'll be moving into the new shopping centre when it opens.' So he went to Mr Feeney's office and asked Mrs Richardson to write a letter to Maureen offering her the shop. But she wouldn't do that, not right away, because she said she would have to wait until the birthday card lady said she was going to move out. Then he could offer it to a new tenant if he wanted to.

Then Scobie came home so that was nice. It was soon after Valerie Fish had told Bunderlin that he only needed to see her once a month now and she'd said he could send a letter or a card to Martin and he wouldn't have to go back to prison so long as he didn't start doing his thing with the notebooks and the lists like he used to. The police don't like people to do that sort of thing.

'Don't you fret, Mr Bundy,' said Scobie. 'Don't you fret. I can do that for you.' And he did. He got all the notebooks he had started before he went into prison and he borrowed Bunderlin's camera.

He took photographs of everyone called Latham in Lostock until at last Bunderlin thought that one of the people he had found might be the real Martin.

One morning Scobie came round with the van and Bunderlin squeezed himself into the passenger seat with his bag of biscuits and two apples and his penknife, just like he always did when he took Klaus and Ulla. 'Now I can't guarantee nothing, you know, Mr Bundy, but it's my guess he'll show up,' said Scobie. They left the van near the library and went into the park from there because there were some benches among the trees and bushes from where they could see who was coming in to the park.

'Here he comes, Mr Bundy,' said Scobie at last. 'Here he comes.'

A white bull terrier with brown and black patches came shambling along, nosing the gravel and the grass and the leaves. It approached within a few yards so Bunderlin cut off a piece of apple and threw it forward. The dog went to investigate and quickly gobbled up the titbit. Bunderlin threw another and the dog took that as well.

Then a man came into view. He had a neat beard, so that was right. And he was wearing cord trousers and a checked shirt and he had a jumper draped over his back with the arms hanging over his shoulders and hugging him round the neck. 'Samson! Samson, come here!' he called and the dog ran over to him. They went off towards the gardens and Bunderlin knew he was the real Martin and they were going to be friends again, so that was nice.

Forty

Greta Bunderlin's Diary. Selected entries.

Wednesday 3rd April 1935. Trude says that we are safe now with her friends. They brought a doctor to see me and I slept for a long time after we got here but I am well now. Franz has gone back to get money from Papa. I am afraid that Papa will give him nothing and he will stop him coming back to me. Trude wanted me to let her go with him and take my baby so that Mama can look after him. Really she is very kind but I must keep him. I will call him Peter. Nobody in the family has that name.

Trude has good friends. They let us stay with them in this big house and I have my own room but I do wish Franz would come back so that we can have our own house.

Friday 17th May 1935. Franz came back tonight. Papa has put money into a bank in Holland so we can buy a house and Franz can buy tools. He will not tell me about Joachim but I think something bad has happened. Franz is covered with bruises. I think Joachim did it to him but Franz says that Joachim cannot hurt me now and Lotte is safe. He says that we will have to stay here for a long time.

Sunday 9th June 1935. Today I went to the church because I wanted Peter to be baptised. I promised Franz that I would not tell the priest the name of Peter's father. I would say he is Peter Bunderlin, the same as the boy. I did not think he would do it today but when I asked him at the end of the service he said to me, 'Where are the godparents?' It made me sad because I had to say I do not have any friends. So he told me to wait. He came back and asked me to follow him. There were two people waiting near the font and the priest told me they would be the godparents. Then he said to me, 'Name this child,' so I told him. He took Peter from me and splashed the cold water on him but he had his back to me and I could not hear the words he was saying. It was done in only a minute. He wrote our names in his notebook and hurried away. Then the lady who was godmother said to me she was sorry the priest was so unfriendly. Her name is Dorothy and her husband is Jack. They are nice people. I will keep going back. Just because the priest is unkind it does not mean I should not go to church. Maybe Dorothy will be my friend.

Wednesday 14ᵗʰ August 1935. We have bought a nice house. Franz borrowed a handcart so that we can go to the big shop to buy furniture. We have pushed the cart up and down the road many times today and tomorrow we will do the same. But then we will be finished. Trude is not with us now. She has gone home to Koblenz but Franz made her promise not to tell anyone where we are. I do not think Papa knows she came with us. I wish we could go home.

Monday 30ᵗʰ September 1935. Today I went for a walk behind the house. There are allotments with little sheds and vegetables growing. I could not go very far because the path is rough and it was too hard to push the pram. When I came back there were lots of children at the school with their mothers.

Christmas Day 1935. Today I cried all day.

Thursday 16th January 1936. I go to the shops and buy everything we need. I do not speak English very well and everybody thinks I am stupid. We have a wireless so I listen and I try to understand and learn, but Franz always wants to find the German stations. I like to hear it but it makes me wish I could go home. I said if Joachim was not there any more maybe it would be safe for me to go home, but Franz got angry and said we can never go home.

Thursday 23rd January 1936. Peter can crawl now. He is going to be a very big boy like all the Bunderlin men. He is happy but he does not know what happened before he was born.

Monday 9th March 1936. Franz has a shop now. He is out all day so I am very lonely. When he comes home he is all the time in his workroom.

Tuesday 17th March 1936. We have a nice house. When I go into the garden I hear the children playing in the school. They sing and shout and laugh. One day my Peter will go to the school and he will learn to be an English boy and we will forget where we came from. Dorothy told me about someone who has some goats which she cannot keep. Franz says we can have them. I am happy. It will make my garden like home.

Friday 20th March 1936. Today I had a letter from Lotte. If Franz knows about it he will be very angry with me because he said that I must not tell anyone where we are. He said that it would not be safe but I do not understand what he means. I wish he would tell me what happened when he went home.

The letter had been tucked into the notebook at that page:
'Bauernhof Bunderlin, Dumpelwald. Thursday 12th March 1936.
Dear Greta, I miss you so much. I do wish you could come home but please do not try, because Papa is still so angry. He would make

you tell him where Franz has gone but nobody must know. I do not know what would happen to Franz if he came back again. He is very brave and I know he did it for Berthe and me as well as for you. Dear Franz is the only one who believed us. But there must be more because some girls in the village said they feel safe now that Joachim is not here any more.

'In the summer Berthe will be starting work in the dairy. She wanted to go to the ladies' college in Koblenz but Papa said there are undesirable people there. I wish I knew what he means. He has become secretary of the Party so he is very proud of himself and people treat him as if he is the mayor.

'Opa has been very poorly. He coughs all through the night and sometimes I think he might not wake up in the morning. I wish he was strong again like he used to be, but he is more and more like a very old man.

'Please do not write to me again because Papa must not find out where you are. He said I must forget about you. But I will not forget. One day I will come and find you and we will be together again. Give Franz a big hug for me. Your loving sister, Lotte.'

There was only one more entry, several months later, in that notebook.

Tuesday 8ᵗʰ September 1936. The long summer holiday has finished and the children are back at school. I like to hear them laughing and shouting at play but some of the mothers scowl at me if I am in the garden when they take their little ones home. I wish I knew why they do not like me. I try to be nice.

Perhaps there were one or two notebooks missing for the second one begins three years later. It continues in Suetterlin script but most of it is in English.

Tuesday 26ᵗʰ October 1939. Two policemen came today and

took us away in their car. They took me into a room with the policemen and some other people and kept asking me questions about our home in Germany. And they asked why did I come to England. They called me an enemy but I am not an enemy. Then they told me to go home and look after my little boy. But Franz they did not send home.

Friday 27th October 1939. Franz came home today. He does not want to tell me what they said to him.

Monday 15th January 1940. I am very frightened. The two policemen came back this morning while it was still dark and took Franz away. I think they tried to tell me why they were doing it but they shouted and swore and my dog was barking. I could not tell what they were saying.

Wednesday 17th January 1940. Where is Franz? I do not know where they have taken him. Today I went to the police office and asked the sergeant. He told me it is because we are enemy aliens and he said I would be sent away as well if I did not have to look after my little boy. I said we are friends. We do not hurt anyone, we do not want this dreadful war. We do not want Herr Hitler to come to England.

23rd December 1940. There was bombing again last night and it was so frightening. It came so close. Some of the houses at the corner were hit and today there is just a pile of bricks and stones. Thank God nobody was hurt. I was in my garden this morning and the man from down the road called to me. He said he thought I would be happy because I wanted it to happen. I never wanted this to happen. Why would I want it? It is horrible. So many children have had to go away to live with families they do not know because it will be safe for them. I do not want that. Peter, he is laughing and singing when the bombs come but my goats, they are so frightened. I bring them into the house and we sit together in the kitchen but my poor, poor goats, they do not understand.

Monday 8th April 1940. Today I took Peter to the school. I think he will like it.

Friday 2nd May 1941. The people at the greengrocery want someone to clean the shop in the mornings. I said I could do that job for them now that Peter is going to school. This afternoon Dorothy Latham came to see me. She works at the Post Office next to the greengrocery and said they want me to start going there on Monday morning. That is good because I need to earn some money while Franz is away.

Sunday 18th May 1941. Today I went to church. I go because I think I should. At home we always went to church on Sunday morning so that is what I do here. I thought it would be good for Peter to go into the Sunday School. It would help him to learn. But today the priest said I must not bring him any more. It is not because we are German but because Peter says silly things and makes the other children laugh. What silly things? I do not know.

Thursday 7th August 1941. Some people are kind. Dorothy from the Post Office came today with Jean, her little girl. Her chickens have been laying well and she brought me some eggs. She gave me some flour bags. They are very good. I will make her a nice blouse and if I can find some cottons I will embroider flowers for her

Wednesday 28th January 1942. Today I had a visitor. I was afraid because he was German and I thought Papa had sent him to bring us home. He told me his name was Heinz Gershman. He was with Franz in prison on the Island of Man. They have taken so many German men because they believe we are all spies. Now they are letting people come home so Heinz came with a message. They do not let Franz write to me. Franz too will come home but maybe he will have to wait until the war is ended because Papa is an important man in the Party. Heinz told me Franz said I must find someone to rent his shop. It will give me a little money to replace what Franz cannot earn while he is a prisoner on the island. Heinz said go to Mr Feeney in Saint Mary's Street. He is sympathetic. He will find us a good tenant.

Selected entries from the second notebook.

Saturday 22ⁿᵈ April 1950. Today I am so happy because I had a letter from Lotte. I was so worried when the Post Office returned to me the letter which I had sent to her two years ago. I thought something dreadful had happened to her. I was frightened to tell Franz about Lotte so I was worried for Franz and I was happy for Lotte. And when I was singing to my goats Franz said to me, 'Gretchen, why are you up and down happy and sad?' I started to cry and then I showed him the letter. 'But this is so wonderful,' he said. 'You must go. You must take Peter and go. I will look after the animals.'

'Hotel Loewe. Monday 17ᵗʰ April 1950.
Dear Greta,
Do please forgive me that I have not written to you for so long. For so many years I was frightened that Papa might learn where you are and send someone to look for Franz. It is safe now. You could come to me and nobody would hurt you and nobody would hurt Franz and you would not even have to see anyone who knew us because I am a long way from Koblenz. If Franz is still with you, tell him I miss him. There is only me left. I do not like to talk about what happened but one day I will tell you. It would be so lovely if you could come to me or if I could come to you. Peter will

be a big boy now. I hope he is like Franz.
Your loving sister, Lotte.'

Sunday 23ʳᵈ April 1950. Today Franz told me what happened when he went home. I thought Papa had given money for us but that is not right. He refused to help us and said that Franz must bring me home. So he went to Joachim and told him that he must help us but he kept saying that it was nothing to do with him. When Franz called him a rapist he got very angry and attacked him. He beat him and beat him with a stick and poor Franz thought he would kill him. But then Joachim fell down and when Franz looked at him he was dead. He knew he had to get away very quickly so he got Joachim's big van and went into the house and took all the silver and as many of the paintings as he could get into the van. He sold it all in Switzerland. He says to me it is only what I should have because of what Joachim did. That is why Franz says the house and the shop must be mine and then Peter's but never his.

'Hotel Loewe. Tuesday 16ᵗʰ May 1950.
   Dear Greta,
   I was so happy when I had your letter. I know you will like it here and so will Peter. The mountains are so beautiful and so are the lakes. I am sorry that Franz will not be able to come with you but, of course, he must stay and look after your animals. But when you have to return I will come with you and see him in England.
   Your loving sister, Lotte.'

Friday 30ᵗʰ June 1950. It is so good to be here in Germany, even though this is somewhere that I never knew at all. I am so happy for Lotte. It was so good that Papa sent her away before the war.

Sunday 1ˢᵗ July 1950. Today we went to Dumpelwald. Lotte did not want to come but I said we must go. Werner took us in his big car and we stopped in the market square near the Kirche. It is so different. A lot of the old houses and shops are still there but so much of it is new. I do not think I would have known that it is Dumpelwald. We had our meal in a little café near the new post office and then Werner drove us to Bauernhof Bunderlin. Lotte and I, we both cried when we saw it. The big house was pulled down after the people from the village had broken into it and destroyed it. Joachim's house is still there with the small barn beside it where he used to take me and tell me never to say anything about what happened there. There are four new houses and a big showroom in the old dairy where they sell tractors. The barns and cattle sheds are being used for a timber yard. We did not go in. We did not look for any of the people we used to know.

Tuesday 11th July 1950. Franz was so happy to see Lotte when we came home. All the years we have been here he has been sad, but now he laughs and sings. It is like when we were all at home before the bad things started to happen. Lotte says she thinks our home is like a tiny little piece of Dumpelwald but I know that she has forgotten about keeping animals. She has been so long working in her hotel. When she goes home and tells her girls all about our home here in Lostock, they will think what a very strange Aunt Greta.

Forty-one

The final piece completes the picture.

'I wish Gran had been with us longer,' said Emma as she pushed her carefully ironed clothes into her rucksack ready to return for the spring term. 'I mean long enough to hear more of her story. She must have had lots to tell.'

'She never was the sort of person for saying much,' Martin replied. 'Just turned it all over in her head and kept it to herself. Your grandad's even worse.'

'And Greta Bundy. She must have been a fascinating person.'

'She was.'

'And it was Gran who started her off with her goats. I wonder what that book was. The one Auntie Jean said she gave Peter when Grandad said it would be silly to give him a Prayer Book.'

'Haven't a clue. We'll probably never know.'

Emma zipped up her rucksack and took it out to the car. 'Just had a thought,' she said when she came back in. She ran upstairs and Martin waited by the door with his keys in his hand.

'Yes!' Emma shouted excitedly. 'Got it,' she said when she came down and thrust a book into Martin's hand. 'You're priceless, Dad. You've had this how long now? And you haven't looked at it properly at all. Look at that!'

It was one of Bunderlin's six copies of Palgrave's *Golden Treasury*. Martin opened it and saw for the first time the inscription on the flyleaf:

To Peter with all my love and prayers as you start at your new school. I am sure you will enjoy reading these poems and that you will find some favourites to treasure all your life, just as I have done.

Auntie Dorothy.